MURDER BY THE BOOK

J.L. CAMPBELL

WWW.BLACKODYSSEY.NET

Published by
BLACK ODYSSEY MEDIA
www.blackodyssey.net
Email: info@blackodyssey.net

Library of Congress Control Number: 2025916805
First Trade Paperback Printing: June 2026
ISBN: 978-1-957950-91-4
ISBN: 978-1-957950-92-1 (e-book)

Cover Design by Ashlee Nassar of Designs With Sass

10 9 8 7 6 5 4 3 2 1

Manufactured in the United States of America

Distributed by Kensington Publishing Corp.

The authorized representative in the EU for product safety and compliance is
eucomply OU, Parnu mnt 139b-14, Apt 123
Tallinn, Berline 11317, hello@eucomplianceprtner.com

Dear Reader,

I want to thank you immensely for supporting Black Odyssey Media and our ongoing efforts to spotlight the diverse narratives of blossoming and seasoned storytellers. With every manuscript we acquire, we believe that it took talent, discipline, and remarkable courage to construct that story, flesh out those characters, and prepare it for the world. Debut or seasoned, our authors are the real heroes and heroines in *OUR* story. For them, we are eternally grateful.

Whether you are new to J.L. Campbell or Black Odyssey Media, we hope that you are here to stay. Our goal is to make a lasting impact in the publishing landscape, one step at a time and one book at a time. As always, we welcome your feedback and kindly ask that you leave a review. For upcoming releases, announcements, submission guidelines, etc., please be sure to visit our website at www.blackodyssey.net or scan the QR code below. And remember, no matter where you are in your journey, the best of both worlds begins now!

Joyfully,

Shawanda Williams

Shawanda "N'Tyse" Williams
Founder & CEO, Black Odyssey Media

CHAPTER 1

CASEY MITCHELL

YOU CAN'T CHANGE *your mind now.*

That time was past. She'd taken the first step, which couldn't be reversed. Not after waiting years for this opportunity.

At lunch, Casey barely ate, but if her stomach didn't settle, the little she'd swallowed would reappear at any moment. She swiped her forehead with the back of one hand but didn't look up from the laptop screen. *Breathe!*

Aside from the tapping on the keyboards, the hum of the air conditioner broke the silence around the team of five writers. Emily Smalling, their editor, also sat in the space that doubled as a dining room. The villa in Ocho Rios, Jamaica, was luxurious, but they'd barely sampled any of the amenities since landing yesterday afternoon.

Their trip was supposed to be a treat from their employer, Addison Comstock. Or so she said. Nothing Addison said ever turned out as simple as it seemed on the surface.

As though Casey's thoughts summoned her, Addison walked into the room. Her black hair, threaded with blond highlights, formed a bun at her nape, and the color in her cheeks almost matched her rose-pink shirt and loose pants.

The air thickened as she cut a direct path to Madelaine Ebanks and flung a file jacket on the table. The printed sheets inside fanned across the glass in a wide swirl. Nobody moved as she spat, "This is garbage. I need something exciting, fresh, and you dare to turn in this crap?" She pulled in a sharp breath, then added, "A five-year-old child could do a better job than this."

Emily's hand went to her throat, and the color seeped from her face.

The movement caught Addison's attention. "I don't know how this load of rubbish made it past you."

Addison probably didn't know what writing involved anymore. Why would she, with a stable of minions churning out stories at her disposal?

Maddy, a mousy thirty-two-year-old slip of a woman, gathered her rejected work in a jerky motion. None of them dared to twitch in their seats for fear of having Addison's wrath turned on them.

"This rubbish should go in the shredder." Addison gestured toward the far corner and the equipment she'd hired along with the villa. "And I should fire you on the spot."

They all knew she wouldn't. Or couldn't. Aside from being skilled and trained to deliver their work in Addison's style, each writer and editor operated under a strict contract. Maddy's would run for another ten months. Despite that, nobody wanted to face Addison when she was in a mood.

"Are you suffering from burnout?" Addison screeched. Her face darkened when she faced Maddy across the table. "Did. You. Hear. Me?"

Maddy nodded but didn't speak. If she responded verbally, Addison would find a reason to continue her rant.

Settling her weight on both hands, Addison leaned on the tabletop. "Rewrite that chapter. I need it this evening."

A collective gasp hung in the air. Usually, she gave them grace to rewrite the assignment overnight, but not this time. Something was up. It was almost six p.m., the end of the workday. At this rate, Maddy wouldn't finish until nine or ten p.m.

Casey glanced at Maddy, who tipped her head back and sniffed. While willing her not to cry, Casey mentally went through what she'd submitted yesterday. When Addison's gaze settled on her, Casey fought not to hunch in her seat. She loathed herself for shrinking from a bully.

"Your chapters weren't bad, but they weren't good either. They need to be tighter. Your pacing could be better." Waving with one hand, she continued, "The rest of you better be sure your work is reader-ready before I lay eyes on today's writing."

"And you…" Addison's gaze shot to Emily as she approached the doorway, "ensure you do what I'm paying you for."

Addison had to be blind not to realize Emily was unwell. Typical.

With one hand covering her mouth, Emily released a hacking cough that Casey was certain tore at her lungs and chest. When she stopped, the pronounced wheezing was loud enough to worry Casey. Would she, or wouldn't she die today?

Emily's face was white and resembled crumpled tissue paper. The woman was fading before her eyes. Thanks to her sister, who was a nurse, Casey was more aware than most when it came to other people's well-being.

Frowning, Casey asked, "Are you okay? Shouldn't you lie down?"

The older woman's mouth gaped, and she scrabbled for the inhaler inches from her hand. As her fingers closed around it, she crashed face-first onto the glass surface.

Casey sprang from the seat, rushed to Emily, and slid the inhaler aside as she raised her limp wrist. "Her pulse is weak, but she's still with us. Have the butler call an ambulance."

No one moved to follow her instructions until she spoke again. "Somebody help me lift her off the table, and get Addy back in here. Now."

Maddy scooted out of her seat and ran from the room. The unnatural stillness sent a chill down Casey's spine. Emily's possible demise should have made her happy. The woman made their lives hellish while catering to Addison's endless demands, but now she was nothing but a pale sack of skin and bones.

The *tap-tap-tap* of Addison's heels on the marble tiles broke the spell Casey was under, and she stepped aside. She realized then that none of the men tried to help. Emily's vacant eyes forced Casey to take her pulse a second time. With her stomach still in revolt, Casey whispered, "She's gone."

Grabbing Emily by the shoulder, Addison yelled, "Emily, wake up! You can't die on me. I won't have it."

CHAPTER 2

ALECIA COOKSON

FOR NO REASON Alecia could pinpoint, Addison turned on her today. Nothing she wrote was good enough. Broderick, the main character, felt wishy-washy. Rita, his girlfriend, was too stupid to live on the page, and Alecia's descriptions were as bland as a bowl of tasteless grits. All according to Addison.

If she had another option waiting, she'd have told Addison to shove her book and her abuse where the sun couldn't penetrate.

From where she sat on the double bed, Casey said, "Hey, stop wearing out your brain with what's gone. It's not helping."

"True." Addison's abuse always made her feel worthless, and she hated it. Her gaze followed Casey, and she sighed. "And I'm not the source of her problems."

Casey scooped the hair away from her face into a fat ponytail, then crossed the room and turned the door handle. "None of us is."

Earlier, it had taken every shred of self-control not to burst out crying at the table. She'd never been so humiliated in her life.

Addison raged at her, using curse words and insulting her skill and mental ability. The threats galled her because Addison couldn't let her go on a whim.

Proximity to Quentin Young was what kept her on the team. The irony was, their "situationship" was going nowhere. She'd sacrificed one year and didn't have more time to waste. The toxic work environment made escaping one of her top priorities. She simply hadn't found an "out" as yet. She had money but no way to void her contract. That's if she dared to do it.

If she was sure of him, she wouldn't think twice about walking when her contract came up for renewal. She was in love with Quentin, and working for Addison kept him within her sight, if not within her reach, in the way she wanted.

Quentin did double duty as one of Addison's editors/writers, and the scuttlebutt around the small group claimed they also had a sexual relationship. None of the men was exempt from Addison's insatiable appetite. He'd admitted nothing, but Alecia was suspicious. All he'd said when she asked about it was, "D'you believe everything you hear?"

She thanked God he hadn't come. The time here would be easier if she didn't have to think about him being in Addison's bed and unable to do anything about it. Still, an ultimatum was necessary. Thirty was staring her in the face, and so was the deterioration of her viable eggs and a chance at motherhood. Quentin wasn't the perfect man, but would be a decent candidate for any babies in her future—if this job didn't put her into an early grave first.

She picked up her phone and went to the messages they'd exchanged. The last one came early this morning. Scrolling through them, she realized that no matter what she said about Addison, Quentin never responded with negative comments. As though she'd share any of them with someone else. Or maybe he believed she'd betray him to Addison.

That's where that witch drove them, to being unsure of each other. None of them liked Addison, and no one wanted to be caught in the whirlwind of her meanness.

Alecia chewed her lip, debating whether to call Quentin. Nothing was stopping her, so why was she hesitating?

Because you doubt him.

She sucked her teeth, then sighed. Either she was going to do it, or she wasn't. Before she could change her mind, she speed-dialed the number, hoping it wouldn't cost a fortune. He picked up after the third ring.

"Hey, love. You got off early today."

"You call this early? For your information, we were at it right up to dinnertime."

"Well, it's not like you didn't know what to expect."

She chuckled and muted the television. "True that. You know what's what."

The shuffling of papers accompanied his words, "So, how is Jamaica?"

"It's here, not that I'll get to see it," she groused.

"Guess it's a no-go on seeing the relatives, huh?" His smooth bass and soothing tone made her long for him.

A ball of discontent rolled into her throat, and she swallowed it down. "I didn't need that reminder."

"It would be a pity to fly in and not visit them."

"Yeah." She pictured his dark eyes and easy smile, wishing she'd stayed in Orlando. Shifting to stare at the fifty-four-inch television screen on the wall, she sighed. "I miss you. If you were here, the trip would be more bearable."

"Before you know it, you'll be back home."

She pressed her lips together to hold in a comment, but couldn't resist saying, "But first, I have to walk through the fires of hell with you-know-who."

She didn't mention Emily's passing since he'd seen it in the group chat.

"Take your mind off Addison," Quentin whispered. "Dream of me instead."

Alecia's antennae went up because she could have sworn she heard a woman's voice in the background.

"Where are you?" She winced at her suspicious tone.

"Home. Where else would I be? We have deadlines, woman."

His response made her smile. Maybe she'd heard the television. After all, Quentin had never given her the impression he was a wild one. But with men, you never knew.

After a sappy goodbye, she threw the cell phone on the sheet and wandered around the room. The décor was cheerful, with bright splashes of colors in the drapes and matching sheets to combat the heavy mahogany furniture. They even had a blooming spathiphyllum, or peace lily as Mama called it, on the balcony.

When she circled back to the bed, she caught a flash of red peeking from under Casey's pillow. She glanced at the doorway, then back to the journal. Casey had been writing in it before she left. Since Emily's death and today's blowout, her vibe had been weird. Alecia wondered if something specific had upset her. Of course, Addison's tirade had thrown everyone, but the journal might reveal more. She'd been silent and preoccupied for much of the afternoon.

Alecia noted how Casey left it before flipping the latch open. The heavy pen fell out, and the point jabbed her foot. She giggled and shook her head. Stupid of her to be so nervous, but anyone would be at the prospect of invading their friend's privacy. Especially someone who trusted her.

One cryptic sentence on the otherwise blank page in Casey's scrawl made her frown.

A long time coming, but Mommy will get the recognition she deserves.

Casey's mother had died years ago, so what was she talking about? Raised voices made Alecia cock her head, and instead of flipping to the previous page, she closed the journal and shoved it under the pillow as she'd found it. If Casey caught her snooping, she'd have no acceptable excuse.

Drawn by the sound of voices, she peeked through the drapes.

Casey's slender figure loomed over Addison, who lounged on a floater at the shallow end of the pool and released a peal of laughter that reminded her of a gaggle of honking geese in a territory war. Discordant and upsetting.

Although Alecia listened, she still couldn't hear the conversation. Not from the distance across the brick-and-cement deck. Casey tugged her ponytail, which she did when she was on edge, while Addison sipped from a wineglass. She guessed Addison was smirking since she couldn't separate that from her regular expression—a cross between her Botox-induced mask and satisfaction from her evil thoughts.

Casey turned toward the house, and Alecia stepped away from the window. She rolled into bed, grabbed the remote off the side table, and increased the volume on the television. The comedy on screen wasn't a favorite, so her eyelids dipped after several minutes. She had settled on her side when the door opened and Casey stepped inside.

"You all right?" Alecia asked, yawning.

"Sure. The night air did me good." She headed for the bathroom, then returned to change into her nightwear.

Alecia slid her feet into bedside slippers, switched off the television, and opened the door. Over her shoulder, she said, "I'm going to get some water."

She heard Addison's voice when she hit the landing and would have gone back upstairs if their eyes hadn't met.

"So, Quentin, what d'you think of the new chapters? God rest her soul, Emily didn't have a chance to scan them before she…"

Whatever Quentin said prompted tinkling laughter that sounded like wind chimes gone mad before Addison lowered her voice. "Quentin, darling, you are the absolute limit."

The Chinese roast chicken they'd had for dinner curdled in Alecia's stomach, and a sour belch erupted behind her hand. She walked into the kitchen, drank some water, and filled the glass to take back to the room. Her hand was unsteady, so a little of the water spilled on the countertop. She wiped the droplets with a hand towel while anger bubbled in her chest.

Alecia took the job with Addison for her own reasons but still rued the day Casey pointed her to that online ad for an opening on a team of well-paid writers and the promise that it would change her life. That part was true. Making it through the interview gave her the proximity to Addison she didn't know she would come to crave. Her money went much further, but her peace of mind had fled.

As she stepped into the living room, Addison chuckled softly. She twirled a lock of hair around her finger, threw it over her shoulder, and walked through the door toward the pool. Her comment floated on the still night air. "…and you don't know what you're missing."

Alecia wanted to wring her scrawny neck. Wasn't it enough that she was already sleeping with two other members of the team? Why did she need Quentin, too? He'd take Jesus off His cross and say he wasn't involved with Addison, but he'd be lying.

Huffing on the way upstairs, Alecia asked herself why she was holding on to Quentin. Aside from adoring him, she couldn't have enough of his lovemaking. Apparently, Addison needed it, too.

Something had to shift. She'd been lax with her plans since joining the team, but the second she landed in Orlando, that would change.

CHAPTER 3

ADDISON

RUDDERLESS. IN A word, that's how she felt. Like a ship that lost its captain in the middle of a voyage. How dare Emily die on her? The old bat knew she was allergic to everything. Why didn't she take better care of herself? It was creepy being in this villa where she'd dropped dead.

She'd need company tonight. Erik or Jon would do.

While pacing the airy living room decorated with overstuffed sofas and colorful paintings, she barked orders at Piper Jennings, her executive assistant. "Find her relatives or her daughter. Contact Rachel and Theo."

Her publicity team would know how to handle this tragedy. Smoothing her hair with one hand, she continued, "I will speak with Theo myself. We need to release a statement once we locate Emily's people. We have two more nights in this place, but if the authorities will let us go tomorrow, book the first flight out."

She sank on the sofa and stared at Piper, who nodded and sat with her pen poised. Her black hair, pale face, and deep-blue eyes made her seem gaunt, especially with that black bag she called a dress swinging around her knees. Her gaze was watchful, but for once, her focus made Addison nervous. The men and alcohol wouldn't do tonight. She needed one of her pills. It would help her sleep.

Tomorrow yawned ahead, and all she could clutch at was finishing the book, the one constant in life that kept her sane. Writing gave her purpose. Nothing else mattered.

She'd always believed Emily hated her, but she was loyal, and that mattered above everything else. Aside from that, Emily was an expert in the publishing business and gave excellent advice. Since they'd arrived, a local station had chased her down for an interview and sent their questions, but Emily warned her about being blindsided and advised against doing it. Addison was inclined to accept because any publicity was good, leading up to the release of her next book.

A drumbeat behind her eyes made her want to scream. She didn't know what to do about anything that needed her attention. Her helplessness fueled her anger.

What did they do when people died in this godforsaken place? Should they make special arrangements to ship Emily back to America? Would the local authorities do an autopsy? The questions flowed together, confusing her.

"S–Should I contact the villa owner to ask him what to do?"

She latched onto Piper's hesitant question as though it were a lifeline. "Yes. That sounds like a plan."

"Okay. I'll figure out what he can handle and let him do it."

With a dismissive flick of the wrist, Addison closed her eyes. "Fine."

The team was still in the dining room, but she doubted they were writing. If they didn't have a deadline, she wouldn't care. No matter what happened, the story had to continue. Nothing stopped because death had visited them. Her publisher wouldn't understand if she didn't have a book to show for the months she'd been in creative mode. With a renewed sense of purpose, she opened her eyes.

Piper had left the room, and as Addison stood, the low hum of voices traveled from the dining room. They knew better than to be lollygagging, rather than writing. A glance at the ugly metal clock with bronze tentacles spreading across the wall told her it was almost nine o'clock. The vehicle from the morgue had been and gone. She didn't know what to do with herself, but that couldn't last long.

A flurry of steps took her into the dining room, where the lifeblood of her writing had pooled and stopped. The team members spoke in whispers to each other, neglecting the work she was paying them to do. If Emily hadn't been so selfish, they would have been wrapping up by now. There was nothing else to do but have them continue.

When she cleared her throat, the group of five raised their heads. "Emily may have left us, but you still have an hour's worth of work to finish."

She ignored their gasps and the eyes that pegged her as the spawn of the devil. "It will be good for everyone," she added as a finger of remorse stabbed her. "Emily would have wanted us to finish today's assignment."

None of them spoke, and their gazes returned to their laptop screens. Another few seconds went by before the clacking of their keypads resumed. She paced the room to be certain they understood she was serious. If she left, they might slack off, although each of them needed to produce a complete chapter for assessment. Emily selected the best prose from each writer, and Piper compiled their work in a fresh file before Addison laid eyes on it.

Everyone except Emily thought her modus operandi was weird, not to mention extra, but Addison was able to produce top-shelf books each time because she had refined her process. Only the best prose went into each chapter and landed in the final manuscript. She didn't mind paying Ellen and Piper to finetune what the others produced. With Emily dropping dead, Addison had to make adjustments to keep the production line moving.

As she passed behind Jon, a handsome ex-footballer with smooth, mahogany skin, she trailed a hand over his shoulder and leaned in to whisper, "You'll have to take over the editing and then hand it over to Quentin."

He nodded and continued typing.

Since she didn't want him worn out and unable to concentrate on this evening's chapters when tomorrow came, her focus went to Erik.

He avoided looking her way, no doubt hoping it would change the situation. The momentary hesitation before he hit the spacebar and the sudden flush to his skin gave him away. A spiteful smile curved her lips when Erik finally raised his head.

His nostrils flared. He'd likely guessed her intention. One thing was sure, Erik had no love for her. That was too bad because she didn't care.

The port hadn't dulled the memory of seeing Emily face down on the pages she'd been editing when her heart gave out.

After Addison shrieked at Erik and Jon to lift her off the table, all they achieved by propping her on the back of the chair was a macabre display. Emily's mouth was a gaping maw that advertised the obvious. Jon had gently tried to close her jaw, but it refused to stay shut.

"Put her in the bedroom. One of you needs to give her mouth to mouth." Addison didn't name anyone when she snapped, "Did someone call the housekeeper or the houseman? Any of them will do."

Both men grimaced as they hoisted Emily from the chair.

Addison marched behind them and opened the door to Emily's room.

When they laid her on the bed, Addison asked, "Who's it gonna be?"

Jon exchanged an inscrutable look with Erik before putting an ear to Emily's mouth. Next, he picked up her wrist to check her pulse. After an interval, he laid it at her side. "That won't be necessary. She's gone."

"Are you sure?"

He didn't answer, and Addison let that bit of insolence slide because of the situation. Jon would know when someone was dead since he'd taken a CPR course. Emily was thorough and ensured that at least two team members knew how to save a life, if it ever became necessary. Pity nobody got the chance to keep her alive.

Now, Addison had to deal with the complications Emily had caused by dying here instead of waiting until they were back in Orlando, including the police.

Addison sighed and raised the glass for another sip, wishing her mind would stay in the present. Her phone pinged, and she would have ignored it, except it reminded her that doing tonight by herself wasn't an option. She opened the screen, barely glanced at the message from her publicist, and dialed Erik. When he finally answered, she kept her tone sweet. "I need to see you. Now."

Taking longer than necessary, he finally entered the suite and stopped short of the bedroom. His muscular body was exactly what she needed. Her libido went into overdrive, although he wore an ordinary gray tee shirt and sweat bottoms of the same color. The hostility oozing from him was palpable.

"Shut the door."

He did, with a backward kick, and remained in the same spot knowing she wouldn't extend a special invitation. Erik could sulk all he wanted, but she wasn't having it. Yesterday was dead, and he ought to get over it.

Addison sauntered up to him, slipped both hands under his tee shirt and met his lips. The kiss she laid on him was long and deep. She gyrated against his hips to put him in the mood faster. She bit his lip, and he let out a yelp that didn't deter her. His response was lukewarm, so she tweaked his nipples hard. Then, with both arms around his neck, she drew him in for another kiss, but nothing happened where it mattered.

Two more minutes of his non-responsiveness, and she stepped back but kept her hold on him. "What's the matter?"

"I don't know." He shrugged. "Guess I must be tired."

She would have believed him, but for the mocking edge to his voice. Two could play, so she led him to the bed. "Get in."

In a teasing display, she eased out of her wrap and climbed on top of him. She helped him undress and let her fingers do everything guaranteed to prime him for their romp, but he remained flaccid. Ten minutes of hard work for nothing made her mad. She propped herself on one elbow to stare him in the face. "Was it what I said to you last night?"

He stared at her, pokerfaced. "Which part?"

She'd said many things, but she didn't owe him an explanation. He worked for her, not the other way around. She clasped him in one hand, kneading him with all the expertise she'd gathered with her many lovers. Her reward was a sticky palm, and she'd only brought him halfway to life—a state that still wouldn't get the job done.

Her breath whooshed from her chest as she fell on the mattress. "Get out."

Erik lay still, and Addison thought she'd have to repeat herself. When she opened her mouth again, he grabbed his clothing, pulled them on, and left.

The door closed, and one hand settled between her thighs, but she was too outraged to finish the job Erik should have done. She was Addison Comstock and shouldn't have to pleasure herself when she had several men available. She changed her mind about ringing Jon, but the phone buzzed and took the decision from her.

Her publicist had sent a message. *Don't cancel tomorrow's interview. You may have to do some damage control. Check your email.*

CHAPTER 4

CASEY

"ARE YOU ACCUSING me of something?" Casey asked, tipping one eyebrow. Her heart thundered while the policeman studied her the way a scientist would examine a newly discovered species.

"I didn't say that." Detective Barham glanced at his tiny spiral notepad, then asked, "Do you have family on the island?"

She forced herself not to assume a defensive pose by folding both hands in her lap. "Why do you ask?"

"Something in your accent."

"Yes." Casey shifted on the ugly leather seat. "My grandmother lives here."

"And have you visited her since you arrived?"

"No. I haven't had the chance as yet."

The slight movement of his eyebrows gave away his opinion, which she ignored. He had no right to judge her, especially since he didn't know her circumstances. She wanted to see Gran more than anything, but Addison had made that impossible for now.

Detective Barham exchanged a glance with the silent detective who'd been watching her when he wasn't scanning the study Addison had taken over since their arrival. Rows of what Casey guessed were romance novels and stacks of lifestyle magazines filled the shelves that stood between two windows.

The second officer, whose name she hadn't caught, leaned forward in the seat next to hers. "I understand you're a writer."

"All of us in this villa are, as I'm sure you know."

After pinning her gaze with his, he asked, "I also understand you had reason to handle Ms. Smalling's inhaler. Why?"

She slowed her breathing and shrugged. "I moved it out of the way when I tried to help Emily."

"Was that the only time you came in contact with it?"

"Of course. What other reason would I have to touch it?"

He had nothing to match her fingerprints against, and it would take time to get information from Orlando, so the policeman was toying with her for his own reasons. After locking her into an unnerving stare-down, he said, "Please give your account of what happened yesterday evening."

The memory of Emily's pale face and sagging jaw rattled Casey, and she closed her eyes. When she opened them, she clutched the pendant at her throat and told the policeman every detail she remembered.

Detective Barham scribbled on the pad at intervals, then tapped it with the pen. "Until we have confirmation from Ms. Smalling's doctor about her condition, you cannot leave the island."

The pounding in Casey's head prevented her from hearing his next words, but she caught on when he flipped the pad shut. "…rule out an autopsy."

"You do know we have lives in Orlando, right?"

His partner's gaze cut to her, and he frowned. "Death is serious business, Ms. Mitchell."

"I never said it wasn't. I only meant we're on a schedule."

"If we find there has been foul play, your schedule won't matter." A half-smile came before his next string of words, which were meant to provoke. "And there's the grandmother you haven't visited."

He waited, expecting her to comment, but she stayed silent and willed herself not to break into a sweat.

"You're free to go." Detective Barham stood, as did his partner. "Our instruction goes for the entire team. None of you is at liberty to step on a plane."

Standing, she cleared her throat. "How long before we hear back from you?"

"Shouldn't be more than a couple of days."

"Thank you."

When she turned the door handle, he said, "Please ask Ms. Comstock to come back in for a second."

Casey nodded and left the room, warning herself to be careful. The policemen might work in a tourist town, but both were focused and observant.

Addison met her coming out of the dining room, and Casey paused. "The officers want a word with you before they go."

Glancing at her watch, Addison sucked her teeth. "I have an interview in a few minutes. What more do they want from me?"

Her question wasn't directed at Casey who slipped into her seat, relieved to be rid of Addison, if only for a few minutes. The others continued typing as though everything was normal, but of course, they would. Their consciences were clear, and they had already talked to the police.

Emily's death had rattled Addison, but she'd seemingly recovered overnight. Though pale and drawn, she still maintained enough normality to drive the team without mercy.

That she-devil cared about no one. They had a couple of days to go and barely had time to sample the pool or walk down the beach. The one dip Casey took was early in the morning. "Before the cock put on his drawers" was how her grandmother referred to ungodly hours.

Casey smiled, though her heart was heavy. Gran would flay her alive if she didn't come to visit before getting back on a plane, which was a distinct possibility. And it was a good thing her bestie hadn't been able to make the trip. Rochelle would have been livid if she came and Casey was locked away writing all day. Because of work, they barely saw each other, but were still as tight as when they were children.

She'd barely laid her hands on the keyboard before Addison appeared with the phone to her ear. "Yes. Let me get comfortable. Thanks for calling back. I do appreciate it."

Any other person would have found somewhere else to speak with the media. Not Addison. She parked herself at the far end of the table with her legs crossed and fabric from the sheer, white skirt draped over her ankle. Not far enough to prevent them from overhearing the small talk and interview.

With one hand, she invaded the dish of assorted chocolates on the table and cushioned the phone between her head and shoulder as she popped one into her mouth. She was diabetic, but no one would know based on her consumption of candy and chocolate.

"I've been in the game for a while with an extensive catalog, but I stay on top of trends and keep my writing fresh."

Casey and Alecia looked up from their screens at the same time and pursed their lips to avoid grinning at Addison's rehearsed response. A peek at the corner of her screen told Casey she was behind on her word count. She had to write faster if she didn't want to be at the receiving end of a rant.

"I don't know where you got that information," Addison snapped, "but I have no connection with anyone here. All my close family members left the island years ago. I saw to that."

Casey paid closer attention, but continued typing.

When Addison placed one foot on the floor, she also lowered her voice. "Yes. I self-published my first few books. None of it was work that belonged to anyone else. Where did you hear that rubbish?"

She went silent, then rose and stood with her back to them. "It would suit you to do proper fact-checking. Let me speak with your editor. If this is the way you do business here, I don't want any part of it. How dare you cast aspersions on my character and work?"

Casey didn't raise her head or act like she'd heard anything extraordinary, but it was challenging to hide a smirk. The conversation had slowed her considerably, so she typed a few sentences, then shot a glance at Alecia, who was too still not to be listening. Letting her gaze bounce between the laptop and Alecia's face, Casey reminded her to keep typing. Alecia winked and picked up the pace.

Addison deserved every bit of bad fortune coming to her. She'd made their stay here miserable with random interruptions and unreasonable demands for more chapters. At the rate they were churning out sentences, their bodies would suffer from the strenuous pace. This wanton cruelty was made worse by sitting at the table where Emily had died.

Aside from her, Casey didn't know anyone who could vouch for the quality of Addison's writing. As crazy as the thought was, her meanness made Casey wonder if she had any talent left and whether she'd had any at the start of her career.

Based on what she pieced together from snatches of conversation, plus articles she'd found, Addison had started her stable after her fifth book blew up.

The same book she'd stolen and was now being questioned about.

When Casey first called her grandmother with the news that she'd landed a job working for Addison, the older woman had asked if she was mad.

"That serpent cost yuh mother her life," she squawked.

Gran's mixture of English and patois confirmed how upset she'd been. Her loud protest jarred Casey, who'd gripped the phone tighter.

Gently, she said, "Which is why I should get close to her. Learn exactly what she did to be where she is now. As you would say, the secrets are at the head of the stream, not where it flows into the sea."

A weird silence fell between them, then Gran sighed and made a ticking sound in her throat. "I will never understand young people. Be careful. She's like a snake that won't hesitate to poison yuh wid one bite. Don't t'ink she won't do it if she knows who yuh are."

"Don't worry. I'll be careful." She'd scanned the living area of the two-bedroom house she called home, then rested her head on the back of the sofa. Her throat ached, and tears flooded her eyes. Hardly a day passed that she didn't remember her mother, whom she'd adored. Losing her early was devastating, but life grew tougher from that point. Learning to navigate challenging situations taught her how to cope during the worst of times.

"Where did you dig up that shit?"

Addison's harsh whisper woke Casey from her mental fog. She backspaced and deleted the last sentence she'd typed, then peered at the outline on her right as though to decide what to add to the scene. Addison's discomfort was so satisfying, though. Try as she might, Casey couldn't make sense of the lines of text on the paper.

In a sudden motion, Addison whipped around to face the room and jabbed the phone screen. "Piper, when I'm done with this call, I'll need to speak with Rachel and Theo. In the study."

Piper's head bobbed as she rose from her seat. "Okay. Got it."

Addison's agent and publicist were about to have a month's worth of work thrown at them. She touched the screen again and stepped outside. "Are you there?" After listening for a couple of seconds, she said, "None of it is true. If you print even a hint of that trash about me, I will sue you *and* that rinky-dink newspaper."

Addison realized how close to the building she stood and walked around the pool to sink on a lounger in the shade.

She raised her head, and Casey focused on her keyboard. Not that her words made much sense. She bit the inside of her cheek, but a smile she couldn't hide refused to stay away.

Addison had a chink in her armor, and she'd found it. A bit late in the day, but this information was useful. By taking them to the island, Addison had given Casey the perfect jumpstart to her plan. Much like plotting a story, she'd outlined the relevant details. All that remained was to pull the threads together.

Her mother's face floated before her, and Casey blinked to refocus. When she cleared her throat and wound her head in a circle, Addison was staring at her.

Fixing her attention on Casey, she stalked around the pool and stopped when she stood in the dining room. "Since you have nothing to do, why don't you tell me why my business is so fascinating?"

Casey's jaw trembled with the effort it took not to stutter as she said, "I wasn't listening to you. Just lost my concentration for a second."

"I'm not paying you to daydream." Addison spat, then pointed toward Casey's face. "Your chapter had better be tight, or you'll be here till midnight catching up."

She was serious, too, but Casey would be damned if she let Addison get the best of her. The time was coming when she'd pay for every threat, every slight, every abuse she'd heaped on them. Everything she was fussing about now would pale in comparison to her comeuppance.

CHAPTER 5

ALECIA

EMILY IS PROBABLY on this flight.

It was one thing for her to die at the villa, which was creepy enough, but to be on the same flight with a dead body didn't bear thinking about. Still, Emily was out of her misery. The same couldn't be said for any of them who'd had to live with Addison's madness.

Alecia cracked a smile. Things were bad when she could envy the dead. One blessing was not having to sit with the team, especially Casey, who they'd been forced to leave on the island. Sometimes she was too much.

Addison's interview had jolted Alecia, and she wasn't ready to deal with her reaction after mulling over some of what she'd heard. Nor did she want to explain why she'd snapped at Casey last night for no good reason. Some things were best kept to herself. For now.

She leaned against the headrest and closed her eyes as the captain gave an update on the weather. The deep breathing she'd been practicing helped settle her mind, until her thoughts turned to Quentin and her favorite fantasy—being at the altar with him, then having his baby. Then the constant niggle in the form of Addison came back to haunt her.

The flight captain's announcement woke Alecia from a half-awake, half-dream state.

"To those visiting for the first time, welcome to Orlando, and for those returning home, welcome back."

Alecia stretched as far as she could and sat up. The doze she fell into was exactly what she needed to avoid the minefield of her thoughts. As she waited for the passengers to retrieve their carry-on, she took her phone off airplane mode. Several messages came in, along with one from Piper to remind them that Addison expected them at seven sharp tomorrow morning.

The woman never let up.

Alecia hung back as people hurried toward customs. If she wasn't processed with the group, she couldn't offer anybody a ride, although she figured they'd all made arrangements for pickup. The shuttle bus from the parking service was approaching by the time she stood outside the airport.

By nature, Alecia wasn't sociable, and on her own, she retreated into herself. Somewhat content, she avoided eye contact with the people who boarded behind her and stared through the window.

Twenty minutes later, she'd lugged her suitcases into her one-bedroom condo in the South Semoran neighborhood. Her home was the same as she'd left it, and she smiled and inhaled deeply when she stepped inside. This was her usual response to the biggest achievement in her life. The other was being part of Addison's team, but she'd gotten over that quickly, and with good reason.

Another ten minutes, and she was in and out of the shower. A half-hour took care of her cosmetics and clothing, then she did a slow spin in front of the mirror. Her sundress was appropriate and could come off with ease. A hint of makeup graced her face.

She was ready for a reunion, but couldn't leave without pulling one of her scrapbooks from the closet. The pictures were a bad idea. They would sour her mood, but she couldn't help feeding what had turned into an obsession. Each photo was a stab to the stomach and spiked her blood to boiling point. Breathing hard, she forced herself to close the book and return it to the shelf. Then tipping her head back, she blinked hard to avoid smearing her makeup and reminded herself to breathe.

In. Out. In. Out. You can do this.

Her mind spun in circles as she rehearsed what she wanted to say to Quentin, that's if she could get past the part where she fell into his bed to make up for the time away.

The minute she parked in front of the two-story building, she flung the door of the SUV open and almost put a dent in the silver paintwork on his Camry. Laughing at herself, she slipped the tote on her shoulder and locked the vehicle. Then she released a bitter chuckle. She'd made the ten-minute trip in seven and almost fell out of the RAV-4 in her eagerness to see a man who wouldn't commit.

The modest two-bedroom unit suited Quentin's personality. He was good-looking, but not flashy. Mostly calm, but not boring. And in the bedroom, that saying about still waters running deep was true. They clicked on every level, which was why she believed he was the one. Quentin didn't seem ready or willing to admit it.

She rapped on the door, and if she hadn't been ecstatic at seeing him, his lackluster smile would have registered. Arms flung around him, she breathed in a strong whiff of the two-hundred-dollar-per-bottle Deep Dark Vanilla—one of the few pleasures he splurged on. The earthy cypress and patchouli notes quickened her blood, and she grabbed the waistband of his sweatpants. She pulled his head down to hers for a lengthy kiss and moved in so close that not even air could pass between them. At first, he matched her heated response until he held her away by both arms. "Hey. I'd love to, but I can't."

Her eyebrows crumpled. "What?"

Quentin ran a hand over his bristly hair and refused to move out of the doorway. "Addison sent me the stuff you guys worked on over the past week and asked me to edit it."

He had a good eye with editing, but his explanation made no sense, so she asked, "Weren't you also writing and submitting your chapters from here?"

Nodding, Quentin tousled the hair at the back of his head, raising it into jagged spikes. "Since Emily passed, Addison bumped me up, so I've been editing more."

Hands to her hips, Alecia said, "So, you're taking Emily's place, not Jon?"

"For the moment." Quentin shrugged. "Who knows how Addison's mind works?"

She *did* know. Matter of fact, they both knew, but she wanted to find out how far he'd take this madness. "So, remind me again why, after a week apart, I can't come into your apartment?"

His hand went back to his hair, a sure sign he was uncomfortable. Funny, the things she noticed when she bothered to pay attention. "*Uh,* she wants me to return some edits to her in an hour."

"This is some BS. You know that, right?" She barreled past him into the living room, where papers covered the dining table in the far corner.

He didn't close the door, but followed and faced her. "This isn't how I want things to be, but you know when Addison says jump—"

"You lower your tail and ask how high." Her tone and words were nasty, but she didn't care. She'd had enough. "Another man would leap at the opportunity to make love to the woman he hasn't seen in a week, but you prefer to work for a witch who would fire you in a moment if the mood took her."

He eased both hands into his pockets. "Alecia, you're being dramatic. You know how demanding she is *and* that I must finish this stuff."

"You always have an excuse for the shit she does." She waited a beat, then added, "I'm tired of it."

Sighing, he sat at the table in front of his laptop. "This is counterproductive. Meantime, the minutes are ticking by."

It was foolish to believe Addison did this to keep them apart, yet the notion settled in Alecia's brain. They had been careful to maintain their professionalism at work, which was a waste of time. Addison was draining the life from their relationship and the children Alecia longed to conceive.

She watched him while her thoughts churned. He'd said nothing about later in the evening when he finished this stint, and that cut like a sharp blade. Alecia approached him as her throat tightened, but she swallowed her frustration and her tears. "What about later?"

Quentin didn't move or turn from the screen. "We can chill out then."

"By that time I might be gone, and that could mean for good, Quentin."

He stood, nostrils flaring and his narrowed eyes flashing. "Don't threaten me."

Several snappy responses came to mind, but she didn't spout any of them. The fire in his gaze went deeper than this conversation. He was angry about something.

His passion excited her, yet she didn't know how to feel about this weird push and pull between them.

Did he believe Addison could fire him if he didn't finish the chapters she'd sent over to keep him occupied?

Alecia wasn't prepared to lose after a week, with mere dashes of hope to fill a journey to hell and back. She marched into the bathroom and removed her dress and lingerie, then released her hair and let it fall around her shoulders. She might be conflicted, but she wasn't above fighting dirty to keep Quentin—or his attention.

She slipped back into the living room, where he'd closed the door and sat hunched over several sheets of paper. With a feather she'd removed from his bedroom closet, she teased the back of his neck. He slapped at his skin, and she moved into his line of sight.

Quentin pulled in a sharp breath, but before he could object, she straddled him and slid her hand inside his waistband. As she covered his lips with hers, and he responded with a groan, a satisfied purr emerged from her throat. She'd been denied long enough.

Addison would have to wait.

CHAPTER 6

ADDISON

"THIS COULD DESTROY everything I've built."

Addison paced the length of the plate-glass windows that let in brilliant sunlight and offered a panoramic view of downtown Orlando. Eight o'clock was early for her, but she couldn't wait any longer for this meeting with her agent.

They had spoken about Emily's passing, and Rachel had opened the paper to the page with the obituary. Addison hadn't spoken with Emily's daughter, but Rachel had contacted her and would take care of any payment owed to Emily for her services and any vacation time she hadn't taken.

"You're making me dizzy." Rachel laid down the newspaper. "I haven't had my first cup of coffee. Where is that boy, Vance?"

The "boy" in question was a brawny thirty-year-old looker. If Addison didn't know Rachel's tastes ran along the paler side of life, she might have thought she had a soft spot for her assistant. She also preferred them young, but didn't indulge herself the way Addison did. He was new and certainly worth considering. His milk-chocolate skin and neat goatee made her fingertips tingle to stroke it, but her mind was on business today.

As if he'd heard his name, Vance walked into the room carrying two cardboard cups. "One Irish and one black."

He handed a cup to Rachel and set the other on the desk for Addison. How anyone could have coffee diluted with condiments so early in the day boggled her mind. She liked hers black and strong enough to take away the taste of all the vices she'd indulged in the previous night. That scenario didn't apply today.

She was on edge, perhaps because she'd slept alone, thanks to needing time to think and strategize. She'd been careful over the years with her literary life—zero scandals and no messy publicity—but what she'd forgotten now threatened to wreck her career.

"Thanks." They both spoke as Vance stepped away and closed the door.

Rachel sipped from the cup, set it aside, and rested both arms on the desk. "So, apart from Emily, what has you so worked up at this hour?"

Huffing, Addison fell into the seat in front of Rachel's monstrous walnut desk. The curved feet reminded her of a bow-legged man well past his prime, and the black glass on top made her think of murky water. Two overstuffed sofas, large oil paintings of speckled foliage, and plush carpeting advertised Rachel's success. As did the wall lined with enlarged book covers featuring award labels.

Addison sipped the coffee, then pulled her purse from the other visitor's chair into her lap. She unfolded the scanned document she'd printed and slid it across the desk. "This."

The glass clock on the wall, with its black face and giant gold letters, mocked Addison. The muted ticking of the second hand made her feel they were counting down to something unpleasant. Her gaze shifted to Rachel, who pulled in a harsh breath.

Her resemblance to Emily hit Addison. Both women were in their sixties, carried themselves well, and wore pixie haircuts. But where Emily had thickened around the middle, Rachel was svelte, thanks to her regular morning routine at the gym. A tinge of guilt came over Addison. Emily hadn't had that luxury because of their schedule.

"How did you come by this?" Rachel asked, lowering the sheet with an unsteady hand.

Addison swallowed to clear the obstruction that sat in her throat, but crossed her legs as if unbothered. "It came in my email yesterday."

"Did they ask for anything?"

"All it said was that it's time to pay."

"Forward it to me." Her intense hazel irises darkened as she continued, "I can have someone track down the IP address."

Addison came close to snorting, but didn't. The slight nausea in her stomach wouldn't allow her to act as though the message hadn't rattled her. "I doubt whoever sent it was stupid enough to leave a trail of breadcrumbs."

"I know that. Forward the email to me anyway."

"Sure." After clearing her throat, Addison asked, "What's the plan for damage control from this past week?"

Frowning, Rachel protested, "I think you're making more of this gossip—"

"Don't treat me like some idiot having a case of the vapors." Pressing a hand to her heart, she continued, "I feel in here there's more to come. There's malice behind that piece of paper. Plus, those pointed questions from that…that wanna-be journalist in Jamaica didn't spring up from nowhere. Someone is driving this campaign against me."

"I understand how you feel, but—"

"No, you *don't*." Addison ground her teeth together, then pulled in a breath and relaxed her jaw. "Your career isn't on the line. Mine is. If my life goes down the toilet, you still have other clients. I'll have nothing."

Rachel eased forward in her chair. "In case you forgot, I gave you the nondisclosure agreement you needed for *that* deal to happen."

"But you're not the one in the line of fire."

Laying both hands on the leather desk pad, Rachel met her gaze. "Let's analyze the situation."

She leaned back in the seat. "We don't know that the person who sent this is doing anything more than bluffing about something they may or may not have. Secondly, there's that nondisclosure agreement."

"What if this isn't from anyone connected to *her*, but someone who somehow got hold of…" She couldn't bring herself to name the document they'd both manipulated to her benefit.

"Didn't you tell me you had the only copy?"

"Yes. She promised me, and I believed because of her situation."

Rachel's disbelieving stare made Addison cringe. Her words sounded like those of someone with no experience in the business world. She'd seen plenty since making a name for herself, including people getting close to her for their benefit and casting aspersions on her, so they would seem decent while leaving her reputation in the mud.

"Okay. Let's work with the assumption that there *may* be a copy of the manuscript somewhere out there. What's the worst that can happen?"

Addison sank lower in the seat and hugged herself, suddenly cold. She refused to imagine the repercussions from any such scenario. Still, she choked out, “It would be a disaster.”

“Is there anyone who could fight you in court over royalties?”

She cast her mind back to the dignified old woman with the smoldering eyes. She was likely dead by now. Her grief hadn’t been obvious while they’d completed their transaction, but it was there, a third presence in the shabby living room.

A watery memory snatched at the edges of her mind, and she squinted until the picture cleared—the whole time she’d been inside that rundown house, two skinny girls who resembled each other peeked at her from the doorway.

She’d ignored them, amused by the way they stared at her through long, frizzy plaits that hung around their faces. No doubt, they’d never been that close to someone well-dressed and educated. Even then, Addison understood how to carry herself as though she had influence and power. Back then, she’d been writing her own books and hoping to make it big someday.

Rachel opened a file, and the movement brought Addison back into the room.

“I don’t think so,” was her belated response to Rachel’s question.

“Theo should be here in another ten minutes.” Rachel nodded, as though they’d reached an agreement. “We can go over strategies to keep your name in the spotlight. In a good way, of course. Maybe some teasers on *Murder by the Book* and what readers can expect. I’ll see if the publishing house will do a giveaway of some kind—something significant that readers will love. If they won’t do it, I’m sure they won’t mind us organizing a give back to your readers. If we send pre-orders through the roof and put you on a list early, they’ll be happy.”

“I’m sure.”

Someone rapped on the door and waited several seconds before opening it. Vance stepped inside and held out a fat manila envelope. "Package for Ms. Comstock."

Her gaze shot to Rachel's before she accepted the mail. It might be nothing out of the ordinary. After all, Rachel's office had received her business correspondence for years. She searched for a postmark, but didn't see one. She wet her lips, then smiled as Rachel anticipated her request and slid a letter opener across the glass.

Addison picked it up, inserted it under the flap of the envelope, and slit it open. She peeked inside, knowing people did the unthinkable for attention. Addison had received countless chapters and manuscripts from hopefuls wanting to put their books in her hands, believing for a breakthrough. She'd also received articles intended to smear her reputation and question the quality of her stories and writing. And sometimes, threats also came.

She eased the sheaf of papers onto her lap, and a chill spread through her body. A copy of the same title page that came in her email now lay in her lap. She flipped the leaf, and a scan of the next sheet confirmed she held in her hands the original manuscript for her first bestseller, *Games People Play*.

A page was missing. The one that could ruin her life.

CHAPTER 7

CASEY

SHE WALKED INTO the sunshine, more at ease than she'd been in the last four hours. While she sat in the Montego Bay airport waiting to board the flight home, every nerve in her body was stretched tight. A continuous reel played in her head. Detective Barham and his partner appearing with handcuffs among the hordes of people to grab her for more questioning.

Nothing of the sort happened, but she remained on edge. Anyone would, after being "advised" by the local police not to leave the island. All because she'd touched that inhaler.

Addison hadn't hesitated to leave her behind, but Casey expected nothing different. All she'd offered was a promise to pick up the phone if the situation turned sticky, but they both understood Casey was on her own if she was officially detained.

Donnette, her sister, honked the horn in Casey's Honda Civic and waved to catch her attention. She scrambled from the car and let out an undignified squeal as she hugged Casey tight and tweaked her fuzzy ponytail. When she stepped back, Casey smoothed the hair, which wouldn't stay flat, no matter what she did with it.

"I missed you more than I figured I would," Donnette said.

"I missed you, too, sis."

"You're lying," Donnette threw over her shoulder as she opened the trunk of the car and hefted the suitcase inside. "Once you were with Gran, you forgot about me."

"I did not." Casey tugged one of Donnette's twists and headed for the passenger seat, hoping she wouldn't have to dodge any awkward questions. Her last few days in Jamaica brought back unpleasant memories, though she'd enjoyed the time with their grandmother.

As they pulled away from the sidewalk, Donnette asked, "Are you going to tell me what kept you in Jamaica?"

"What d'you mean? I said I'd be there a few more days."

Donnette didn't pull her gaze from the road as she shrugged. "The others came back before you, that's all."

"How d'you know that?"

"Alecia has been posting on social media."

"Hmmm." She turned on the radio, then closed her eyes. If she pretended to be tired, maybe Donnette wouldn't ask more questions.

"…an interview I want us to catch."

"Huh?" Casey rolled her head and opened one eye.

"I said…never mind. You'll see when we get home."

"Fine."

The hum of the engine soothed her, and some minutes later, Casey sat up when Donnette squeezed her arm. "Wake up, sleepyhead."

Yawning, she got out to stretch in their front yard. The two-bedroom house in Pine Hills was the best investment they had made, and Casey loved every corner of it. She and Donnette had improved their home each month over the past couple of years. Donnette took care of the garden, and Casey decided on the décor, which satisfied their personal preferences.

After she wheeled her suitcase inside and dumped her handbag and carry-on in the bedroom, Casey peeled off her shirt. She was almost inside the bathroom when Donnette yelled, "Come on. I saved this so we could watch it together."

"What, the interview?" Casey asked as she backtracked to grab her shirt, then perched on the arm of the large sofa in the living room. "Why is it so urgent?"

"*Shh.* It's with Addison."

A familiar logo slid to the center of the screen, and Casey bit one side of her lip. Addison had done this interview while in Jamaica.

"I saw some of it while I was home," Casey said, sliding onto the cushion next to Donnette. The truth was, she'd seen the entire thing.

"Well, I haven't."

"Tell me why I have to watch this now?"

"*Because.*" With a dramatic eye-roll, Donnette added, "We'll both get busy and forget."

Casey raised both hands in surrender while Donnette fidgeted with her laptop, which she'd connected to the television, and increased the volume.

The host on the Jamaican cable station greeted and introduced Addison, then exchanged small talk in the first couple of minutes. Her smooth hair, pulled into a bun at her nape, emphasized her flawless, deep-caramel complexion.

"Shall we begin? I'm told your family's originally from Jamaica. Is that so?"

"Yes, in this very parish." Addison cheesed the way she did whenever she boasted about helping her relatives. "But none of them live here anymore."

Addison and the interviewer sat facing each other at a horseshoe-shaped desk. The station's logo provided a colorful backdrop, but didn't overpower either woman.

"What would you say to your local fans about your success?" The hostess stared into the camera. "Specifically, those who want a career in writing?"

"Learn the craft. That way, you can earn a lucrative deal."

"And what about those hopefuls who are not sure who they can trust with their book babies?"

A frown creased Addison's brow and went so quickly, Casey would have missed it if she'd blinked. "I'd say go through the proper channels. As with everything else, there are always predators."

"Speaking of which, Ms. Comstock, there are people who believe you fall into that category."

Addison released a tense chuckle. "I'm sure you didn't bring me here to blindside me with accusations that have no basis in reality."

The hostess, who went by Jenny Z, glanced at the card in her hand. "Of course not, but if there's no truth to the stories, can you say why they have persisted?"

Addison sat straight in her seat. "You assume I know what stories you're talking about."

Jenny Z tipped her head to one side and smiled. "Surely you're not so insulated that you don't know what's being said about you on the internet?"

"I don't pay attention to naysayers and gossip, Miss..." Addison paused, pretending she'd forgotten the other woman's name.

Jenny Z quirked her lips but didn't respond to the slight. "To go back to the question—"

"Can we focus on something else, especially the book coming out next?"

"We'll come to that shortly. Our viewers appreciate hearing about the personal aspect of our guests' lives—"

"I'm here to talk about the book." Addison's smile was a grimace, and anger bubbled under the surface.

Casey identified the signs. Her boss's eyes flashed, but she held herself still to maintain control. Addison had served up a humiliating dose of her ire when she thought Casey was listening to her on the phone. It didn't take much to blow her hair-trigger temper.

The show cut to an insurance ad, then the station's logo came into focus. The interview had been recorded live and streamed on the internet concurrently. At the time, Casey texted Rochelle and told her where to find it online. She didn't think to include Donnette, guessing it would upset her too much. So much for that.

Donnette sucked her teeth and increased the volume again. "Bet if she understood it was a live interview, she wouldn't have gone."

Without looking away from the screen, Casey chuckled. "She'd have turned up, anyway."

"True. She loves the limelight."

Casey leaned in to catch the parts of the conversation she'd missed while texting with Rochelle when the interview first aired.

"Is it true that your first big break came from a project not written solely by you?"

The interviewer was good. Though the question could be considered accusatory or offensive, she kept a pleasant expression.

"*Nothing* is further from the truth. That book—"

"*Games People Play,*" Jenny Z supplied helpfully while shooting a glance at the card in front of her.

"Yes. That book came during the time I returned to Jamaica for a visit. I guess the island's beauty inspired me." Addison's smile was smug.

Casey wanted to slap the satisfaction off her face. Same as the first time she'd watched Addison lying. *The nerve!*

"What's interesting is the fact that *Games People Play* was the first mystery you wrote."

Although she nodded, Addison's expression was wary.

"Before that, you were writing romance, correct?"

"Yes, I was."

Jenny Z shifted, and the camera zeroed in on Addison. "What changed? How did you go from publishing a romance months before, to writing such a hard-hitting mystery? How did you hone those skills overnight?"

Addison laid one hand on top of the other and maintained a half-smile. "Well, I wouldn't say it was overnight."

"It certainly seemed that way. In fact..." Jenny Z shuffled the interview cards until she found the one she wanted. "Barely two months passed before you put out that other novel."

"And it took off like a rocket into space." Addison rested against her seat, a queen on a throne. "And look where it took me."

"Yes, indeed." Jenny Z smiled into the camera and continued, "We'll now take a break. Don't touch that dial. *Island Moods & Views* will return in a moment."

"That's exactly what I expected." Donnette rose from the sofa and sucked her teeth again. "She doesn't have one humble bone in her body."

As Donnette disappeared into the kitchen, Casey remembered she hadn't been able to sit still while watching Addison. She gave in and texted with her cousin, Michelle, a production assistant, who worked with the interviewer.

She'd responded in thirty seconds. *You worry too much. Everything will go as planned.*

When the show's logo flashed on the screen, Casey yelled, "They're back."

The two women remained in shadow until the theme music faded. Between them sat a black, circular device that wouldn't have seemed out of place on a spaceship.

Donnette took her seat while Jenny Z welcomed and updated the audience, then focused on Addison.

"There's talk that you met with an acquaintance and got hold of a manuscript you promised to assess so you could help with the publication process. It's said you didn't keep your word. Did you put that one aside to follow your own path, or did it help you further your career?"

Casey had never seen Addison rendered speechless and was as taken aback now as when she'd witnessed it last week.

Her silence lasted until she gathered herself and drew a breath. "Where did you hear that garbage? I want to know the source of that drivel."

Jenny Z laid a hand on her interview cards as if they held secrets. "My research team promised anonymity."

"Only a coward would throw accusations they cannot substantiate."

"I agree with you, but you know the nature of our program. We search for human-interest stories that affect our celebrity guests—"

"And damage their reputation," Addison spat through trembling lips.

"That is never our aim." Jenny Z straightened her cards and smiled at the camera. "It's your turn to interact with our guest.

Ask your questions and get the scoop from the horse's mouth—in a manner of speaking."

Her gaze returned to Addison. "Are you ready?"

She flashed a tight smile. "As ready as I'll ever be, but I have limits. There are certain questions about my writing I can't answer because of confidentiality clauses."

"We certainly understand that. The lines have been flashing for a while, so let's get to it." She reached toward the device on the desk and pressed a button. "Welcome, caller. Go right ahead."

"Hello. I'm an aspiring writer, and I want to ask Ms. Comstock about her process."

Addison leaned forward and clasped her hands. "Much has changed over the years, but now I employ a team to research and collaborate on all aspects of my stories—the setting, the timeline, the editing. Each team member deals with a specific area."

Casey and Donnette glanced at each other, amused by the canned response.

"Thank you. Can I ask one more question?"

"Certainly."

"That all sounds good, but people are saying you no longer do any of your writing, that your team does it all."

Addison wore a fixed grimace for a smile, but her eyes blazed. "There's no truth to that rumor. People will say anything to tear down others. Thank you for being a faithful fan."

"You're welcome."

"Let's take another call." The host pressed a button and allowed the person to speak.

"What would you say to those who want to follow their dreams, despite their limitations? For instance, we know you turned your back on your infant daughter and went off to America when you got your lucky break, and…"

Casey's breath caught while Addison sat as though carved from stone.

"Thank you, caller." Jenny Z addressed Addison, who put a hand to her throat then lowered it to the desk. "So, are you saying you still do *all* your writing? You've never really confirmed or denied that you do or don't. Plus, is there any truth to that question about a baby?"

Addison shot to her feet, her skin flushed and blotchy. "I'm ending this farce of a show. You'll be hearing from my lawyers."

The host closed out the segment by apologizing to the audience and moving to a KFC ad.

Frowning, Donnette motioned toward the screen and pressed the remote. "That's it?"

Before Casey could respond, Donnette's phone pinged. She grabbed it off the center table, swiped the screen, and squinted at it. In slow motion, she shifted sideways and held the phone out for Casey to see. "Look at this. Why is my sister on social media? You didn't tell me the police stopped you from coming back."

A shiver gripped her body, but Casey didn't move. *What the hell?*

Laying the phone aside, Donnette pulled in a deep breath. "Do not lie to me, Casey. What did you do?"

Nothing she said would satisfy her sister's curiosity, so Casey held her silence.

CHAPTER 8

ALECIA

EMILY'S DAUGHTER DIDN'T resemble her, aside from the stony set of her face. She was striking, with a blunt-cut bob framing her startling blue eyes. Marion resembled her brother, but he seemed older and even more self-absorbed. He continued checking his watch, making it obvious he didn't want to be in the chapel connected to the funeral home. And he had to make it through the burial.

The team attended, but wouldn't linger. Addison's frequent glances at her watch confirmed her obsession with the time they were losing, even though they were ahead of the delivery date, thanks to their slavish schedule. Since Emily's death, Addison filled the hours by being the worst version of herself.

Neither Quentin nor Jon had ever been as vicious with their editing pen as Emily, which was another reason for Addison to harass them.

"This book has to be perfect, which means rigorous editing," she'd bleated all week.

Aside from trashing their writing, she'd been gorging on sweets. Emily would have reminded her to stop trying to kill herself, but none of them dared break her almost manic consumption of chocolate-covered nuts. Her constant pacing set everyone's nerves on edge.

As soon as the officiator said, "Amen," Addison was on her feet. She hurried to where Marion stood and murmured in an apologetic tone.

A sneer twisted the other woman's face. "Emily gave you the last few years of her life and forgot she had a family, and you can't even wait for the ground to swallow her."

Addison reached out, but Marion sidestepped her hand and spoke over her shoulder. "Thank you for taking care of the arrangements. I'll give your apologies at the repast."

"Time to get back to the grind," Alecia whispered out of the side of her mouth.

Casey nodded and stood, smoothing her stylish gray pantsuit. "Let's go."

They walked toward the door with the other team members behind them. In the harsh glare of the Orlando sunlight, Casey tipped her head back before joining her inside the RAV-4. While she waited, Alecia turned on the radio, and lively salsa poured from the speakers.

Casey chuckled and settled her purse on her lap. "How you enjoy music you don't understand is beyond me."

"Music is universal." Alecia threw her scarf on the back seat. "The words don't matter. It's the beat that speaks to my bones and gets me moving."

Laughing, Casey waved one hand. "Whatever floats your boat."

The flippant comment made Alecia grin—until she spotted Addison getting into Quentin's Camry farther down the line of vehicles. The saliva dried in her mouth, and she grimaced as though she'd sucked on a lemon.

Casey glanced at her, then said, "I'd question it, except she's doing everything to ensure this book doesn't run behind schedule."

"Somehow, I didn't think she'd ever ride in that thing."

"It sounds as if she could catch a disease from being inside it."

A spiteful smile hovered around Alecia's mouth. "If those seats could tell what Quentin and I have done on them…"

"TMI, my friend. Keep that to yourself." Casey giggled with one hand over her mouth. "I bet she's hounding him about every aspect of the story. Plus, she stays busy with Erik and Jon."

"I guess you're right." Her half-smile was meant to satisfy Casey, but Alecia wanted to scream. No man was safe from Addison.

Last weekend's interlude kept her satisfied for the past couple of days, but she had concerns—for instance, that conversation he'd had with Addison while they were in Jamaica. These days, she favored Quentin, which was a mystery—unless she was buttering him up to assume Emily's role at a cheaper rate. Addison was wealthy, but she didn't waste money.

As hard as she'd pushed on Sunday, he said nothing about his promotion. A week apart made her want him more than ever, but his overriding concern was finishing Addison's chapters. Eventually, she gave up and went home to sulk.

On Monday morning, dark circles ringed his eyes. Quentin resembled someone who'd been in a train wreck, but Addison hadn't been screaming. Alecia figured he'd stayed up all night to fine-tune the edits. More and more, she wished for an ordinary life and someone of her own. She'd been so certain sliding into Addison's life was right, she didn't consider how it would mess with her emotional health. Being close to her was the only thing that mattered at the time.

The rumors that she hired people to write her books were simply that to Alecia, until she answered an ad to submit a writing sample. Casey had shown it to her, but warned her not to let on that they were friends.

They had met several years earlier at a salon and discovered their families were from the parish of St. Ann. The love of their original homeland, pampering their bodies, reading, and writing formed the basis of their friendship.

Both of them had blank spaces in their history. She peeked at Casey, realizing she knew nothing about her early life other than that her mother died young and her grandmother took her in, along with Donnette.

Some friendship they shared. Neither of them had ever revealed the dreams and secrets that bonded truly close women.

She'd never told Casey that Mama wasn't her biological mother, nor that her sisters weren't blood relatives. The lack of people who belonged to her through blood was the reason she craved all she could have with Quentin, if he'd act right.

What she'd settled for was a facsimile of a relationship that came under pressure with each of Addison's demands. Their last proper date was over three months ago. This slow route to anything resembling commitment was unacceptable, and her eggs weren't getting any younger. She let the air out of her cheeks at the same moment Casey imitated a weird sound from the music.

Despite mere tolerance for salsa, Casey rocked in time with the music as she stared through the open window. That was another thing they both enjoyed: the preference for fresh air over the car's air conditioning. Alecia reached up to sweep a strand of hair off her face, but instead adjusted the rearview mirror.

Quentin's car was behind them and even from here, his and Addison's grins were obvious. What on earth was so amusing? The festering resentment and uncertainty crawled down her throat and sat in her chest. She continued watching them, but didn't fool herself. If Addison wanted Quentin, nothing would stop her from having him.

She laid her foot on the gas to put space between them. Watching the two together at a distance was what she needed to assess what was happening, if anything. Alecia was so preoccupied, she almost mowed down the automatic gate as it swung away from the SUV.

Tim, the security guard, playfully saluted them. "Someone had a little too much to drink at that function."

She forced laughter while waiting. "At a funeral? I should be that lucky."

After easing into the spot next to Casey's Civic, she grabbed her purse. "Come on. I need a bathroom break before I sit in front of that laptop."

"Haste makes waste, as my grandmother used to say."

Alecia scoffed. "You and your proverbs."

"You gotta admit there's one for every situation."

"*Mmm.* Meet you in the studio." She hurried upstairs to the ladies' room, did her business, then stared into the mirror. She hated that her existence revolved around two issues—blood relatives she didn't have and making a life before she was too old to enjoy one. Like it or not, it was decision time.

She turned away from her reflection in the white-painted space. Her pale skin and the shape of her brows reminded her of Addison, but she'd treated herself to a cosmetic procedure and did all she could to accentuate what God had given her. And yet, she wasn't satisfied.

She reapplied her lipstick and walked into their writing space with confident steps. Her start in life had destroyed her self-esteem, but she'd recreated herself by reading numerous self-help books and articles, memorizing affirmations, and following feel-good podcasts. She wasn't where she wanted to be mentally, but was determined to shift her mindset.

She removed her phone and dropped the small purse on the seat while she greeted Maddy and Erik, who'd arrived earlier. Casey was probably snagging a sandwich in the kitchen.

Their boss left nothing to chance. Even their lunches were specially prepared. "I refuse to serve junk food that will turn your brain into sludge," she declared while scarfing down chocolate.

Alecia's pace was casual as she crossed the room to the large windows. The blinds were drawn, but the blades were open, allowing her to see the parking lot below. Quentin stood on the marble driveway, holding the passenger door like a chauffeur. Addison stepped out and put one hand on top of his, smiling seductively. She leaned in and whispered in his ear, while her other hand snaked out and cupped the front of his pants.

She squeezed, and instinctively, Alecia snapped several shots with her phone camera.

A tic started near her eye, which she couldn't massage away. Of all the vulgar things to do in public, and for Quentin to stand there smirking as if she'd paid him the biggest and best compliment. The blood rushed to Alecia's head, and she turned her back on them. Another bathroom trip was necessary. She couldn't face Addison without calming herself first.

At the doorway, Casey grabbed her arm. "What's wrong?"

Her lips parted in a fake smile. "Nothing. Be back in a minute."

She raced into the ladies' room and sank onto a padded bench covered in white leather. On the counter across the room, the colorful dahlias crowded together in a crystal vase. Alecia's existence was the same. Her family, the team, and Addison stifled her.

This woman was so wrapped up in herself, she couldn't see beyond her nose. Nor did she care who she hurt. Addison had set her sights on the one man Alecia wanted, but she wouldn't let him go without a fight.

"I'll see her dead in hell first."

She yanked the door open and walked into Addison, who stood on the other side. Heat flushed her face and neck, and if she could have gotten away with it, she'd have shoved her to the floor and delivered a swift kick. Instead, she stepped aside and mumbled an apology.

"Where are you going in such a hurry?" Addison asked, but didn't wait for an answer.

To deal with your boy toy.

CHAPTER 9

ADDISON

SHE'D GONE WITH her instinct to hire a private investigator, but regretted including Kirkland Maynard in this meeting. His faded buzz cut, watchful eyes, and the cupid's bow mouth were distracting. He was a handsome man who tickled her libido.

Having him present while she met with her agent and publicist wasn't the smartest thing she'd done this week. Theo was distracting enough with his headful of curly black hair and deep-brown eyes. She'd wondered about his sexuality but hadn't confirmed whether he was gay or simply effeminate. He'd given her the eye a time or two, but she hadn't bitten. She preferred her men taller and thicker. If Emily were here, she'd warn her to focus on business. The memory worked as well; it dampened her desire.

"I think we should start with a giveaway." Theo uncrossed his legs and lowered his portfolio. "It will grab your fans' attention and help them forget that other business."

"I agree." She'd discuss the gift package with Piper, who was good at handling those details. The gifts to staff for their birthdays and anniversaries didn't matter, but Addison was hands-on with her fans. They kept her living the high life, so were worth splurging on. She wouldn't go overboard, though. She was a businesswoman, not a charity.

An invisible weight settled on her shoulders as she shifted in the seat. The glass wall between her office and the studio gave her an unobstructed view of her team. She might not be in the room with them, but could tell at a glance who was slacking off and who was productive.

The dedication page that hadn't come with the manuscript delivered to Emily's office turned up earlier today at this address—the place where she lived and worked. Pity she didn't have cameras pointed at the street. Otherwise, she'd have known who had dared to come that close to her property. She'd remedy that in the next few hours after a call to the company that installed the surveillance equipment on the perimeter of the grounds.

She'd searched her mind and couldn't understand how this was happening. The woman tied to that manuscript had died, and everything connected to her should have disappeared. The room faded, the surrounding voices became a low rumble, and the years fell away.

Seventeen, to be exact.

Luck brought Yvette Finch, another writer, into Addison's orbit, and she capitalized on the younger woman's plight. She hadn't thought about her in years, but the innuendos and mud-slinging meant considering a problem she'd never anticipated.

Theo leaned forward, and his garish, canary yellow shirt jarred Addison from the trip into the past.

"I'll ask your social media manager to start some blasts," he said, moving his ankle in a tight circle.

Rachel, who'd left the room to take a call, came back inside. "Sorry about that, but I'm sure you didn't miss me too much." She claimed the seat she'd had previously and placed her cell phone on the edge of Addison's desk.

Theo glanced at the private investigator, then strutted toward the door with more swing in his step than necessary. "Talk to you later, Rachel."

His display was all for Maynard's benefit, and Addison's lips twitched. Her amusement lasted until she remembered the paper concealed in her purse. She'd shoved it in there and locked the drawer after she'd read it. It might contain fingerprints, but if she brought in the police, what would she tell them? There was no stated threat.

When she opened the envelope, Piper was sitting across from her and may have noticed her reaction. In the two years of her employment, she'd been discreet, but Addison couldn't afford to be careless. Not now, when she was at the pinnacle of everything she'd ever wanted.

During the last few days in Jamaica, she'd mulled over the media attacks. Her blood reached near boiling point when she recalled how that talk show host ambushed her. She'd been bold enough to do that because few people in Jamaica ever sued over defamation of character.

Hiring Maynard resulted from her frenzied brainstorming, and it galled her to waste money investigating the people around her. It might not be the best strategy, but it was necessary.

"Rachel tells me you come highly recommended."

He nodded once. "I did a stint in the police force and then went into business for myself as a PI."

He was the sort of professional Addison despised—the ones who followed people around and dug into their business. But he was exactly the kind she needed to ferret out the enemy in her midst—if there was one.

She'd been generous to her people and given them a start in the writing world, but each of them was talented and could do well on their own. That's if they opted to do the work involved and were in the right place at the opportune moment. She hoped that wouldn't happen. While she didn't often admit it, she needed them.

Although she had nothing to tie any of them to the gossip being spread about her, one couldn't be too careful. If someone on the team intended to ruin her life, now was the time to lay a trap and oust them.

She selected a chocolate from the crystal bowl, then eased it toward Rachel.

Both of them had diabetes and another common enemy—candies and chocolate.

"Are these safe?"

"You ask that every week." Addison wagged a finger. "Because of you, I don't indulge the way I used to. No walnuts, no cashews."

Every other Friday, they met in Addison's office to discuss her work-in-progress. They also strategized, discussing the books that were doing well and those that might be in a slump. Their exchange about the chocolates was also a ritual. Piper placed a standard order, specifying the mix to purchase and the reason. The missing element was Emily, who'd have shaken her head in disapproval.

"Good girl." Rachel fished out two of the chocolates, unwrapped one, and popped it into her mouth.

Addison helped herself to another while studying Maynard, who eyed the wall of book covers, similar to the one in Rachel's office. As far as the team was concerned, she'd hired a new writer and editor. Rachel had interviewed him, and they organized this briefing to explain his assignment.

A gurgle made them peer at each other, then at Rachel.

She clutched her throat with both hands, and her eyes were pulled wide. Horrifyingly wide.

Panic. Terror. And something Addison didn't dare to name hovered in the office. She sprang up from the seat, fearing the worst. "Rachel. What is it?"

She said one word as a red tide spread across her face and neck, then released another hoarse cry. "Car," she croaked.

Addison couldn't make sense of her garbled speech, but Maynard did. He grabbed Rachel's key fob off the desk and bolted through the door.

She rushed to her agent's side, with her heart pulsing at a frantic rate.

The whites of Rachel's eyes were a terrifying sight as her body convulsed.

The signals between Addison's brain and limbs stopped, and she couldn't move.

Something between a gasp and a moan came from Rachel's throat before she flopped forward and went still.

CHAPTER 10

CASEY

WHO WAS THE man who'd been in the office with Addison, Theo, and Rachel?

The furtive glances from those who wrote facing Addison's office gave away their curiosity. They didn't know what happened, but sat to attention when the stranger ran through the door as if the apocalypse had started and nightmarish creatures were chasing him.

Some froze in their seats, and others gaped while Rachel's seizure and collapse unfolded like a macabre stage production. By the time he raced back into the office and stabbed Rachel in the leg with an EpiPen, Addison's theatrics were well underway.

"Someone call the paramedics," the unidentified man commanded.

That's when Piper scrabbled for the phone and did as he ordered. The team sat in silence while Addison screamed and cursed. No one was sure whether to continue their chapter or act the way regular human beings would and commiserate with one another. The choice was easy since they couldn't keep their eyes off Rachel.

Ten minutes later, the paramedics rushed in. After checking her vitals, one of them left the building and returned. The pair zipped Rachel inside a body bag and rolled her out on a gurney.

Addison stormed out of her office behind them and left one instruction. "Keep writing. I'll be back to check on your chapters."

She reappeared in the afternoon with the new guy, walking with a spring in her step. "Everyone," she said, standing in the center of the room, "this is Kirkland Maynard. He'll be joining the team and will work alongside Jon and Quentin to get our chapters reader-ready."

None of them reacted to the news. Emily hadn't been gone two weeks, but the wheels of Addisonville kept on churning. Casey's lips twitched as she wondered whether Addison had bedded the recruit during the interview process.

The moment their eyes met, Casey figured he was someone to watch. His gaze was direct and sharp, and of course, he was striking. Addison wouldn't hire him otherwise.

"Happy to meet you all. You can call me Kirk." His grin was disarming, open and friendly, except for the assessing way he scanned each person in the room. She could be wrong, but Casey's sixth sense told her something deeper existed between Kirk and Addison that wasn't obvious this minute.

A welcoming chorus rippled through the studio before Addison clapped twice. "Let's go back to it. We're six weeks out from turning in *Murder by the Book*. Let's not drop the ball now."

Kirk nodded to acknowledge her command, then sat at Emily's desk and opened a file.

Without another word, Addison left, and blissful silence fell.

Shelving her curiosity about Kirk, Casey eased her laptop aside and pulled the story bible in front of her. She read the synopsis, memorizing where she was supposed to go with the current chapter. The housekeeper was the next victim to fall prey to the killer.

She spun to the research material that applied to her death while she considered how lucky she'd been that the Jamaican authorities hadn't insisted on an autopsy to rule out foul play in Emily's death. Her heart still clenched when she remembered Detective Barham.

Technically, nothing was suspicious about her death. Emily's chronic asthma left her vulnerable, and in a place where flowers bloomed everywhere, she'd suffered from the moment she'd landed in Jamaica.

If the pathologist had examined her body, they would have concluded that her sickness weakened her heart, and the bronchodilator was ineffective. One could use an inhaler for so long before the body grew accustomed to it, and the doctor changed or adjusted the medication. Knowing Addison, she would have shared Emily's condition with the police to ensure she left the island on schedule.

Chewing the side of her lip, Casey recalled their second evening at the villa. She'd pointed Emily to the delicate peach angel's trumpet that occupied one corner of the yard. "I'm certain I saw at least four colors."

Emily wasn't interested, but humored Casey because she loved plant life. She'd flapped her wrist and agreed. "They're beautiful."

Dragging her to the other varieties was unnecessary. The smell wasn't overpowering, but a dash of jasmine mixed with citrus. Emily backed away from the bush laden with blooms while fumbling for the pocket of her skirt. Two pumps from her inhaler reduced her panic, and she'd scuttled toward the patio as fast as her feet would carry her.

What Emily didn't know was that a little angel trumpet dust went a long way.

Casey brought her mind back to her writing and focused on finishing the scene. The memories would keep.

An hour later, she drove home to lie down and clear her mind. The drama at work and the inability to breathe freely after Rachel's passing left her with a tension headache.

Donnette had arrived before her and started dinner. The scent of curried chicken filled the living room and made Casey's mouth water, although she wasn't hungry.

"Don't get comfortable," Donnette warned, sticking her head out from the kitchen doorway. "We're eating in twenty minutes."

True to her word, she yelled for Casey to come to the table. After saying grace, Donnette encouraged her to dig in.

"You've been quiet since you came back from Jamaica." Donnette spoke with her fork poised in the air. "You've barely even talked to Rochelle, and the two of you can chat up a storm."

"Guess I'm tired. We had several marathons at the office to compensate for the time we lost when Emily died."

Donnette shook her head as she chewed a mouthful of chicken. "I don't know why you continue to work for that woman. She's going to suck the life out of you."

The fork fell to the plate with a clang, and she gathered the scattered rice grains off the placemat. Donnette's words struck a chord and reminded her of things she didn't want to think about, so she quipped, "Not if I have anything to do with it."

"You can't say I didn't warn you." Donnette sipped carrot juice then asked, "So, how is Gran, really?"

Donnette's shift at work and Casey's schedule meant that sometimes they didn't have proper conversations for several days. This was the second evening they'd eaten together since she'd flown in, and Casey hoped she wouldn't regret it.

"Same as always. I can't believe she's eighty. She hasn't aged at all."

"Weird, isn't it? It's like Mommy's death brought her to this point and no further." After another sip, she wiped her mouth with a napkin. "How are Denise and Michelle getting along with her?"

Casey laughed and picked up her fork. "You make her sound difficult. She raised them, same as she did with us. Why would they have any issues?"

Her mind went to the days after Mommy died, when they lived in the four-bedroom house overrun with cousins. In Jamaica, it was common for grandparents to raise their grandkids while their parents tried to build a better life—sometimes in the capital city, Kingston, or overseas.

"Yes, but we weren't there for long," Donnette insisted, as if it changed anything.

Neither of them had a problem returning to their original home before Mommy married and moved out.

"True, but it suits them to stay with Gran. Less money all around for us to contribute."

Donnette nodded, but didn't speak.

The visit with their grandmother raised memories Casey tried hard to suppress, and she struggled to block the images that visited at all hours of the day and night. Donnette was her heart, but being around her meant walking through a roomful of broken glass each day. When something was wrong in Casey's world, she sensed it and was persistent with her questions.

"You still haven't explained why the police thought you were involved in Emily's death."

The rice Casey was about to swallow sat at the back of her throat and refused to move. She gulped carrot juice to move the obstruction before she said, "I told you all about that."

"But you never explained why you didn't tell me when it happened."

Sighing, Casey replaced the glass. "You know why."

"I hate it when you shut me out."

She didn't waste her breath with an explanation. Although Donnette was two years older, Casey had assumed the role of leader and protector when they were girls. Some things they never spoke about—with good reason—and Casey didn't wish to remind Donnette of issues she'd never dealt with and likely never would.

"Hey." Casey let out a heavy breath, uncomfortable with the way her chest tightened. She hated when they had disagreements. "I'm sorry."

"Yeah. You always say that."

"I didn't want to burden you with something that was easily explained."

"Right. Since you took that job, sometimes I worry about you." Donnette picked apart the napkin without taking her eyes off Casey. "You and I know what we've been through, so I can't help praying you won't do anything you can't come back from."

Casey stabbed at a piece of chicken and stuffed it into her mouth, although her throat ached with unshed tears. Donnette's anxiety and concern were enough to unravel her. The growing pile of napkin pieces said more than her sister would admit, which worried Casey.

Years ago, Casey discovered her compassion had an on-and-off switch. She was fiercely protective of Donnette due to their history, but when it came to other people, she preferred to remain detached.

She'd made a few friends, including Rochelle, whom she met at school when she first arrived in America. Rochelle was fun-loving and up for all kinds of shenanigans, but best of all, she was loyal. Rochelle was the one person who had any insight into their terrible home life and history with Addison.

Casey kept her circle small because she never forgot the pain of losing her mother because of poverty. Independence meant everything, and so far, she and Donnette were winning. Mommy had been a giver, and Addison and Emily were takers who didn't deserve sympathy.

Losing her most valuable employee left Addison scrambling, but she'd replaced her easily enough. Emily was privy to the details of Addison's wrongdoing and co-signed her thievery. Why should she continue to enjoy life when their mother's had been cut short through no fault of her own? Emily had gotten exactly what she deserved. Pity she hadn't suffered the way Mommy did, growing weaker every day and unable to afford the care she needed.

With a shaky hand, Casey brought the fork to her mouth. "It's hard to leave things as they are when we know what those women did."

Donnette grabbed her arm and leaned in, clenching her jaw. "I can't afford to lose you. Casey, listen to me. We have a good life. Don't let hate cost us more than we've already lost."

CHAPTER 11

ALECIA

HER PALM STUNG when it connected with Quentin's cheek, but she didn't regret hitting him. His breathing was so heavy, she swore he'd forget himself and give her a black eye. Thank goodness he wasn't the kind of guy to retaliate, but push a man too far, and anything was possible. Stepping back, Quentin cupped his jaw where her handprint stood out against his creamy skin.

"Have you lost your mind?"

"Do you give a shit?" she said and pushed past him into the apartment.

Yesterday afternoon, he disappeared with Addison after an impromptu meeting, which meant one thing. Quentin returned within an hour with his clothing neater than when he left, and he wouldn't acknowledge Alecia, no matter what she did.

That was telling.

She still wanted to vomit at the idea of sleeping with the same man as Addison.

"What is your problem?" he asked, closing the door.

The sweatpants and tee shirt hugging his muscles would have her salivating on any other day, but she'd stewed in anger last night into this morning when he wouldn't take her call. Avoiding her didn't mean he wouldn't have to deal with her at some point.

"You, Quentin." She poked him in the chest. "You are my problem."

He clamped one hand around her wrist. "Don't come around here giving what you can't take."

"Tell me what I'm supposed to do if you keep humiliating me with the games you're playing with Addison."

"I don't know what the hell you're talking about."

"That's about right." She cut her eyes at him. "You never know what's happening between us, but I bet you know the way around Addison's bedroom."

He shifted his feet and sighed. "I'm in the middle of reading yesterday's stuff. I don't have time for this."

"Isn't this your weekend off?" she asked, propping both fists on her hips.

"Yeah, but—"

"But nothing. You're so far up Addison's ass, you can't remember we have a relationship."

He opened his mouth, then shut it as if he might say the wrong thing. Quentin's breath came in ragged puffs that warmed her face.

Anticipation shifted through her.

"Listen," he snapped, "you know how this thing between us started."

"And?" The heat from a moment ago evaporated like dew under the morning sun.

Quentin shrugged. "It was a matter of…"

With her head tipped back, she asked, "A matter of what?"

He shoved both hands into his pockets and rocked on the balls of his feet. "Convenience. We got together because of that."

A crushing weight on her chest made it difficult to construct a complete sentence. "So, all this time…"

Quentin rubbed the back of his neck then sighed. "I'm not saying you aren't special to me. The…"

Her mind spun in circles, and she lost track of his explanation. His platitudes meant nothing. If he'd stabbed her with a knife, the wound would have been less painful. For weeks, they had flirted before finally having mad sex in the shower of the men's room. She wasn't proud of it, but each time she remembered the heat and their passion, she wanted him all over again.

He wasn't demonstrative, but was a fiend in the bedroom. That, in some ways, made up for his lack of affection and commitment. She'd allowed that to be enough and built fantasies around this man who didn't care about her. "I must be blind or stupid," she muttered.

Heat flooded her face and neck while she cursed herself for being a fool. Her reluctance to go through the dating routine with anyone else and plain laziness combined to bite her in the ass.

Quentin wasn't handsome in the conventional sense of the word, but was quite attractive. His African-American mother and Asian father had given him the best of their genes, but on an emotional level, he lacked depth.

His detachment was why he'd said nothing bad about Addison. Plus, he didn't want Alecia as a partner. She'd simply been a way to scratch his physical itch—a willing participant in this fiasco of a romance.

Twelve months out of her life was too much to give up for nothing. How had she not seen the signs? Alecia shook her head, knowing she'd ignored the obvious.

Addison grabbing Quentin's crotch shouldn't have surprised her, but it did. She'd shown no interest in him openly, so her gesture knocked Alecia sideways. Not only was it crass, it implied Quentin was a liar—always denying he was messing with her. He was too comfortable not to have been in her clutches before yesterday. And how did he feel, knowing he was servicing Addison like a farm animal, along with his coworkers?

She pulled back her shoulders, ready to ask where they stood. But that would have been stupid. They were exactly where they'd been all along—holding a hovering pattern. Her mouth tasted bitter, the way it did when she was dehydrated.

His face softened. He was about to apologize, but she held up one hand. "It's fine. I finally received the message you've been sending all this time."

Alecia stalked out of the apartment, slamming the door behind her. When she sat in the SUV, she rang Casey. "Hey. Where are you?"

"Downtown doing a little shopping. What's up?"

Staring across the street at another apartment block, she said, "I need to talk."

"Okay." Casey drew the word out, and Alecia understood her response.

Heart-to-heart talks were not their style. Their conversations revolved around the studio, with little or no mention of the happenings in the real world.

A short blast of a horn interrupted Casey's question, and Alecia struggled to hear her words. "Where d'you want to meet?"

They settled on a café downtown, and on the way, Alecia couldn't decide what to tell Casey. Rejection was ingrained in her DNA, making it difficult for her to share her feelings with anyone else. Now, it was too late to change her mind, so she entered the café and chose a table where they'd have some privacy.

Confiding in her two sisters was impossible. Maxine's marriage was rocky, and Ophelia couldn't stay in a relationship to save her life. Their mother's example hadn't been stellar, since none of her affairs lasted beyond six months. Evadne Cookson had turned into something of an expert at choosing the wrong men. Aside from those reasons, Alecia kept her business private because her sisters had always hated her. Adulthood hadn't changed their attitude.

When the wind chimes tinkled, Alecia closed her manicured fingers into a fist. Despite not having a life, she maintained a semi-regular routine at the hair and nail salon. Popular wisdom said if a woman took care of herself, she'd also feel good.

Casey stood on the welcome mat, scanning the area, and smiled when Alecia waved.

"Thanks for coming," Alecia said. "I hope I didn't frighten you with my sudden call."

Shaking her head, Casey took the opposite seat. "I figured it was something important, so here I am."

"I need to bounce some of this madness off someone who can give an unbiased view."

Casey rested a hand on top of hers. "Don't apologize. You never know when you'll need someone's help or advice. What's up?"

"Let's order before I give you the 411."

They chitchatted about what they'd been working on the previous day and how the recent deaths affected the group until the waiter delivered their coffee. The café was at the back end of the lunch hour, so the scent of fried chicken, oxtail, and rice and peas assaulted them, but Alecia wasn't hungry for food.

Finding words took a while, but she explained the problem while Casey listened in silence. To wrap up, she added, "I know this sounds crazy and sad, but it is what it is."

Curling a lock of hair around her finger, Casey frowned. "Let me get this straight: Your relationship with Quentin is over because he's been messing with Addison, correct?"

His apologetic expression filled her memory, and Alecia cursed herself again for being a fool. How was it possible to verbalize their mess and still think he was worth her time?

She sighed and moved the cup in a circle. "Yes, in a nutshell."

"That's awkward." Casey raised both eyebrows and moved her head from side to side.

"As hell." A burst of laughter from a group two tables away startled Alecia. "I should have figured he wasn't exempt. I don't know how she does it."

"It takes a certain type."

The chocolate reminded her of the times Quentin had served it to her when she woke in his bed. Why did those who took everything have more, while other people were forced to survive on nothing? Aside from having him as a plaything, Addison didn't need Quentin. She was simply greedy, which riled Alecia up again. Every bit of loss and nastiness that came to her over the last few weeks was exactly what Addison deserved.

Lying through her teeth to save face, Alecia declared, "While Quentin is no enormous loss, I hate the fact that Addison ruined our relationship."

"Yeah. That sucks." Casey lowered her chin and clasped both hands. "But why do I feel you don't want it to end there?"

Alecia bit her lip, fighting not to speak, but the words escaped from her. "I'm so tired of life passing me by, and now..." Her voice cracked, and she grabbed for the mochaccino to cover her gaffe. No man deserved her tears, least of all Quentin. She sipped, barely tasting the warm brew, but her words were cathartic and refused to be suppressed. "She's taken even the little I had. I should..."

"You should what?" Casey leaned in, her expression wary.

Smirking, Alecia continued, "I have a juicy bit of gossip she wouldn't want the public to know."

Casey didn't ask what it was, but warned, "Whatever you do, be careful. If she knows you have anything on her, she'll make your life hell."

"Tell me about it." A bitter smile twisted Alecia's lips. "But if things go south, I can stay afloat for a while."

"She'll do everything so you never write on another team or sign a book contract. You know that, right?"

Alecia shrugged and scanned the surrounding area to be sure no one was listening to their conversation. "She may have powerful friends, but she isn't God."

"True dat." Casey raised her cup and touched Alecia's while they laughed at her slip-up. They hardly used patois, even when alone together. "If you need any help, just ask. You already know how I feel about her."

One sip later, she added, "Be careful, though. There's something about the new guy."

Nodding, Alecia sat back in the chair. "Yeah. There's more to him being there than what she told us."

"Exactly." Casey's eyes flashed, and her vehement tone made Alecia wonder what she wasn't sharing.

Talking to Casey took the edge off her anger, but she was far from satisfied. She'd given Quentin the impression she was done with him, but her heart said she was far from finished. As she raised the cup, her phone rang. She lifted it from her lap and swiped the screen.

Quentin was calling.

CHAPTER 12

ADDISON

PIPER DIDN'T BLINK while she sat with the phone pressed to her ear.

Sometimes, the glass wall was more curse than blessing. Addison picked up the buzzing intercom and avoided the open studio when Piper announced, "Mikhail is on the line."

"Good. I need to speak with him."

Her social media manager lived across the country and was highly skilled at his job. Mikhail created engaging posts for her various accounts and kept the conversations going in the comment section. The biggest plus was that he kept the Negative Nellies and their poison to a minimum.

"We have an issue."

Addison raised one eyebrow. "A greeting would have been appropriate since we haven't spoken this week."

"Why waste your time? You're a busy woman." Amusement colored Mikhail's deep voice, which was at odds with his slight build. A Grenadian native, he still sounded as though he'd never left the island. When they first met, she'd teased him about having a Russian name.

He'd laughed and quipped, "Don't you know Caribbean people swipe names from everywhere like it's nobody's business?"

Her mind returned to the present, and she frowned. "Right. So, what made you pick up the phone instead of texting?"

"I guessed you'd prefer to hear what I have to say."

She stared through the glass, paying scant attention to the men and women working in the next room.

"There's an influencer, Island Gyal, who's thrown out a broad hint that she has some dirt on you, which she plans to share later this week. She's hinting it's about your roots."

The back of her neck tightened, but Addison didn't massage the spot. She was sick of keeping up appearances. Too many things were happening at once. She wasn't ready for anything else, but when did life ever stop?

"She probably needs some kind of payday," she spat. "Wanting us to reach out to see what she knows."

"Actually, she's independent. Doesn't take any kind of endorsements. Buys her own books and claims she doesn't want to be obligated to any publisher."

Addison scoffed. "Everyone has a price."

"Do you want me to contact her?"

"How else will you find out what she's after and what she believes she knows?"

"Okay. Consider it done. I'll circle back soon."

"Sure. Do that."

She sat and hung up the phone. If she were alone, she might have screamed in frustration or—much better—knocked back some port.

Her attention shifted to the top drawer of the desk, where she stashed the document she'd kept to herself. That dedication page from *Games People Play* haunted her, and she hadn't come up with a strategy to fight the mess on the horizon.

She had the safety net of a nondisclosure agreement to fall back on, which didn't comfort her, but thank God she'd been smart enough to cover her bases. Early in her career, she'd learned the importance of contracts and built her success on them. Emily was brilliant and had worked with Addison's lawyer to secure her intellectual property. Only she knew how much she missed the old bat.

If losing Emily put her at a loss, Rachel's dramatic exit shook Addison to the root of her being. Where would she find another agent who went to the lengths Rachel did to keep her name in front of her audience? Theo was decent at what he did, but Rachel had brilliant ideas and guided her publicist to important people in the industry.

Addison didn't relish the task of engaging new support staff and wanted to hurl a few choice words, plus anything within reach. Her hand fell on the crystal plaque to one side of her desk, and she lifted it.

That first award came from a large book club in Miami. The well-to-do bunch of women fell in love with *Games People Play* and invited her to their weekend conference. From there, Lady Luck had smiled on Addison, and word spread about her book. Her small backlist was suddenly awash with paperback sales, and she couldn't write fast enough to keep up with readers' demands. After years of scribbling, scrimping, and sacrificing, she'd come into the light.

She'd also climbed far enough to hire a stable of talented writers, which she handpicked after interviewing them and reviewing their writing samples. That decision was made for her when the demand for her books exceeded the supply on the market. She started with two hungry male writers, and the first documents they received were samples of her writing. She trained them until they could replicate her style and voice.

Her employees had never been family, but they were efficient and produced on demand. With success came expansion and more bestsellers. She hadn't done right by the people who served her, but their generous compensation made up for her faults. That was the best she could do. And now, someone was plotting to destroy her.

She hadn't slept well since Rachel passed. The police had grilled Piper and her, and neither of them could explain how or why wrappers with the same brand of chocolate-covered cashews made their way into the bowl on the desk. Piper always ordered from the same supplier, who provided a standard order. The team was questioned but couldn't provide any answers, so the case remained open, and the investigation continued. Thank goodness she and Rachel were on good terms, otherwise she might have been their number one suspect.

She replaced the crystal and rose to pace the office. Although Theo told her not to worry about the live interview she'd done on the island, something about it unsettled her. That woman, Jenny Z, was overly familiar with her history, but who was her source?

Too many years had passed, and she'd made too much progress to have ghosts raising their heads. She lived a thousand miles from who and what she'd been before her big break and didn't need any reminders. Maybe she'd call the station because she *was* Addison Comstock. That alone should have been enough to make the woman hesitate before asking those ridiculous questions.

"I'll be back," she announced, striding past Piper's desk with her cell phone in hand.

She kept walking until she pushed open the door of her living space and made a beeline for the sofa. Grabbing her iPad, she tapped in her password and opened her social media page on the network she preferred most. Giving anyone full charge of anything that had her name on it wasn't Addison's style. She was more than a name. She was a brand, as Theo often said.

While browsing the last of the two other networks she understood but never logged into, she zeroed in on a comment posted under a carousel of her books. *For all we know, she's a fraud.*

Addison shot to the edge of the seat, fumbling to hide the comment. Frustration grabbed her by the throat when she couldn't do so because she didn't know the password for that account. She typed a blistering comment, then deleted it when she remembered the advice from her team not to respond to reviews or any negative comments about her books or her.

After a spin around the bedroom, she returned to the living area of the suite and dropped onto the sofa. Emily would have listened to her rant, but she no longer had that privilege. For the first time in years, Addison was lonely. She loved her own company, but would have given anything to share the issues bothering her mind with someone who understood her fears. Life wouldn't be worth living if her world ever crumbled.

If her fans turned against her, she would die. Their adoration was what she lived for, and the one thing that kept her grounded. For most people, family mattered. For Addison Comstock, the hill she'd die on was her readers' adulation. Some folks would consider that pitiful, but not her. Family had wounded Addison too deeply for her to ever heal.

She was halfway through writing a message to Rachel when she remembered her agent was gone. Laying the phone down, she took several deep breaths before copying what she had written and sending it to Mikhail. One comment could snowball into a hailstorm of innuendo directed at her. People could be small-minded and nasty about others' success. She'd lived through enough of what Jamaicans called "bad mind" to know it was true.

As hard as she tried not to revisit the comments, she failed. Several fans defended her, which lifted her mood. She noticed the wine bucket by the bar and the half-empty glass of port she'd been sipping last night. The port would be warm—or as warm as it could be in the air-conditioned suite. She'd had more than enough then, but this madness would drive anyone to drink.

One last scan of her account dropped a ball of anxiety laced with anger into her stomach. Some know-it-all commented, *I've heard stories about her, and I bet there's proof if we dig deep enough to find it.*

Instead of pouring fresh port as she had intended, Addison grabbed the glass off the counter and smashed it against the mirror behind the bar.

CHAPTER 13

CASEY

"MISS MITCHELL, WHY did the Jamaican police detain you?"

"They questioned me, along with everyone else." Casey maintained eye contact with the officer across the table and kept her hands clasped in her lap. "I wasn't detained."

"Didn't they stop you from leaving the island?"

"They requested that I stay until they completed their investigation."

The harsh light pinpointed the thinning spot on the policeman's head and reflected off his glasses. "Why?"

Casey shifted and kept her hands hidden. They trembled from the chill of the air conditioner and fear of what might happen if this officer found a link between Emily and Rachel's deaths. She pushed aside the sensation of an invisible hand squeezing her heart.

"Fingerprints." She tipped her head in a slight motion, admitting to her action. "I moved Emily's inhaler out of the way while helping her, but I'm sure you know that."

Detective Ince rubbed the side of his nose and silently tagged his partner, who lounged against one wall. The officer straightened and stood next to his partner across from Casey.

"I wonder what we would find if we asked that Ms. Smalling's body be exhumed for an autopsy." Detective Robinson pulled out the other chair and lowered himself into it. Unlike his partner, he carried more body weight and a full head of brown hair.

She took her time before responding, knowing she had to be careful. In her arrogance, she'd forgotten about them after their initial visit to the studio and was rattled when they turned up at the office that morning. After a conversation with Addison, they asked to speak with her again—this time, at the Orlando Police Department headquarters. Since she wasn't handcuffed, she assumed they were doing their due diligence but didn't lower her guard.

She searched her mind for the question she'd been asked, then said, "I'm certain they would find she died because of an asthma attack."

"And you had nothing to do with her death, Ms. Mitchell?"

"None at all." Casey smiled faintly. "I may write about murder, but I'm not a killer."

"That remains to be seen." Detective Robinson shifted his attention over her shoulder, then asked. "What about the chocolate-covered nuts we found in your handbag on the day Rachel Maxwell died?"

Once more, she cursed herself for not being as thorough as she could have been. Shrugging, she answered, "They're around the office. Addison doesn't mind us having them."

"Are you sure about that? Because she made a point of telling us how expensive they are."

"We don't overindulge, so it's not an issue."

"*Hmmm.* You stood out because no other employee had any of the chocolates among their possessions."

"I'm partial to them," she lied and gave him a bright smile. "Matter of fact, I may have one inside my bag right now."

The chapter she'd left unfinished crossed her mind, but she'd put in extra time to catch up. That didn't bother her. What did, was the heavy silence that fell over the team as she'd left the studio. They would whisper about her, but the worst part was losing Addison's trust. If she believed Casey was in any way responsible for Emily or Rachel's death, she would crucify her. That couldn't happen. She had so much more to do.

"Excuse us for a moment, Ms. Mitchell."

She nodded to acknowledge Detective Ince's request, conscious they'd be watching her from the other side of the two-way mirror. Hugging herself was out of the question, so she let her mind spin back to the day they first interviewed her. She'd come close to hyperventilating while describing what she saw during Rachel's collapse. When Detective Ince asked if she knew the cause of death, she massaged her forehead and mumbled, "From what I understand, it was an allergic reaction."

"To what exactly?" His intense blue eyes glinted behind wire-rimmed glasses.

"I don't know." She shrugged and shook her head at the same time. "But someone used an EpiPen on her."

"Thanks, Ms. Mitchell. We'll let you know if we need to speak with you again."

"Sure." She'd left Addison's office, which they'd commandeered for questioning the staff, and returned to her desk, unable to type another word. Since then, she'd been careful not to speculate with her coworkers. The less she said, the better, and with Kirk around, she was doing herself a favor by not offering any opinion on anything that didn't concern her.

The policemen entered the room again, and she sat up, pulled from that first encounter. This time, Detective Ince carried a file, which he opened when he sat. "Your sister is a nurse, correct?"

A sharp pain stabbed her chest as she inhaled, but she refused to focus on the paperwork. They were baiting her. "What does she have to do with this?"

"Nothing." Detective Ince raised one hand, and his thin lips curved in a half-smile. "Except for the fact that she would know the effects of a food allergy and be able to advise what to do if you wanted to hurt someone."

Her heart lurched then sped up, competing with a runaway train, and her jaws hurt with the effort not to grind her teeth, but she held on to her composure. "My sister wouldn't harm anyone. She's not that kind of person."

"But you are?" Detective Ince lifted one eyebrow in a taunt that made her want to rake his face with her nails.

"I never said that." She reached for her handbag. "If you brought me here to harass me about an unfortunate incident that has nothing to do with me, then you're looking in the wrong direction. I have to go back to work."

The thought of the studio dropped a boulder in her stomach. How would she explain why the law considered it necessary to scoop her up for questioning? She wanted to rub away the sudden tightness that gripped the back of her neck, but wouldn't give them the satisfaction of knowing how close she was to panicking. None of this was supposed to happen. Why were they trying to blame her for what was clearly an accidental death?

"You might want to hang around, Ms. Mitchell." Detective Robinson glanced at his watch, then added, "We asked your sister to come down. She's on the way here."

"What?" She swallowed to clear her throat, pulled the handbag into her lap, and spoke through her teeth. "Why are you getting Donnette mixed up in this? We haven't done anything."

"Then her interview shouldn't take long."

"This is harassment," Casey spat as her focus went from one man to the other. "You're only doing this because another of Addison's workers died. How is it our fault if they had chronic illnesses or were allergic?"

"Nobody said it was your fault," Detective Robinson said. "We are ruling out the possibilities to satisfy Ms. Smalling's relatives *and* ensure neither of these women was actually targeted."

That was news to Casey, but it didn't improve her mood. Donnette would have her head for this, especially after her warning the other day.

"Why would anyone target them?" she asked, narrowing her eyes.

"You tell me."

She restrained herself from tugging the hair at the base of her skull, then released a harsh breath. "I'm sorry. I don't know."

"You may wait outside while we interview your sister." Detective Ince stood and opened the door to usher her out.

On the way down the wide corridor lit by fluorescent panels, Casey prayed Donnette would forgive her for upending their lives. She thrived on peace and calm and would likely freak out about being questioned. The best Casey could do was reassure her that nothing would come of this disruption—that's if she'd listen.

A uniformed officer came around the corner toward her, escorting Donnette.

Casey couldn't gauge her reaction, but grabbed her hand. "Hey, Dee. I'm—"

"I was at the start of my shift when they called me to come here." Donnette swept her from head to feet in one pass, then hugged her. "I thought they arrested you."

"No—"

"So, why do they want to see me?"

"I—"

"Excuse me." The policeman touched Donnette's arm and pointed toward the interrogation room, where Detective Robinson stood outside the door. "They're waiting for you."

Casey patted Donnette's hand, but what she wanted to do was hug her again. Neither of them was whole without the other, which Casey understood too well. The loss of their mother and distance from the father Casey adored made them closer than most sisters. Her stomach soured when she pictured the man who held her heart until they landed in America.

Her phone pinged, and she scrabbled to pull it from the bag. Piper had sent a text.

Will you be coming back soon? Addison wants a meeting.

Casey rubbed her chest in a circular motion while her throat closed. She lowered herself to the closest seat, distracted by a message from Rochelle that flashed on the screen. She opened it and scanned the picture someone had taken when she'd left the studio. Across the back of her burnt-orange suit, a caption announced, DID SHE OR DIDN'T SHE?

From the angle of the photo, someone upstairs was the culprit. Most likely, Alecia who lived half her life on the internet. She was seriously going to kill her.

You're on social media again. What did you do this time?

Her stomach knotted as her fingers flew over the keypad. How bad is it?

A sly mention of u being questioned by the police about a suspicious death.

She bit her thumbnail, then replied. They're wasting their time with this foolishness. Nobody knows who I am anyway, so there's that.

Rochelle's response was swift. Ha! It doesn't work that way when ur connected 2 one of the biggest writers of our time.

The heaviness in her stomach spread to her limbs, and she prayed the police would wrap up quickly. If they were lucky, Donnette would hold herself together to continue her shift. But later, there'd be hell to pay at home.

Casey chewed at her lip as she typed words she wasn't feeling. Storm in a teacup. It will pass.

From your lips to God's ears, chica.

Footsteps echoed down the corridor, and Casey raised her head after typing a hurried reply. Let's hope so.

The young officer stopped a foot away and cleared his throat. "Ms. Mitchell? Detective Ince asked me to let you know he will be detaining your sister."

CHAPTER 14

ALECIA

ADDISON SET DOWN her coffee mug with a *thunk* that carried to Alecia in the studio. "Piper! Get in here."

She rose from the desk closest to the office door and hurried inside, carrying a pad and pen.

Addison lowered her voice, but her words were still audible. "Get Theo on the phone. Now."

"But he's out of the country."

"I don't care where the hell he is. Find him!"

Alecia knew for sure Addison had seen the snippet in the gossip column. Nothing else would have caused that reaction. She picked up the paper again, crumpled it in her hands, and pressed her lips together, like someone holding back a scream.

Bit by bit, Addison's existence was unraveling, and Alecia wouldn't have missed a minute, although the sight of Quentin each workday lit a fire in her stomach that wouldn't go out, no matter how many affirmations about peace she repeated in her head.

She sent a glare in his direction, which he missed since he was in the middle of editing their latest chapters. Her face burned at the memory of his pity call on the weekend. She'd known she shouldn't have answered, but as always, her neediness exposed her to more humiliation.

"I'm sorry for how things turned out, but—"

She'd lifted a finger and left Casey at the table, ready for reconciliation if that's what he wanted. On her way to the alcove housing the washrooms, she said, "I don't want your *buts* or apologies."

"I understand that, but I–I'm not ready to commit."

A white haze covered the tiles on the other side of the passage as she supported her weight with her back to the wall. "Don't waste my time. That's fairly obvious."

"Maybe we can—"

"Thanks, but no thanks for whatever crumb you were about to offer. I don't need it."

She used a moment to compose herself and returned to the table, where she pretended one of her sisters had called. Casey asked no questions, but searched her face and didn't argue when Alecia said she wasn't feeling well and had to leave.

On the way home, she counted all the ways in which Addison had destroyed her life. Since she'd reeled Quentin into her web, Alecia spent more time inside her head than building the future of her dreams. That was changing because she'd had enough.

She spun the page on the outline at the same moment Addison reached for the phone, then changed her mind and slumped in the seat, still transfixed by the newsprint. She rose, grabbed her cell phone, and walked around the desk. Her next move would be visits to her social media pages.

Shallow and predictable.

Another peek at her stirred Alecia's sympathy. Then she caught herself. Addison had caused her more misery than all the people in her life combined, including her wretched sisters. She'd save her sympathy for someone who deserved it.

Earlier this week, whispers that someone else had written her fifth book made Addison mad as a black mamba. Nothing the team wrote was acceptable. Not even Casey—who usually slid under the radar—got away. She'd fallen far out of favor since the police hauled her off for questioning, with Addison barely acknowledging her existence. Casey seemed too quiet since, and refused to talk about that incident, so Alecia respected her wishes. She didn't see any point in crossing a boundary that might strain their friendship.

Addison's irritable tone cut into Alecia's thoughts.

"Piper, what's taking so long?" She stood in the doorway, phone in hand. Today, she was elegant in a pink suit and black high heels, as if prepared for anything that came her way.

Piper's wide eyes seemed to fill her face. "I–I'm getting a recording from Theo's phone."

"Did you send a text or an email?" Addison asked, emphasizing each word.

Her assistant's voice barely crested to a whisper. "No, but I—"

"Do I have to tell you everything?" Her attention swung to the rest of the room. "In fifteen minutes, I want to see where you're at with your chapters."

A collective sigh fell around Alecia, and she propped herself higher in the chair. They were in for a grueling session, but it didn't matter. Addison's discomfort made up for the pain and suffering she had caused Alecia for what felt like her entire existence.

Addison's voice rang out again. "Get me the editor for that stupid rag."

"Okay."

Piper was aware of which publication she meant because within a few minutes, she transferred a call to Addison, who asked her to shut the door. Piper's mad scuttling reminded Alecia of a scene played out in a comedy, but the woman didn't deserve this level of cruelty and stress.

A pulse beat at the side of Addison's head, same as the one that hammered Alecia's temple when she was upset. When Addison's face flushed and the complaints continued, Alecia wished she could lipread.

Her fingers slowed, then halted, and she quickly continued typing, lest Addison accuse her of slacking off. The staccato beat of the keyboards continued, but not at the usual pace. The air was heavy, and those who'd seen the day's paper had a clue why Addison was in a temper. Lately, the atmosphere in the studio was so tense, nobody gossiped about anything to do with her. That's the toxic environment they now existed in—unable to trust one another or be themselves.

She angled her head to avoid Kirk, who did more listening than speaking while they were on a coffee break or at lunch. That alone marked him as suspect. Plus, he was too interested in what was going on in Addison's office. The man was primed for action, his spine stiff as though expecting her to summon him.

Addison's voice hit a crescendo of garbled words. Then she stomped across the floor and yanked the door open. "Kirkland. I need you in here."

When he stood, she added, "Bring your notes."

He gathered his papers, stuffed them inside a folder, then sauntered into the office.

The door barely closed behind him before Addison laid one hand on the newspaper and waved him into a seat. Although she'd calmed down a bit, her cheeks were flushed, and she kept a chokehold on the pendant between her breasts.

Alecia would have given anything to hear what was being said. *Murder by the Book* was the furthest thing from Addison's mind. If that were the reason she'd summoned him, they'd have been referencing his notes, plus Alecia was familiar with that expression. The one she wore when dishing out an ultimatum. Whatever she'd hired Kirk to do wasn't being done to her satisfaction. It was time for him to act or face termination. With one finger, Addison jabbed the newspaper, then flicked her wrist in Piper's direction.

Her explosive reaction was priceless, but as Casey sometimes said, "Nothing happens before the time." Additional facts would follow since Addison had way more history than today's revelation. The few tidbits they had dropped would set tongues yakking and minds fired up to know more. The lines of text were burned into Alecia's brain like the tattoo in stylized writing on her hip that read, You are enough.

We have reliable information that suggests the top-tier writer left more in Jamaica than she has ever shared with the media. Aside from losing her long-time developmental editor to an asthma attack, she left a precious piece of herself behind some years ago. Checks have revealed there is truth to this allegation.

Piper shot off her seat and opened the office door the instant Addison declared, "The part about Emily is true, but everything else is speculation and another attempt to ruin my reputation. Why would I do whatever it is they're accusing me of now?"

Alecia's lips twisted in a smirk. *Good question, but the world will know soon enough what kind of woman you are.*

CHAPTER 15

ADDISON

MARION'S UNBLINKING STARE reminded Addison of a snake. She was working her way toward something unsavory and taking her time about it. Addison sensed she wouldn't be rushed. She intended to milk whatever weapon she possessed for everything it was worth. Although she suspected what Marion had laid her hands on, Addison refused to show fear.

Why did it seem everything was conspiring to dismantle her life? She'd avoided this meeting until she couldn't anymore. Now that she was here, Addison longed for this farce to be over.

The rustic outdoor restaurant wasn't suited for the unpleasant business Addison expected Marion to raise. She was not disappointed when she caught a hint of malice in the other woman's gaze. A sip of marocchino provided the shot of espresso and chocolate she needed to settle her stomach, and the hint of a breeze caressing her skin was welcome.

"My mother kept your secrets," Marion finally said. Her black shirt met her smooth jet-black bob, creating the effect of a hoodie. All she needed was a scythe to personify the Grim Reaper.

A fake smile lifted Addison's lips. "Of course. We spent so much time together, it was inevitable."

Marion crossed her legs and settled more comfortably in the seat. "More to the point, my mother gave up her life to you."

"That's dramatic, don't you think?" Addison waited a few seconds before adding, "Especially since the two of you were estranged."

Marion's mouth twitched, and a tic developed around one eye. Her smug expression disappeared. "That's none of your business."

Now that she had something to needle Marion with, Addison ran a fingernail across the plush napkin and let out a small sigh. "I wouldn't say that at all. You see, Emily told me how you ignored all her efforts to patch up your *relationship,* if you could call it that, and how you made a career out of ignoring her."

The closest Emily had come to telling her about the standoff with Marion was to say she was off living her life and doing her own thing, but Addison didn't owe her the truth. Not when it was clear she was out for blood. If Marion thought she was in for easy money, she could think again.

"The situation I'm here to discuss has nothing to do with my mother and me."

"Which makes me curious. What business could you and I possibly have? I paid to fly her body back here and covered the funeral expenses." Addison widened her eyes and laid a hand on her chest. "If you want to discuss what Emily was entitled to, in terms of vacation leave, then you have a legitimate claim. Otherwise..."

"*Games People Play. The Tides of Time.*" Marion's voice was flat, but her ice-blue eyes were laser-sharp.

Other than swallowing, Addison didn't move. The drumbeat of her heart was her business alone, but she struggled to keep her breathing even. She didn't want to believe Emily had been this careless with her files, but Marion had been through her mother's things. That was clear.

"You've named two of my books, but what about them?" Addison lifted one shoulder in a casual gesture and prayed she wouldn't start to perspire. "Emily was privy to some of my contracts. That was part of our agreement."

"There's more to these contracts, as you well know." She paused for dramatic effect, sipping from her cup and playing her hand to the hilt. "And now everything is in my possession."

Addison scoffed and picked up her mug. Before she sipped, she slowly shook her head. "For someone who's been in business as long as you have, I can't believe you think you have any claim to those papers. Everything to do with Addison Comstock, LLC, belongs to me."

Marion glanced at the biscotti she'd ordered but hadn't touched. "Oh, I agree, but if I read some of those documents correctly, there is intellectual property in your catalog that doesn't belong to you."

This time, Addison couldn't hold in her gasp. She slammed the mug on the ivory place mat. "How dare you?"

"You can act all outraged, but my eyes didn't lie." Marion smirked as she delicately bit into the biscotti dipped in chocolate and sprinkled with pistachios.

Addison picked up her purse, removed some bills from her wallet, and threw them on the table. "Any dealings we have are over. You may contact my assistant to collect what's owed to Emily."

They assessed each other until the back of Addison's knees hit the chair as she stood. "If you know what's good for you, you'll erase this conversation from your tiny mind."

Throwing her chin into the air, Marion released a tinkle of laughter. "You amuse me, Addison. Of course you'll be hearing from me again."

Addison licked her lip, searching for a suitable comeback, but drew a blank. She stiffened her spine and marched to the sidewalk, forgetting she hadn't called for an Uber. To cover her gaffe, she put the phone to her ear and stalked around the corner with a purposeful stride. After securing transportation back to the studio, she rang Mikhail.

"Addison, what's popping?"

"You know better than to talk to me in language I don't understand."

She could have sworn he snorted, but she didn't have time to waste berating him. "I haven't spoken to Theo as yet, but I'm going to put out a statement."

After taking stock of where she stood, she walked into the outdoor dining area of a restaurant and claimed a seat.

"To cover what exactly?" Mikhail asked.

"My books, of course."

"Why would you need to do dat?" he asked, losing a bit of the King's English. "I've been talking to Ronique aka Island Gyal, and thought we weren't going to create any waves."

"You haven't told me anything to convince me she can make good on her threat."

"True, but you can't hurry some things. She works full time and has over a hund—"

"I don't care what she has," Addison snapped. "Either she's prepared to tell you whatever lies she's getting ready to post or she's not."

"I'll touch base with her today."

"Do that, or else..."

Mikhail understood what she meant and didn't waste more words before ending the call.

A waitress approached the table and asked to take her order in a cheerful voice that riled Addison.

"Go away," she growled and dismissed her with a wave of her hand.

The brunette's jaw went slack, and she backed away, then hurried inside.

The vehicle Addison requested pulled up next to the sidewalk, and she left the shade and approached the Nissan.

Once the young man identified himself, he stepped out, assisted her inside, and asked for her passenger code. Comfortable in the back seat, she dialed Theo's number. Maybe it would have been better if Mikhail worked with an agency. She'd feel more certain that any moves he made would be effective, although he'd been stellar at keeping her audience engaged. She couldn't think of a reason to doubt him. Except that one week was too long to be dithering with some influencer about what she did or didn't know.

This ominous cloud hanging over her life was nerve-wracking. The malevolence had to originate somewhere, but Kirkland hadn't pointed to anyone inside her team who might be responsible. He couldn't find any evidence connected to Casey, who was the most likely culprit. The police hadn't charged her with anything, but it didn't comfort Addison. If their eyes were on her, it was with good reason.

There was something about her Addison couldn't put a finger on. She was always pleasant, and her face was a neutral mask that reminded Addison of pond water—smooth on the surface, but one never knew what might be lurking underneath. Addison's instincts had never led her wrong, but she didn't waste time examining anything that wasn't a problem.

"Addison, good to hear from you." Theo startled her when he spoke in her ear. His bald-faced lie made one side of her mouth lift. "Do you want me to prepare something before our meeting tomorrow?"

"Yes. I just spoke to Mikhail about putting out a statement as soon as possible."

"Saying what?"

She scanned the rearview mirror to check whether the driver was listening, then angled her head sideways wanting to curse. This mess was making her suspect even strangers. "I'll call you when I return to the office."

"About the statement." Theo paused and cleared his throat. "I don't think that's a wise idea."

"Did I ask for your opinion?"

"No, but if it's to do with what I'm thinking about, drawing any kind of attention will make you seem guilty since no one has made any formal accusation."

In a near whisper, she said, "So, I'm supposed to sit back and allow someone to ruin my career and reputation?"

"I'm not saying that."

"Then what the hell are you saying? Because that's what I'm hearing."

"Why don't you speak with Matteo to be sure you're covering all bases? He can help you decide whether you should say anything."

The mention of the attorney she had on retainer fired up the synapses in her brain, but she'd never admit to Theo that his idea was brilliant. This foolishness had dragged her so far down, she wasn't thinking straight.

Matteo should have been her first stop since this madness unfolded, but she'd been caught up with feeling in the dark for an enemy out to ruin her. God knew she'd done some suspect things over the years, like the number she'd pulled on her first two writers, David and Tavoy. She met them at a writing workshop where she was a presenter more years ago than she cared to remember.

After assessing a one-page sample, she contacted them the following week. Both were young, eager, and willing to hone their skills. Six months later, while on her payroll, the two co-wrote an action-adventure-romance novel during their downtime, which they asked her to read and pitch to her agent.

Three chapters in, and Addison was salivating. The story was well-plotted with superb pacing and drama on each page. She did as they requested and asked Rachel to assess the manuscript.

"This is another surefire winner," she'd commented in their telephone call. "How did you get so lucky?"

"I asked my team to write it," she'd lied glibly.

Suspicion colored Rachel's voice with her next question. "So, you own this material?"

"Just as soon as you draw up a contract for it," Addison said smoothly. "They know I'm ready to take it off their hands. I'll need a nondisclosure written in, of course. A binding one."

A tense stretch of silence forced Addison to hold her breath until Rachel said, "I hope this time around you offered them something more generous than you did with your latest chart-topper."

"Of course." Addison released the air from her lungs in a gentle exhale, then, as adrenaline shot through her veins, she added, "How soon can you have it ready?"

"Two to three days. Meantime, don't do anything I wouldn't."

Her veiled reference to *Games People Play* didn't make a dent in Addison's good mood. She wasted no time and immediately called David and Tavoy into her office, a rented space in downtown Orlando that fell short of the studio she visualized having someday.

Both young men were babies really, which worked to her advantage. When they settled into the bucket seats on the other side of her desk, she stared at them in silence, then let out a deep sigh.

"I'm sorry, guys, Rachel doesn't think your manuscript is up to standard in its current state. In fact, it needs extensive work to make it ready for publication."

They shared a disbelieving exchange—one pair of eyes dark brown, the other hazel—and slumped in their seats. Between them, they barely had chin hairs and wouldn't add up to three hundred pounds if placed on a scale together.

She let them stew in their disappointment for a moment before addressing them, her elbows propped on the desk as she studied them over her laced fingers. "I know this is disappointing, but you have time on your side and the opportunity to learn more from me."

Neither of them responded, so she continued, "If you want, I can buy the manuscript from you, polish it up, and see if I can't do something with it further down the road." The room went quiet until she added softly, "I'm prepared to make a generous offer, but there are certain conditions."

She explained what she was prepared to give, and they reluctantly signed the contract, which she rushed Rachel to complete the following week. The advance reviews were everything Addison expected and more. Twelve months later, her publisher released *The Tides of Time* to rave reviews. The awards came as time passed.

A week after the book's release, David and Tavoy submitted their resignations, effective immediately, with no explanation.

They made no accusations and asked no questions. Their anger and contempt may have meant something if the book flopped, because she would have capitalized on it in vain. But she was riding high on the exhilaration of hitting number one on several charts before release day.

They had no recourse after her lawyer at that time demolished their attempt to sue. She didn't care because her energy was focused on putting together a new, expanded team. The letter from their legal aid lawyer caused a hiccup, but she swore she wouldn't take that path again. Now that her brand was established, it was too risky. Plus, her attorney had warned against the appearance of impropriety. "It can destroy your career," he'd warned, peering at her through his glasses.

Considering that he was familiar with her business, she waited a while before seeking other legal counsel. A clean slate made sense.

She hadn't given in to her opponents then, and wouldn't now. She'd fight to the death to keep her name and life's work from being destroyed. That portion of her past didn't serve her, so she'd make the best of the present and look to the future.

Squaring her shoulders, she shook off the cobwebs of decades past, scrolled to the number she wanted, and dialed Matteo's direct line.

"Addison. What a pleasant surprise."

She forced herself to hold in a sigh. Men were such liars.

"I need a meeting with you. Today, if possible."

CHAPTER 16

CASEY

PIPER BURST INTO the ladies' room weeping.

From one of the stalls, Casey peered through the wooden slats, then walked out and washed her hands at the sink. By that time, Piper sat sniffling on one of the padded benches.

Casey threw the hand towel in the bin, then approached the other woman. She bumped her gently with one leg and squeezed her shoulder while lowering herself to the seat. "Come on now. You've been doing this job for a while. You can handle anything."

With facial tissue pressed to her nostrils, Piper blinked hard and pulled herself upright. "I know, but lately this job has been so much worse."

Wincing, Casey searched her mind for something to comfort her, but didn't know what else to say. As usual, Addison lashed out when she felt threatened and didn't care who she hurt on her rampage.

Piper was stronger than she appeared because ninety percent of the time, she was the one who endured Addison's sour moods.

For her to have a breakdown meant someone told Addison no, or she was in a nasty mood.

Just another day at the circus.

"It comes with the territory." To Casey's ears, her words sounded weak. She sat sideways and faced Piper. "This is what we've chosen to do. We are all still here because of our contracts. Maybe now is the time to think about whether you want to renew yours."

Piper's eyes watered, and she tipped her head back. "I don't understand why she gets so riled up over what people think of her and what they're saying. That's what publicists are for, right? To fix the things that go off the rails."

She threw a panicked glance at the door, then back to Casey. "Never mind. I've said too much. Please keep this between us."

"I will." Casey patted her arm, then frowned. "What set her off this time, anyway?"

Piper rose, straightening her black skirt and white silk shirt. "The usual these days. Threats by an influencer to out her over something she did in Jamaica way back when."

At the counter, she studied her face in the mirror, gently poking under her swollen eyes.

Addison had gone through the wringer since the media personalities in Jamaica hinted she had a seamy side, but all she'd done up to now was huff and puff. Besides being in her feelings, maybe it would serve her better to fix her image instead of wearing out her staff.

Aside from accusing her of everything from envy to sabotage since the run-in with the police, Addison ignored her, but Casey realized that was temporary. Meanwhile, she was coping the best way she could—writing and minding her business.

Surviving Addison's madness was akin to walking through a minefield, not knowing when an explosion might rip her apart, and her personal life resembled the after-effects of a tropical storm.

In a teasing tone, Casey said, "We've all had to toughen up, and if I've told you once, I've told you fifty times, never let the devil see your tears."

She nodded and returned Casey's smile. "I'm trying."

With a gentle punch to her arm, Casey whispered, "Try harder."

She left Piper with the intention of having lunch. Her latest chapter had challenged her and took longer than the time she'd budgeted. While the others left exactly at noon, she'd stayed behind.

Once more, she thanked her luck that Addison hadn't installed cameras everywhere on the property. Being in the studio early or late guaranteed privacy, but she didn't spotlight herself by doing that too often.

Everything was about details and planning, which ensured she bought Addison's favorite brand of mixed chocolates at a local in-bond store during her time with Gran. Mixing them into the containers around the studio the evening before Addison met with Rachel was relatively safe. That way, it wouldn't seem as though Rachel was a target. The pair of gloves she'd brought from home had long been discarded.

Her mother's smile, the touch of her hand, and her embrace were where Casey ran when the world grew overwhelming. Time and circumstances dictated how much longer she'd be a planet revolving in Addison's crazy galaxy.

Reality intruded when she stepped into the kitchen, which was empty, except for Kirk who sat at one of the two six-seater tables and nodded to acknowledge her.

She greeted Randolph, the chef, at the counter. Fiona, his assistant, offered a bright smile and a greeting. "We have sandwiches, as well as chicken salad today."

"Sounds good. I'll have the salad."

"I knew you'd say that." A grin broke over Fiona's freckled face. She took pride in learning all their preferences. Casey ate lightly at work because a full meal and sugar made her sluggish. "Give me a moment."

After Fiona plated her lunch, Casey turned away from the counter separating the kitchen from the eating area. Kirk waved her over. Knowing it would be rude to reject his invitation, she pasted on a smile as she approached and took a seat.

"Seems we're both on the late train today," he offered instead of a greeting. "My meeting with Addison took a while. What kept you?"

"My chapter." She unwrapped the cutlery and laid the napkin to one side.

"Mmm." He bit into one half of his sandwich without taking his eyes off her.

"Is something wrong?"

"Not at all." Kirk wiped his mouth and dropped the napkin out of sight. "Just making conversation."

"Oh." Let him read into that whatever he liked.

He'd rolled his shirt up to his forearms, which carried a sprinkling of dark hair. From his wide shoulders and muscular arms, she guessed he had a rigorous workout routine. His goatee and hairline were neat, as if he'd left the barber's chair an hour ago.

While she studied him, he quirked well-defined lips, which probably made other men jealous, yet he didn't seem overly conscious of his looks. Those intense, inquisitive eyes warned her to be careful of him.

He ate another bite of the sandwich, then asked, "How long have you worked for Addison?"

"Long enough." Her cryptic answer was meant to shut him up.

She picked at the tasty chicken salad and avoided him. If he were as smart as he seemed, he'd understand the message. Casey told herself Kirk was dense or determined because a moment later, he came from another angle. "How did you become part of the team?"

She considered her answer, fighting to keep a smile off her face. He was trying hard. "Same way I presume you did. Or not. Someone posted a link to the ad on a writers' forum. I answered, got an interview, and voilà."

"Impressive. Being here tells me you're good at what you do."

She chewed a forkful of salad, sipped from the water glass, then said, "All of us on this team are good."

"Touché." He grinned, revealing a row of even teeth. "I meant no disrespect."

"I should hope not." She lifted her fork, but deliberately paused. "How did *you* get hired?"

He shrugged, and his smile widened. "My story is the same as yours: an opening came when the previous editor died."

"You appeared as fast as a whirlwind, so I wondered." Her careless lifting of one shoulder was designed to convey idle curiosity.

She wasn't surprised when he quipped, "I have my grapevine, same as you."

"Clearly."

They ate in silence while Casey wondered whether he was being honest, or if there was a deeper motive for his presence. Her instincts said yes.

Addison never shared more than they needed to know; that was standard.

If Casey didn't have information she wanted to protect, her mind wouldn't be up in her boss' business, seeing shadows that might not exist. No matter what Kirk said, she'd be foolish to lower her guard.

Her appetite hadn't returned since the fiasco with the police, which was ongoing, so she gave up on finishing the salad. Dredging up a pleasant expression, she dabbed her lips. "Good talking with you."

"You, too."

She edged the chair back to rise, and Kirk cleared his throat. "Can I ask you one more thing?"

Casey raised one eyebrow. "What's that?"

"Since I'm the newbie around here, what advice would you give?"

"Mind your business and write your chapters. Or edit, *if* that's what you're here to do."

Kirk's smile was playful as he tilted his head to one side. "Anything else?"

Oh, he was clever, trying to pull her out. She rose and smoothed her skirt. "Maybe, but that depends on whether you're the next boy toy or stool pigeon."

A tic squeezed one of his eyes, but he didn't respond.

Let him wrap his brain around that. He understood well enough and would be a fool to repeat what she'd just said. If he were in the studio to ferret out information, they'd know because whatever he uncovered, Addison would use to attack them.

She'd given him enough to indicate she wasn't clueless. As she stepped away, she threw another bone over her shoulder. "And by the way, be careful of the company you keep."

The tension headache that blossomed behind her eyes during the day was now in full bloom. Casey released her hair from the band that held it together, but relief didn't come. For the first time since she'd been on Addison's team, she hadn't been able to focus. Maybe because her mind kept straying to the schemes and plans she'd approved and rejected over the years while she laid tracks to the person who could have saved her family, if she'd cared.

Eyes closed, she lounged on the beige leather sofa, ignoring the comedy she'd been watching. Kirk intruded on her mind, which was disturbing. She couldn't explain her attraction to him. Maybe it was the aura of confidence that surrounded him, or the sense that he was dangerous.

The last time she was this taken with anyone was five years ago, and that hadn't ended well. Now, she couldn't afford to feed what might become an addiction. Not when she was close to achieving her biggest ambition. All of that could wait, and none of it would include him. She'd be reckless to chance it with Addison in the picture.

As much as she didn't deserve it, Addison was due some grace. The empire of lies on which she'd built her career was slowly falling apart, which had to be devastating.

Plus, Addison's treatment of the men she slept with, her mood swings, and asinine behavior were enough to put Casey off romance in any form. No man would deal with her random hours and the stress she sometimes took home from work. And to think, her job was making up stories.

On a practical level, Casey was in no position to maintain a healthy relationship and never had been. She carried too much baggage. After her stint with Addison was over, she'd think about finding a good man and enjoying life. For now, she'd stay focused on the most crucial task she'd set for herself since landing in America.

Donnette set the dinner tray on her lap, then returned with her own meal. "You okay, sis?"

"Sure." Casey stretched and smoothed her hair. "A little headachey, but I'm fine."

Acting as though she'd had a random thought, Casey knitted her eyebrows. "What happens when there's too much insulin in our bodies?"

Donnette lifted her fork with a sliver of chicken breast and stopped halfway to her mouth. She laid it down and focused on Casey. "Are you having issues with your sugar levels?"

"No. I'm not diabetic or anything."

"So, why are you asking?"

Casey grabbed the first thing that came to mind. "The other day, after I ate that huge chunk of sweet potato pudding, I felt a bit off."

"Really? You seemed all right to me. That was Sunday."

"I chased it with nearly a gallon of water, so I was fine after a while, but…" She left her words hanging.

The nurse in Donnette picked up the thread. "Hypoglycemia, or insulin shock, which can lead to organ failure if glucose isn't fed into the body." She narrowed her eyes and pulled back to ask, "Are you sure you're okay?"

With a flick of the wrist, Casey nodded. "You worry too much."

Donnette stabbed a small chunk of tomato, then lifted it to her lips. "Can you blame me, especially after that session with Detectives Ince and Robinson? And they made sure I understood this isn't over."

"Didn't I say to let me worry about them?"

"That's the problem with you. You think you're superwoman." The fork hit the plate with a clang as Donnette asked, "What am I supposed to do if you mess around and the police lock you up?"

"Nobody's getting locked up. Trust me." She reached for her sister's hand, but Donnette pulled away.

"Trust you? Do you know the level of embarrassment this caused me at work? In fact…" She released her breath on a huff. "HR called me up on it. Do you understand that a *private* medical facility takes every precaution when hiring people? And any hint of trouble with the police affects me? I could lose my job over this." She rubbed the muscle on one side of her neck as her voice turned shrill. "And meantime, your reputation is in tatters. Yes, I know what's being said on the internet. Casey, whatever you're doing, let it go before it destroys our lives. Please."

"Donnette, why d'you think I—"

"Save it. Let's talk about something else."

Their conversation was dead because Donnette wouldn't listen to anything she said. She'd withdraw into herself and emerge when she was ready.

Casey massaged the back of her head as the pain intensified and spread to her eyes. The guilt that racked her while waiting three hours before the police released Donnette was overwhelming. She hadn't given up hope, which paid off. The police didn't keep her overnight. As she suspected, they were baiting them for their own reasons—typical behavior when they had nothing on people they considered suspects.

Her jaw hung slack after Donnette walked past her on her release without speaking. She'd followed her into the parking lot, which was a waste of time because she drove away without uttering one word.

After trailing Donnette to work and watching her walk into the building, Casey went home to lie across her bed in the darkness. Before she fell asleep, she rolled off the mattress and sat cross-legged in the closet, staring into space. Eventually, she removed a lip gloss container from one of the shoeboxes. Her legs were stiff when she rose, carrying the plastic tube.

On an earlier trip to Jamaica, she took back a few angel's trumpet petals for their album of mementos. Anything from home was precious since Donnette hadn't returned in some time.

"Too many painful memories," she always said.

When the blooms dried, Casey crushed a couple of them to powder, being careful to wear both gloves and an N95 surgical disposable respirator. She funneled the dust into a lip gloss container that went into her handbag and back to Jamaica.

Emily had trusted her to help when she didn't feel well, which made it easy to doctor her water and sprinkle a pinch of dust inside her pillowcase. None of it gave Casey any pleasure, then or now, and she sighed while emptying the canister into the toilet. She'd dispose of the plastic tube on the way to work. Thanks to Donnette's earlier reaction, she could forget about anything that involved insulin.

Yesterday, Donnette finally spoke as though nothing had happened, but Casey understood the way she communicated and the need to distance herself while managing her emotions. They stood together through everything, and her sister hated change with good reason.

Casey startled and shuttered her thoughts when Donnette stood but didn't leave the room. She waited for Casey to raise her head before she spoke. "If you do anything to destroy our lives, I'll never speak to you again."

"Dee, please." Casey heard the tremor in her voice and sucked in a breath to calm herself, but Donnette wasn't finished. "Addison Comstock has taken enough from this family, but if *you* cause me to lose this job, you're dead to me."

CHAPTER 17

ALECIA

"YOU SHOULDN'T BE in here." Quentin stood back from the heavy walnut door to the men's room and crossed his arms. "Are you stalking me?"

She avoided his question and rested a hand on her hip. "You're the one who dragged me in here, remember?"

"I didn't drag you anywhere. You came willingly."

"When you grabbed my arm and treated me the same as a Neanderthal would?" She puckered her mouth and assumed a sour expression while scanning the granite countertop and marble floor. "But I understand. You don't want a certain someone to see us talking."

"I won't dignify that rubbish with a response."

Alecia released a dry chuckle and raised both hands. "Of course not, because what could be wrong about two people discussing their relationship inside a bathroom *at work*?"

"That's not what we're doing."

"But here we are. Why?" She inched farther into his space, inhaling the musk and vanilla in his cologne. "Could that be because servicing the boss is more beneficial?"

He retreated, shaking his head as though she were something to be pitied. "Not that again?"

"I'm not stupid, but we'll see who's gonna be the fool when people know you're sleeping with the woman who pays you, and that you and other coworkers are bedding her."

Quentin sucked in a harsh breath, and his face darkened. "You wouldn't dare."

"Oh yes, I would."

"Even though you know that's a lie?"

Forcing another chuckle, she tipped one eyebrow higher. "Where's the lie?"

As his frown deepened, Quentin ran a hand over his hair. It had grown out and was now at the stage where it stuck out in all directions unless he kept it moisturized. He'd sprouted stubble, which she found sexy, but that wasn't for her benefit. He was probably trying to keep Addison's attention now that another man was on the scene. But why was she even curious about their business? She had her own private concerns.

His snub nose flared, and his dark eyes bored through her. "So, about you stalking me."

"Get over yourself, Quentin." She lowered her chin to prevent him from guessing the truth, which would humiliate her once more. No woman with a drop of sense would admit to stalking her ex. "I drive past your place to and from work."

"You watch my apartment at night. What's up with that?"

"Do you have proof of these accusations? I'm not the only woman who drives a RAV-4."

"But you're the one person I know with that custom shade of burgundy."

Alecia spread her hands and shook her head even as her stomach sank. "D'you know how many people live in Orlando?"

"That's irrelevant. What's relevant is this sick obsess—"

The door swung inward, and Addison held it open with one hand. A shiver coursed through Alecia's body, and her stomach did a nosedive to her heels. The worst scenario in this awful situation had materialized.

"What are *you* doing in here?" Addison asked, her tone icy.

The question Alecia wished she could ask was why Addison was visiting the men's room.

No doubt to get her freak on.

The corners of Alecia's mouth twinged the way they would if she bit into a lemon. She was in for another dressing down.

Addison faced Quentin, who now stood sideways with a flush coating his neck. The glare he turned on Alecia would have deterred another woman, but not her. She'd had enough of being a fool. It wasn't her fault that he'd confronted her in the passage outside. Since yesterday, she'd been getting some bad vibes from him, but he hadn't approached her until now.

The truth was, she'd been outside his condo at least three times in the past two weeks. Only God could tell why she ran that risk, but it galled her soul to be in this situation. Even after making up her mind, she couldn't seem to move on. But how could she when they were locked into this madness of pretending they meant nothing to each other? She couldn't be intimate with someone for a year and walk away as if nothing had happened. It wasn't possible.

"I need to speak with you." Addison addressed him, but flayed Alecia with her eyes. "I'll see both of you in my office."

Alecia lifted her chin and swept past Addison, wishing she could mow her down. Her heart pounded, and her stomach threatened to eject the lunch she'd eaten a half-hour ago. She swallowed and laid one hand on her tummy, praying she didn't disgrace herself by upchucking in Addison's office. The she-devil deserved the inconvenience, though.

Neither of them walked with her, and Alecia stepped into the studio, noting that only half the team was present. When she stood at Piper's desk, she said, "Addison wants to see me."

"Sure. Go on in."

Piper's wan smile made Alecia feel she was going to the gallows. The dark circles under the other woman's eyes underlined Addison's toxic effect on everyone. She'd come down hard on Piper in the last week, blaming her for everything from missing files to moving the items on her desk. The poor woman had had several breakdowns, and as badly as Addison disrespected Alecia over her last chapters, she'd been relieved when her attention turned elsewhere.

Since her troubles started, Addison had the effect of all the disastrous forces of nature combined—an unrelenting maelstrom that destroyed everything precious.

Before she left Piper's desk, the muted *whoosh* of the door opening and the rhythm of her shoes across the floor alerted Alecia to her boss's presence.

Quentin followed and, like a wuss, wouldn't acknowledge her. He waited for Alecia to fall in step behind Addison before moving toward the office.

Over her shoulder, Addison commanded, "Piper, no interruptions."

"What is going on here?" Addison asked, taking her seat.

She didn't invite them to sit, which was precisely what Alecia expected.

"Alecia?"

She held her silence, still stuck on what Addison wanted to discuss with Quentin that was so important she had to track him down in the bathroom.

"Since neither of you knows why you were meeting in the men's room, let me guess." She rolled a thin silver pen between her fingers. "I've never laid down any rules about fraternizing at work, but I figured everyone understood it was off-limits."

She let the silence stretch, punctuated by the clock behind them. "It causes complications and can become nasty if things go sour."

Alecia forced her eyebrows not to contract in a frown. This hypocritical bitch was forbidding them from having—or continuing—their relationship because she had the power to do so. Tears scalded her eyes, but Alecia willed herself not to let this witch snatch her self-control. The nerve of this woman. All she did was devastate. It didn't matter who or why. She didn't care about either of them. She simply wanted to know Quentin was under her thumb exclusively. And being a coward, he wasn't man enough to stand up for himself. To be fair, he had his job to think about, but still…

A haze passed before Alecia's eyes, and whatever Addison said went unheard. The fog cleared when she asked, "Do you understand?"

Addison grimaced and leaned in when she didn't respond. "I asked if you understood what I said."

The tight, painful vise squeezing Alecia's throat barely allowed her to whisper, "Yes."

"You're free to go." Addison's smug half-smile confirmed she'd satisfied the need for control.

Alecia stalked past Quentin, wanting to kick him in the calf. At the doorway, she filled then emptied her lungs, but it didn't stem the anger tearing up her insides. When she sat and raised her head, Casey asked a silent question.

Her concern almost made Alecia break down in tears. Although she'd posted about Casey's dilemma with the police on social media, she hadn't cut her off totally. The truth was, sometimes Alecia acted before she assessed all the possible consequences. When she tried to apologize, Casey brushed away her excuses with a strange comment. "I've been through much worse."

What could be worse than going viral under suspicion of murder?

Alecia dismissed that question and nodded slightly to let Casey know she was okay. But she was far from being all right. She hadn't been born in the best of circumstances, but now she'd made it past the pain and rejection of her past, and Addison Comstock had ripped everything away. All. Over. Again.

That didn't sit right with her, and as the words on the screen formed an illegible jumble, a lone tear tickled her cheek and lodged in the crease between her lips. Another followed, but she refused to give in to the indignity of drying her face.

Casey shifted to catch her attention, then slid a napkin to her. She thanked her with a tiny smile, then glanced at Quentin, hoping he hadn't witnessed her lapse. In any case, he wouldn't care.

The scrapbooks in her closet brought a measure of comfort, which she'd enjoy soon enough. Half the workday remained, but before she went home, she'd stop at Mama's house and confront her about the gaps in her history she'd stubbornly refused to fill.

CHAPTER 18

ADDISON

THIS COULDN'T BE her life. Addison rubbed her chest, where her heart pumped in deep, painful beats. She half expected it to plunge from her chest and fall at her feet.

Breathe, Addison.

She sat back in her ergonomic seat, which for the first time was more of a hindrance rather than a comfort. The back was too tight against her spine, and the arms irritated her skin, perhaps because she'd been restless all morning and couldn't sit still.

She'd given up on any of the idiots around her coming up with any workable solutions, and Matteo was taking his time about going through her files and scheduling a meeting. She wanted to talk with him now, but he was busy doing only God knew what.

To add to her anxiety—if that's what she was experiencing—he insisted that she not release any statement before they had a proper meeting. Her retainer should have guaranteed her a meeting the moment she asked for one, but he'd been busy frustrating her by not agreeing with her wishes.

She focused on the man sitting across from her, reading her laptop screen. If she were prone to tears, she would have been sobbing all day.

"Why would anyone make these claims against you?" he asked, turning it to face her. "By the way, I sent the message to myself and took a screenshot of the claims from that influencer."

"How would I know any of that? This one has been the wildest accusation yet."

"Is there any truth to it?" Kirkland asked, watching her as if she were a criminal under investigation.

She assumed her don't-try-me face to intimidate him. "I didn't hire you to ask questions."

"How do I know what is true when you're blocking me? The least you can do is help with my process of elimination."

Running both hands up and down her arms to warm herself, she scoffed. "And what exactly are you trying to eliminate?"

"My job is easier if I know the truth."

He was making her uncomfortable without trying, and it unsettled her. "Have I told any lies that you know of?"

"No, but you're not making my job any easier."

"I didn't hire you to do *easy*, but let's just say none of that rubbish is worth my time." She sat straighter and held her head high. "They're lying."

She spun the diamond ring on her middle finger to its proper position to give herself a moment. When she first hit the *USA Today*'s Best-selling Booklist, she'd celebrated with a gift. The twenty-four-carat oval-cut diamond set in white gold was a fitting tribute to herself. Since then, she'd surpassed that accomplishment by far and didn't deny herself anything she desired.

Rachel's and Theo's advice made sense, so she donated to several children's homes because she understood that some folks had a hard life and needed every possible helping hand. Surely, with all she did, losing face to a bunch of envious people wouldn't be her lot.

Kirkland cleared his throat, which plunged her back in the middle of this latest round of drama. Someone had sent her a sheet laid out to resemble newsprint, in which they accused her of stealing *Games People Play.* They also threatened to expose her if she didn't confess to manuscript theft. Whoever came up with that sick joke included the language she was supposed to use for her announcement.

"Is there anything about this manuscript that would raise doubts that you wrote it?"

While she struggled to find a response, Kirkland watched her.

"You *must* have proof this book was yours from the beginning. What about the exchanges between you and your agent? The ones with your editor? The submission to your publisher?"

"I'll have to ask Rachel." She wrapped her fingers around the gold book pendant and closed her eyes. Rachel was dead. "Sorry. I'll ask Vance to send over those documents from her office."

Her thoughts ping-ponged, and she rubbed her forehead to buy some time. How could she have forgotten to contact Vance about her files. She picked up the handset and held up one finger to silence Kirkland.

"Piper, get Vance on the phone. Now." To Kirkland, she said, "My copy of the files is at the bank in a security deposit box, so I can't put my hands on them now."

She'd have to sanitize her papers before handing them to him, but that wasn't happening today.

The second the phone buzzed, she snatched it up. "Vance, I need all my files, including a copy of my contract with Rachel."

"I'm sorry, but I can't release them to you immediately."

A vise strangled her throat, but she managed to protest. "I must have heard you wrong. What do you mean? Have you lost your mind?"

"I have not. Miss Maxwell had a silent partner, and he—"

"I don't give a shit about what kind of partner she had." Her temples pounded, and an ache started low in her back. "I'm demanding my files, and I want them today."

"Miss Comstock—"

"Vance, don't play with me."

"But—"

"Where is this partner, and who is it?" she spat.

"Marcus Ryder."

The name sounded familiar, but she couldn't place it immediately. She pulled in a short breath as an agonizing pain stitched across her chest. "Is he at the office? I need to speak with him this minute."

"He's out of the country this week."

Why did everything conspire to frustrate her? She avoided Kirkland by watching her staff over his shoulder. Alecia was bold enough to eyeball her as if she were a blank wall before she scoffed and went back to typing.

Addison's focus returned to Kirkland, who watched her over steepled fingers.

"Miss Comstock, do you need anything else?" Vance asked.

"Your new boss's number. I hate repeating myself."

"I'm not at liberty to—"

"I'm going to hang up and give you an hour." She stopped to calm herself and rephrase her demand. "When I call back, you'd better have that number."

She ended the call, threw the handset on the desk, and faced Kirkland. Despite her unacceptable behavior, his bland expression didn't change. His opinion didn't matter anyway. He was there to do a job and had nothing to show for the hefty retainer she'd paid him.

"What do you know about Alecia Cookson?" she asked.

"From her résumé, she seems to be exactly who she says she is." He opened both hands, and the citrus and lemon aroma in his cologne floated to her in a distracting tide. "She lives a quiet life."

"What about any romantic relationship?"

"I'm sure you know she was seeing Quentin Young."

"*Was* being the operative word. D'you think she could be behind these social media issues?"

"I'm not entirely sure, but I'll dig deeper."

"This can't take all year." She swallowed her annoyance and reminded him, "I have a reputation to think about."

"And what you're asking me to handle is a delicate matter. I can't be heavy-handed in my investigation."

"Agreed, but I don't see *any* results, and you've been here for two weeks."

"These things take time. Trust me to deal with this in the way I see fit."

Massaging her chest, she said, "Hard to do when my life is falling apart."

"I have to build trust with your people…and that's also hard to do."

She skewered him with a glare. "Need I ask why?"

"We both know you're not the easiest employer or person to deal with."

"If I needed your opinion on how I run my business and how I treat my staff, I'd have asked for it."

"Both affect what's happening to you now, but of course, you didn't pose any questions."

He didn't raise his voice or speak with any attitude, but his defiance was exhilarating.

Few men dared to cross her, yet here he was sticking it to her without losing his cool. She studied him, noting his neat facial hair and sun-kissed skin, also the muscles hidden under his pale-yellow shirt, which he'd paired with khaki pants and brown ankle boots. Some private time with him was exactly what she needed to forget her troubles for a while and put her world back on its axis.

"Walk with me." She rose from the chair and slid her cell phone into her pocket.

He followed her out of the office, and as they went past Piper's desk, she instructed, "I'll be back soon. No disturbances, please."

Conscious of Kirkland's light footfalls behind her, she put an exaggerated swing in her hips. At the end of the corridor, she went left toward her suite. She tapped in a series of numbers on the keypad, and the door opened. Stepping inside, she faced him, sweeping a hand across her hip and letting the light fabric of her skirt float in the space between them. She reached around him to close the door and whispered, "Do you know why you're here?"

Kirkland didn't return her smile. "I can guess."

Slowly, she walked around him then ran both hands over his chest. "Since you know what I want, what are you waiting for?"

Instead of grabbing her around the waist as she'd expected, he circled her wrists with both hands. His breath was a minty wave when he said, "This isn't a good idea."

"Why not?" She pouted and tugged to get him to release her hands. "I'm not asking for anything in return for your...services. It's a no-strings-attached arrangement."

"I'm sorry, but I can't." With a gentle shake of the head, he continued, "This isn't why you hired me, and it will complicate our relationship."

Addison raised one eyebrow and maintained their eye lock. "Yet, you came here with me."

"I wasn't sure whether you were going to show me something related to your case."

She ground her hips slowly against his, triumphant when his penis stirred and then hardened.

"Your reaction makes more sense than your explanation," she whispered. Her victorious smile faded when he stepped back. "Mixing business with pleasure doesn't matter that much."

"It does to me." His faint smile was an irritant, and she wanted to ram her fist into his nose when he added, "Thanks for the offer, though."

As if he's refusing a leftover sandwich.

Clenching her jaw to stop herself from telling him off and embarrassing herself, she moved farther into the suite. "Get out."

Kirkland nodded once and turned away, leaving the door open.

He had some nerve to refuse her. Pity she couldn't fire him, but he was right. Sleeping with him would have put a different spin on their business, especially since he wasn't a pushover. These contracts she insisted on signing would be the death of her.

The phone buzzed against her hip, and she debated whether to check who or what needed her attention. She kicked off her shoes and crossed to the sofa in the sitting area. After sinking on her back, she swiped the screen and squinted at it. Mikhail had reached out with an urgent message that included an image. She opened it and jackknifed into an upright position.

Aside from speculation about her books, someone had posted a picture of her and a child they claimed was hers. She studied the image, clutching the phone until her knuckles hurt.

This can't be real!

A scream tore its way from her throat, and she flung the phone across the room. It clattered on the floor as she sank onto the cushion, gasping. The ceiling blurred and went out of focus as tears scalded her eyes. She had done everything to disassociate herself from the woman she'd been. What would anyone gain from dragging her into the past and wrecking the life she'd created?

CHAPTER 19

CASEY

ALECIA'S SWEAR WORD startled Casey. She twisted to watch Quentin, who was on his way to the counter.

"I'll see you in the studio." Alecia rose from the table and stalked through the door.

When Quentin was served, he cracked a smile, then pulled out a chair and sat with Jon at the next table.

Casey didn't blame him. She wasn't one to interfere in other people's spats, but he wouldn't know that.

Alecia continued dropping spiteful remarks, and the atmosphere around her was toxic. The other team members avoided her, and during their brainstorming sessions, even Casey tiptoed around her, afraid she'd either spit verbal poison darts or burst out bawling.

She was halfway through her meal when the door opened again and Kirk entered. After scanning the area, he gave her a half-smile, which she returned, though she wasn't feeling it. Two weeks, and he'd fallen into Addison's web.

Disgusting.

Several minutes went by before he slid into the seat across from her.

"How's it going?" he asked, unwrapping his cutlery.

Good, until you showed up.

"Depends on what you mean. If you're talking about my writing, that's fine."

"What else would I be talking about?"

"You tell me." She sipped water, waiting for his comeback.

He popped a sliver of beef into his mouth and chewed slowly without taking his eyes off her. When he swallowed, he said, "I feel you have something against me."

"You're new to the team. What could that be?" Before she took the next bite of stewed fish, she added, "Unless you know something I don't."

Her attention strayed to the bottom edge of his collar, where a smudge the color of Addison's lipstick marked the yellow material. She focused on it long enough to be certain he noticed. "Then again, I see maybe you do."

Nothing and no one was off-limits with Addison. One thing about her, she ran true to form. A day ago, she'd given Alecia and Quentin hell over their romance, and here she was bedding another member of her staff. Gran would call it having "white liver," or an insatiable appetite for sex.

"Whatever you're thinking, you're wrong," Kirk said, interrupting her thoughts.

"What *I* think doesn't matter, but now I know for sure what *you* are."

His jaw hardened, and his lips barely moved when he spoke. "I don't care what you think, but for the record, I'm nobody's boy toy."

"Keep fooling yourself." She stood, threw down the napkin, and left the lunchroom, more annoyed than she should have been. Denying she found him attractive was useless, but somehow, she hadn't expected him to fall so quickly into Addison's clutches.

She still had twenty minutes left of her lunchtime, but went back to the studio and sat scrolling on her phone. One social media platform was enough to satisfy her need for connection, but she wasn't a fan. She'd seen too many lives destroyed by unauthorized photos, speculation, and innuendo.

Kirk's scent alerted her to his presence—something herbal and aquatic that stirred her senses and made her want more, which was a no-go.

"Why do I feel you want something?" Casey asked, sliding the cell phone to her left, farther away from him.

"Why would you say that?" he asked, slipping into the chair beside hers.

"Well, when you're sneaking up on people…are you trying to catch me out?"

She'd been scanning the picture of Addison and a baby on the pages of social media influencers who were part of the literary community, so it was good that she sniffed him out before laying eyes on him.

Addison's story had caught fire, and people speculated whether she was the mother of the little girl. They also wanted to know the toddler's identity. Addison was in a tough place because some would not let go. They would dig deeper. The next thing might be a feature story that included the girl's life and location, if someone found her.

"Maybe you're suspicious because of everything that's happened."

Kirk's comment pulled Casey out of her head, and she gave him a side-eye. "I'm not sure what you're calling everything."

"Come on." He intended to charm her with a friendly grin, but she wasn't fooled. "You can't tell me you don't know about Addison's issues."

"I never said that, but I've learned to mind my business and stay out of other people's affairs."

"Where in Jamaica are you from?"

The change in direction was disarming, like his grin. She arched one brow and took a deep breath to restore her balance. "Who told you that's where I'm from?"

He waited several seconds before saying, "Unlike some who try their best to integrate, your accent stands out."

"Kingston," she said, hoping she wouldn't forget that blatant lie if the subject came up again. As far as she was concerned, he was fishing for information to feed Addison.

She'd been acting weird lately, closeting herself with Kirk under the guise of discussing chapters. But there were few significant changes to their submissions and no over-the-top ranting from Addison, so they had to be talking about other matters, like who was exposing her personal business and making life miserable.

Kirk was now the most valuable person on Addison's team, aside from her lawyer and publicist. He was hiding something—or more to the point, keeping Addison's secrets. That made him the enemy, and Casey wasn't one to act stupid or careless around him.

"And you lived there all your life?" he asked, cutting into her thoughts.

She spun the chair to face him. "Why don't you ask Addison to show you my file since you're obsessed with her employees?"

"That's a strong word, and anyway, I'm not interested in all of them." He let that sink in, while scanning her face. "I'm asking you."

She turned back to the laptop, unsure of what game he was playing. "Here's the thing: I don't know why you're so curious about me, but you won't find whatever it is you're seeking. I'd suggest you mind Addison's affairs and let me move on with mine."

"Is it so far-fetched that I'd be into you?"

Her mouth pulled into a pucker. "You forget I know about you and Addison. I'd be a fool to give you the time of day."

A shadow crossed his face, and his eyes narrowed. "I told you—"

"Don't bother. I prefer to rely on what's obvious."

Kirk's nostrils flared, and he pulled in a sharp breath, while she bit the inside of her cheek. She'd hit a nerve.

Maybe he'd leave her alone since she saw straight through him.

That wish died when he said, "My strongest trait is that I'm tenacious."

She propped her elbow on the desk and supported her cheek on one fist. She wasn't certain if he meant a personal or professional level, and it jolted her. "Good for you."

Now, she really was done talking with him. To press home her point, she sat closer to the screen and read through what she'd written before lunch, then continued typing. She was conscious of Kirk's presence at the neighboring seat. He seemed to be reading, but she couldn't tell if he was spying on her.

What he didn't know was that Casey had enough focus for both of them. Once she hit her stride, she forgot he was at her elbow. As the other writers trickled into the room, he greeted them. When he rose and entered Addison's office, Casey's fingers slowed, and her gaze followed him. She shifted her attention to the screen quickly since Addison sat facing the studio. Damn her for this silly idea of rotating their station each week.

"It prevents stagnation," she claimed.

Stagnation, my ass. It's all about control.

She was deep in the words she was stringing together when Addison yelled, "Piper, get Matteo on the line."

Addison's stress served as a source of distraction, if Casey allowed it to be. Her boss definitely wasn't as interested in *Murder by the Book* as she was in her social platforms. Poor Mikhail had to listen to her day in and day out, and also convince her not to respond to every comment made about her, especially if it wasn't affecting book sales. She sometimes forgot her door was open while she paced the office, yelling at either him or Theo.

Writing the scene where the police questioned one witness after the murder scene made Casey's heart skip several beats. The police hadn't called her back in, but she was uneasy, not eating or sleeping well, waiting for something unpleasant to take her by surprise. And, of course, the police could be watching her. If Casey were locked up, Donnette might not survive without her, and the thought of it was almost enough to unravel Casey. But she couldn't bring herself to do nothing about righting their world. She'd be letting herself and Donnette down, no matter what she said. None of this would end in her incarceration. It couldn't. They deserved justice.

Emily came to mind, but Casey shut that down. As Addison's editor and confidant, she knew where all the proverbial bones were buried. And, Rachel, in her role as agent, helped Addison shaft people out of their work. Together, they were an evil triad. They deserved to lose everything. Same as she and Donnette had lost their home, family, and identity.

How many other people had Addison treated the same way, making promises and then stealing their manuscripts? If the details of a story weren't exact, in most cases, they came close.

If it nuh go so, it near go so, as her grandmother would say.

The words flew from her fingertips, which amazed Casey, as always, that she could pour onto the page while malice occupied her head. At 5:05, she tapped on the glass tabletop to get Alecia's attention. She wriggled her fingers, indicating that Casey should go without her.

"I have some stuff to finish up."

Casey translated that to mean she was staying behind to torment Quentin. Every day, Alecia found new ways to provoke him. Her attacks were mainly verbal, but the other day when he believed he'd mislaid stationary items, Alecia had taken them. She also left a sticky liquid on his desk, which messed up his shirt. He'd been swearing more than normal, but hadn't reported her.

"See you tomorrow." Casey picked up her handbag and left the chilly studio, looking neither left nor right. At the bottom of the stairs, she rolled her shoulders, then tipped her chin toward the sky when she stood next to her ride.

Working for Addison had always been demanding. Now that her world was crumbling, it was time for Casey to think about her next steps. The phone rang, and she dug it out of her bag. "Hey, Donnette."

When she didn't answer, Casey checked the screen to be certain she was still connected. Frowning, she went to handsfree. "What's the matter, sis?"

"Thanks to you, HR decided to suspend me."

Casey massaged the bridge of her nose and sank in the seat. "That doesn't make sense."

"Well, it does to them. They can't afford to have their reputation tainted by any hint of scandal."

Donnette's bitter delivery hurt Casey, but she understood. How could she not?

"I hope you're happy, satisfied, or whatever the hell you're supposed to be."

"But—"

"Not another word, Casey. Leave me the hell alone."

"I'm sorry."

"Save it, because the only person you care about is yourself."

Her words were a gut punch that sucked the air from Casey's lungs. Family was everything. Each action she took was meant to benefit Donnette and herself, but none of it mattered if her sister couldn't see it. She folded both hands under her head, leaned on the steering wheel, and let her tears fall.

A tap on the glass reminded Casey she hadn't left Addison's property. She dragged one hand across her eyes and sat back.

Kirk stood outside the open door. "Are you okay?"

"Do I look like it?"

He rested his hand on the door frame. "I'm trying to help."

"Thank you, but I don't need anything from you."

She yanked the door, but he didn't release it. Instead, he pulled a hanky from his back pocket and held it out to her.

Eyes closed, she debated whether to accept it. "If I take it, will you let go of my door?"

He cracked a smile. "Maybe."

The soft cotton held the scent of his cologne. She dabbed her eyes, then muttered, "Thank you."

Nodding slightly, he stepped away from the car but continued watching her.

A heavy mass weighed on her chest and stole her breath when she drove toward the gate.

The security guard waved to her, and she swiped at another tear that trickled down her cheek.

CHAPTER 20

ALECIA

"WHY DO YOU want to hear about that again?" Mama forgot the television screen long enough to acknowledge Alecia's question. "How many ways can I tell the same story?"

"Well enough so I understand it."

"Why yuh come over here when I watching my show, eh?"

Slipping into patois was Mama's way of letting Alecia know she was super-annoyed. After returning home from her job at a daycare center, she insisted on "peace and quiet" while watching every version of *True Crime* that ever aired, even if she'd seen them before. She never tired of yelling at the screen, helping the detectives and lawyers with unsolved crimes.

"I don't see you for weeks, and you prefer the television over talking to me?" Alecia sat next to her, balancing a tray of red peas soup on her lap.

"Don't say dat," Mama snapped, and her small eyes disappeared into the creases of her angular face, which had grown fleshy over the years.

"What am I supposed to say when you act like old crimes are more important than my life?"

Evadne Cookson hit the remote and stopped the film. "What yuh really want?"

"You know you're something else, Mama? You're not even watching a live program. It's something you can see any time."

"And I'm free to see it on *my* time, but here yuh are demanding some of it for no good reason."

Out of spite, Alecia chewed slowly on a piece of pigtail, making Mama wait until she swallowed. "I have a good reason."

"Yeah, the same one that had yuh searching up my t'ings when yuh didn't even know what yuh wanted to find."

That was true. Every parent had a place where they kept birth, death, and vaccination certificates, school reports, and other family records. Plus, documents they didn't want everyone seeing or handling. Alecia had never found Mama's secret stash. She'd been thinking about it in recent times and had an idea she hadn't explored yet.

She lifted her gaze to the ceiling. "You don't forget anything."

Mama yanked off the wig, which was cut in a bob, and dropped it on the sofa. "You've always been sneaky. Maxine and Ophelia never—"

"Whatever, Mama." Alecia raised her hand with the spoon in it to ward off Mama's comparisons and complaints. "I was searching because you never told me what I wanted to know."

Mama shook a finger at Alecia as her cheeks reddened. "You're so ungrateful. I took you in, gave you a home, and two sisters—"

"Who tormented me until I learned to fight."

"Toughened you up, didn't it?" Mama taunted, cutting her eyes back to the television.

"And you wonder why we're dysfunctional," Alecia grumbled.

"We're *dysfunctional* because yuh refuse to leave the past where it belongs."

They'd had this argument for the last two years, and Alecia was sick of it. She dropped the spoon, which clanged against the side of the dish. "Who is my father?"

Mama sank against the sectional, which Alecia bought for her last birthday. She was sixty, but her smooth yellow-brown skin and the wigs she wore made her seem younger. The weight gain and gray hairs that peeked from under the stocking cap reminded Alecia of her age and the struggles they'd been through over the years.

"Have mercy. Dis again?" Mama shook her head. "Gyal, yuh sickening."

"And yet you refuse to tell me what I want to know."

Spreading both hands, Mama yelped, "How can I tell yuh what I don't know?"

"So you keep saying." Alecia's lips curled as she looked straight at Mama. "But I don't believe you."

Mama huffed and rose from the couch. She went to the kitchen and returned minutes later carrying a glass of water with lime slices floating inside. Alecia was sure she'd doctored it with Wray & Nephew White Rum, a staple in her house. Mama took a long swallow, then asked, "How is it going to change yuh life if yuh know who fathered yuh? Yuh doing good for yuhself, and yuh have a family. What more yuh want?"

Alecia skimmed the smoked-glass center table, which would have fit better inside a nightclub. Mama insisted on having it, so Alecia had bought it, same as she did whenever she hinted at wanting anything, no matter how expensive. Now, she wanted to smash it.

Alecia sighed and laid the tray on the table.

"You know who *your* father is, Maxine and Ophelia know theirs. Even so, you still decided to give everybody your last name." Alecia sucked her teeth and added, "But it seems I dropped from the sky on my birthday."

"Cut di foolishness. Yuh need to move on. First, it was yuh mother. Now it's yuh father." She gulped more of her drink, then sputtered, "Y–Yuh believe my answers will change depending on when yuh ask?"

"No, but I'd move past it if you'd tell the truth."

"I provided everything yuh needed since yuh were a year old, yet yuh still can't satisfy?" Her hand shook while she rubbed the space between her eyes. "Ophelia soon come home. Yuh should leave. I can't take another argument."

"Nice excuse." Alecia slid her feet into her sandals. "But don't think this is the last time I'll ask about this stuff. You're hiding those documents, and even if it's on your deathbed, I'll find out your secrets. All of them."

Mama reached forward with an unsteady hand. She missed the table, and the glass fell on the area rug. She sprang to her feet, cursing. "The reason yuh come over here is to ask these stupid questions. Instead of being grateful for what yuh have, yuh keep wearing me out." She pulled back her shoulders and stood at her full height, such as it was. "It shouldn't matter who yuh mother is, but I can't tell yuh."

She sighed and lowered her voice. "As far as you and I are concerned, she's out of the picture. She. Is. Dead!"

Alecia's upbringing conditioned her to submit to Mama. She wouldn't disrespect her by responding to her rant, so she picked up the tray and her handbag, then marched to the kitchen. Washing up was out of the question in her state of mind, so she left everything on the counter. Better to leave instead of saying something she might not be able to take back. Frustration made her throat tight, but she forced out a farewell as she went past the sofa to the front door.

"See you later."

Mama didn't respond and was still, as though she'd been turned to stone.

Ophelia pulled up behind Alecia at the sidewalk seconds before she drove off, but they didn't acknowledge each other. There was no point. Her two older sisters weren't any worse than other people, but hadn't moved past their childhood. Bringing a new baby home when they lived in Jamaica was one thing, but they refused to understand why Mama left them behind when she moved to Orlando and sent for them later.

Explaining to them that Alecia was a baby and needed her more than they did meant nothing. They'd been insecure and petty their entire lives, and Mama had done nothing to improve their relationship, aside from laying down rules that made it impossible for them to get along.

They reminded her of Addison, but what kind of start did she have to make her that mean? Come to think of it, there was hardly any information about her early life online. Alecia knew because she'd been researching. She had her suspicions since one article mentioned Addison's hometown was near Ocho Rios. Other than that, it seemed she'd planted herself and blossomed after she touched down in America.

She took her mind off Addison's business long enough to drive home without causing an accident. The first thing she did was to pull down her scrapbooks and study each in detail before shelving them in the closet. Sitting cross-legged in bed, she called Mama, who opened the line but said nothing.

"Mama, I know you're there. I just wanted to say sorry for harassing you."

She sucked her teeth, then spoke loudly into the cell phone. "If yuh was going to be sorry, why yuh do it?"

"You wouldn't understand how it feels to not belong anywhere."

"Child, don't be chupid," Mama shouted.

Alecia clapped a hand over her mouth to prevent her laughter from escaping. *Chupid* was Mama's way of emphasizing just how stupid Alecia was acting.

"Yuh belong in *this* family. Sometimes, it's better to let the past rest in peace. What yuh goin' to do? Confront di people who gave yuh life? Trust me, Alecia, leave it alone."

The finality of her tone forced Alecia to switch the subject, but she wouldn't stop searching, no matter what Mama said. Her parents might have had a million reasons for giving her up, but she wouldn't rest until she understood their why. People didn't simply walk away, leaving a defenseless baby without compelling motivation. If Mama knew how much Alecia had discovered by researching, she'd be horrified, but Alecia didn't plan to tell her anything.

"To make it up to you, I've arranged a spa treatment for this Saturday. They'll pamper you from head to toe, and you'll be a new woman when they're done."

"Alecia, you don't have to do this."

Mama loved going to the salon, but hard times conditioned her to think that spending money on self-care was a waste of resources. Her idea of a beauty treatment was to buy a bottle of nail polish and have Alecia paint her nails.

"This is good enough for me," she'd said in the past, spreading her toes and nodding her approval when the job was complete.

That snapshot from yesteryear made Alecia smile. "Don't worry, Mama. I can afford it, if that's what you're worried about."

"Okay. That sounds good."

"I'll take you to the salon and back home."

"That's good, because Ophelia is going away for the weekend with her boyfriend. She's leaving that same morning."

Alecia's heart leapfrogged into her throat as an idea settled and snowballed. She couldn't pass up this opportunity, no matter how bad she felt about deceiving Mama.

CHAPTER 21

ADDISON

SHE SMOOTHED A sheet of paper under her trembling hands and swiped her lip with her tongue. Nothing seemed to calm her nerves, but she had to make it through this visit.

Breathe, Addison. You can do this!

The enclosed space where she sat inside the bank, going through her contracts, reminded Addison of a tomb. Her life had been precisely that before she escaped from the hellhole of her father's house.

Some people would say she was ungrateful, but she'd call herself resourceful. A nose for excellent investments created her wealth. Born in a backwater town where farming was the main economic activity, running away was the only path to recreating herself.

As of yesterday, her mother had been in that nursing home in Hanover for five years. Nobody in that parish knew their family, but as long as she sent the payment each month, all was well. Why her mother wouldn't die was beyond Addison. Her mind was gone, and nothing remained in the shell of a body that had borne three daughters as unalike as morning, noon, and night.

The heavy metal door swung open, startling Addison. The securities manager, a thin, pasty man with a ghostlike presence, asked, "I'm checking if you need anything, Miss Comstock."

She waved him away. "I'm fine, Jonathan. I won't be much longer."

His glasses glinted under the fluorescent light as he tilted his head. "I'm not rushing you."

"Thanks." She gave him a grateful smile, which took a chunk of energy. "I didn't think you were."

He withdrew, leaving her to finish.

She swept both hands across the papers in the open file and let her mind drift to her eldest sister and their childhood.

Janet believed in God and went overboard whenever they played church. She always wanted to be the pastor. As the congregants, Giselle and Addison sat on a rickety bench under the mango tree, dodging droplets of spittle that flew while Janet preached. Her theatrics, as she jumped around imitating their preacher, made them break into giggles. Wielding the mic that was the broken-off arm from Addison's doll, she yelled about the fires of hell and damnation.

Their amusement earned them threats of going there for sacrilege in God's house. Reminders that the church they sat in was their front yard irritated Janet, who'd asked to be re-baptized when she was fourteen. Giselle was twelve, and Addison, ten.

Janet lived her conviction, but wasn't a walkover.

Their father's escalating abuse changed their lives during one of their mother's frequent absences to attend a church service. That day, Addison hung over the window ledge, dreaming about places she'd never been, while Giselle lay in bed reading a library book.

If she hadn't been holding on to the flaking wood, Addison would have fallen on the grass outside when her father yelled, "Honor yuh father and mother."

Addison abandoned the window to sit next to Giselle, who stuck her finger inside the book to mark the page.

Janet's response had been, "If there was anything honorable about you, I would."

"Just 'cause you get some education, you think you're an adult. You're still my pickney, and under my roof, you do what I say."

"I am *not* going into your room," she answered in a firm tone. "What would Mama say?"

Giselle and Addison drew closer to the half-open bedroom door. Addison peeked out, but couldn't see down the corridor that led to the living room.

"She gone to church. What she have to do with anythin'?" Papa asked.

Addison caught his meaning. From Giselle's shell-shocked expression, she also understood.

"Mama is your wife, not me."

"I'm not tellin' you again."

A whack echoed along the walls, then the thunder of running feet followed. The loose boards in the wooden floor created the effect of a herd of runaway cows coming down the passage. Their door burst open, throwing Giselle to the floor and hitting Addison in the face. The blow stunned her, then her vision cleared in the next moment.

Janet ran into their cramped room with her lip bleeding and Eustace Black's handprint on one cheek.

The creaking floorboards gave away their father's approach. He stood in the doorway, his shoulders heaving and both hands balled into fists. He reminded Addison of a gorilla about to go on a rampage.

When they rose from the floor, Giselle and Addison huddled around Janet who pushed them to the side. "You can beat me all you want," she declared, "but I'm going to tell Mama."

"And what she goin' to do?" Papa asked.

Standing akimbo, Janet spat, "Make you stop."

Papa lifted his chin and laughed long and hard. "This is *my* house, and no woman or pickney goin' tell me how to run my show."

The two of them exchanged fierce glares until he turned away and stomped down the corridor. Neither Janet nor Giselle had to tell Addison the reason for the argument. She'd seen the way Papa's eyes ran over Janet's curves when Mama left for church in the evenings and told her to serve him dinner. Addison hadn't understood what it meant until now, and it sickened her. Surely, Mama would put him in his place and their home would be the way it had been before tonight's fight.

Their parents had never been affectionate, but the girls had one another, and they made it enough. Church activities occupied Mama, but she didn't have the joy of the Lord Janet preached to them. Instead of happiness, Mama's face reflected resignation. Creases etched her pale skin, especially her eyes, and her mouth fell into a permanent downward curve. Addison believed she'd taken on their father's sour personality.

His source of happiness was the flask of white rum and the cow's milk he mixed in the evenings. After swirling his finger in the glass, he'd suck the milk from it and smack his lips. He'd drink for a while, staring at the pasture across from their house. Then he'd rise, unsteady on his feet, and go to bed.

When they were little, he'd give each of them a taste of his favorite drink. Each sip had been an explosion on Addison's tongue, with the milk lost in the rum's potency, which brought tears to her eyes.

Mama would yell from a safe distance. "Don't give them any rum!"

But Papa's roar of laughter delighted them, and they all squealed during the jockey rides on his knees. His large hands hugged them close, and they'd squabble about who sat where as they rode in the rocking chair their grandfather built for their mother.

On the evening he slapped Janet, they waited for Mama, not talking but hugging their knees and whispering while Janet mumbled prayers that had no ending. After the span of what seemed to be a lifetime, Mama's shoes crunched over the gravel Papa had laid in front of the house.

Janet shot off the bed the moment the front door opened. "Wait," she said, when they tried to follow.

They wanted to hear what she told Mama, but Janet wasn't having it. As soon as she disappeared, Addison gently turned the brass handle and cracked the door open.

Their mother sounded defeated when she said, "It must have been a mistake."

In a sharp tone, Janet replied, "You know what he was trying to do. It's wrong, Mama!"

Addison didn't hear her mother's next comment, but Janet yelled, "This is your job, and I don't know why the two of you don't sleep together no more. If that man ever touches me again…"

Janet marched toward the room, and they pushed the door shut and scampered into the bed they shared.

Without so much as glancing at them, Janet collapsed on her knees in front of her cot praying as if she were alone. When she finished, she changed into her nightwear and pulled the covers up to her shoulders.

A week later, she stuffed her backpack and walked to school with them as normal. At dismissal, they waited for Janet, but she never showed at their meeting spot under the rose-apple tree near the gate. They waited an hour then hurried home, twisting their ankles countless times on the rutted track that ran alongside the asphalted road.

Janet was not there, and the scream Millicent Black released when she put all the clues together stayed with Addison for years. She never returned, and Giselle became Papa's plaything. Soon, she was pregnant.

The soft buzz of her cell phone on the table brought Addison into the present, and she closed her eyes. The horror of her teenage years haunted her. She banished the memories, but sometimes they crept back and wrapped around her like ghosts condemned to wander.

No wonder Mama lost her mind.

Disappointment in her husband, losing a daughter, and the disgrace of having a pregnant teen made life unbearable. Aunt Millie, as everyone called her, turned into a rabid evangelist who spent more time tending to the church's affairs than her own.

Addison's father didn't spare her from his wandering hands, and after Giselle died, she became his next prey. Telling her mother was a waste of time because Mama refused to face the truth. Instead, she accused Addison of lying and slapped her in the face for that sin. The armor she wore, including layers of shorts and tights, didn't prevent her father from taking what he wanted.

On the night she decided one of them wouldn't rise from her bed alive, her life changed again. The crime of threatening him with an ice pick resulted in eviction. At sixteen, she left home with her clothing and the five hundred dollars her mother pressed into her fist.

"If I didn't need this money, I'd tell you to keep it." She picked up her duffle bag, staring into her mother's careworn face. "You let him do this to Giselle, and you didn't protect me. Janet left for the same reason. The two of you never should have had any children. And you're going to church four days out of seven. I hope the two of you burn in hell."

Her mother gasped, and tears welled in her eyes. "You ungrateful child!"

The words meant nothing to Addison. "Maybe if you'd been giving your husband some sex instead of going to church every night, my sister wouldn't be in her grave."

Mama's hand whipped out and delivered a stinging blow to Addison's cheek.

She didn't give her the satisfaction of flinching. When her eldest sister vanished, the Black clan knew their father—a stern man with an ever-present scowl—was the reason she left home. Whenever they spoke of Janet, the whispers and affirming nods sickened Addison. All of them were aware of Eustace Black's habits, which started with his younger sisters when he was a young man, but nobody cared enough to help his daughters.

Addison didn't know how or when her father would be called to account, but his time would come. She recalled then that Giselle, her older sister, died at fifteen in their mother's bed giving birth to her father's child.

Her gaze traveled around the sterile space as Giselle's screams echoed in her head. Sweating. Red-faced. Tormented. Chattering like a madwoman as agony held her in its grip, Giselle yelled during the home delivery, "Take it out of me! It goin' kill me!"

But the baby would not come. Drops of sweat rolled off Mama's forehead while she helped the midwife to bring her grandchild into the world. After five hours of effortless pushing, Giselle lay with her eyes closed as if she'd passed from life. One more round of coaxing from their mother to push harder forced a terrible shriek from Giselle.

The infant finally tore out of her and fell into the midwife's hands. A sea of blood arrived with it and soaked the bed, while Addison bit down hard on her lip to prevent her sobs from escaping. She'd never seen so much blood before and was certain Giselle had none left to live. The baby's head was a weird, elongated shape, and no matter what the midwife did, including holding it upside down, it wouldn't cry.

Meanwhile, their mother couldn't decide whether to change the sheets or massage Giselle's stomach for her to expel the placenta. When Giselle's eyes closed, Mama shook her by the shoulder. "Wake up, child."

Turning watery eyes on Addison, Mama ordered, "Run to the square and ask Dr. Bryson to come. Emergency. Tell him dat."

Sniffling and dashing away tears, Addison pulled on her good sandals and walk-ran to the village. The doctor was on his lunch break, and she rode back with him in his blue-and-white Morris Oxford. She took no pleasure in one of the few rides she'd had in a car up to that point.

The doctor arrived in time to pronounce both Giselle and the baby dead and agreed to advise the morgue when he returned to the village.

As Addison helped the midwife and Mama remove the bloody sheets, her tears wouldn't stop falling. When Giselle was clean and her clothing changed, Addison slinked to her room and lay on her bed. The one across the room was a blur as she wept. Eventually, she fell into a doze, praying Giselle's ghost would haunt Mama and Papa in their bed where she died.

The funeral was a bleak affair with Giselle and the baby buried together. To look at her father, people would think he was an upstanding man and a decent father. Nothing was further from the truth. Addison's disgust festered and turned into hate as she watched him pretend to be something he wasn't.

The memory faded, leaving an ache in her chest. Massaging her forehead, Addison swallowed hard and cleared her throat. The trip into the past left a load on her shoulders, and she barely had the energy to gather the records she needed. She returned the other files to the vault, then pulled out her phone and scanned her task list.

Life took its own sweet time, but it had been good to her. Nothing and no one could destroy her after the hell she'd already been through. If that man Ryder would call her back, she'd have one more base covered. But Vance didn't have any news, so she was stuck, but not for long.

Shoulders back, she headed for the doorway with the folders under one arm. The phone buzzed again, and she was tempted to ignore it, but didn't.

Kirkland had sent a message. *We need to have a meeting.*

CHAPTER 22

CASEY

"YUH SURE EVERYTHING all right, child?"

"I'm fine. Just wanted to hear your voice," Casey rushed to reassure her grandmother, pressing the cordless phone closer to her ear as she sat on the bed. "We could talk more often if you'd move with the times."

"Di internet is not for people my age." Gran cackled, then said, "How is Donnette? I should trust God and not worry, but dat pickney never far from my mind."

"Your brain deserves a rest. She's taking life as it comes." Casey swallowed a sigh and kept her voice light. "One day, the mess from the past won't hit as hard, and we'll all move on."

She didn't believe a word, but didn't mind pretending to soothe Gran's heart and mind. If she closed her eyes, the rasp of Gran's callused palm on her cheek was real. Her touch always brought back the best parts of being at home.

"I've lived long enough to know that time fixes most things."

Casey chuckled, then rose to free the sheer peach curtain trapped on the edge of the wall mirror. "You're far from being a hundred."

"Chile, trust me. Sometimes, I can't tell the difference."

The sad undertone made Casey's chest ache. Whenever she was in touch with her grandmother, it was hard not to miss her mother. Gran was the person Mommy would have grown into if her life hadn't been cut short. They carried an uncanny resemblance to each other—the dark-honey skin, wiry physique, and above-average height.

The villagers used to say Casey and Donnette resembled them, too. Nowadays, Gran confined her hair in two thick plaits, which made her sharp features stand out like a carving. Years of farming cash crops made her flat as an ironing board, but strong and fit.

She didn't need to worry about her grandmother because two of their cousins still lived in the house she and Donnette had improved over the years for their grandmother's comfort. Mommy would have wanted it, which brought Addison and the job to mind.

Gran was thinking along the same lines, as she said, "I'm still glad dat devil's spawn give yuh time to see me."

Her grandmother was still blissfully unaware of the reason she spent two nights under her roof, and Casey aimed to keep it that way. Knowledge of the police stop order would likely have killed her grandmother. She cradled the phone between her ear and shoulder and leaned in to straighten a bottle of perfume on the dresser.

"Trust me, even if I had to stop on the way to the airport, I wouldn't have missed seeing you for the world."

"God bless yuh, and be careful. I lost my one daughter. I don't want to lose you, too."

"You won't, Gran. I live by the stuff you taught me."

The axiom that echoed most often inside Casey's head was, "If you can't be good, be careful." And she'd heeded that advice.

Casey was similar in character to her grandmother, whose streak of independence was unsettling. At eighty, she still prepared meals for the family and tended to her garden. According to her, she'd stay busy until the Lord called her home. She still spoke fondly of their grandfather who died in his forties, but her daughter, Yvette, had been the light of her life.

Perhaps that's why God took her.

Casey scoffed. God hadn't taken her. Addison's greed did.

She replaced the phone in the cradle and wandered into the living room where Donnette sat on the sofa having dinner. Casey didn't try speaking to her since Donnette would ignore her. The television was tuned to a news channel, as always.

Her sister was a current affairs junkie, but with each newscast, she risked mental upheaval. An item about a rape victim, a case of child abuse, or a domestic disturbance was liable to tank her mood.

She was good at masking her emotions, but hid in her room when she couldn't handle the upsetting stories she consumed. Casey didn't know how or when she'd heal, especially without therapy, but each day that went by without a meltdown was a victory.

In the kitchen, Casey hovered over the stove, knowing she wouldn't eat much. She opted for some banana chips and a glass of orange juice and went back past the sofa. Donnette's attention was fixed on the anchor while she dragged her fork through the rice.

Since she'd be ignored, Casey said nothing and returned to her room. She laid the food on the bedside table and switched on her television, but couldn't concentrate. Not when Donnette was worried about her job.

Sliding onto her back, Casey plumped the pillow then lay on her side. Calling Gran may have been a mistake. Reminders of Mommy made Casey sink inside herself, and it didn't help that her actions now affected Donnette.

The past was the past, but the unfairness of it bugged Casey. To Casey, Mommy went downhill fast, but in reality she lasted two years after her cancer diagnosis. Gran shielded them from the truth that Mommy compounded with lies.

"I'll be better soon" was her regular reassurance, but that didn't happen.

Meanwhile, their stepfather, Uncle Pete, had gone from being a supportive husband to creeping into their room late at night to violate Donnette. His eyes had stated his intention long before he laid a hand on her. As the months dragged on and Mommy lost her strength, Uncle Pete took advantage of the situation.

The first time she woke to Donnette's keening, Casey bolted upright and tried to see in the darkness, which was so thick she could grab a handful. Her eyes adjusted slowly, but she didn't understand why the other cot was creaking.

"Donnette?"

Silence fell in the room, and when she eased out of bed to see why Donnette was sniffling, the noise started again. Casey crept across the floor until one of the loose boards squealed under her feet. She gripped the cold railing at the end of the bed, perched on the thin mattress, and tugged the sheet as she whispered, "What happen to yuh?"

A shadow reared up, and Uncle Pete's smell—a combination of cigarette smoke and white rum fumes—twisted Casey's stomach. She clapped a hand over her mouth and squinted, not trusting her eyes. A second later, she knew she hadn't seen a ghost.

He grabbed her arm, squeezing it tight. "If yuh ever tell Yvette I was in here, I'll cut her throat and yours. Yuh hear?"

Sickened by his breath and the whispered threat, Casey bobbed her head and prayed he'd release her arm. He pushed her hard, and she stumbled and fell to the floor. The moment his feet landed on the polished wood, she scrambled onto her cot.

The door squeaked open, and his vicious words filled the room. "Just remember what I will do if yuh ever open yuh mouth."

Casey lay stiff, sweating, and paralyzed by fear, but as the minutes passed, her muscles relaxed. Eventually, she crept into Donnette's bed. She moved closer to the wall to allow Casey to lie next to her. Although the bed still stank of their stepfather, Casey snuggled in and propped her head on the pillow. With her eyes now accustomed to the dark, she traced the silvery trail of tears that marked Donnette's skin as her eyes overflowed.

She didn't know why she was crying, too, but Casey patted Donnette's arm knowing her touch couldn't fix what was wrong. She wasn't certain what had happened, but could guess.

Since Mommy now spent most of her time in bed, they'd been reading her small collection of books. If they came across a love scene in one of the romance novels, Donnette tried to cover Casey's eyes, which amused her. What she didn't tell Donnette was that she'd been reading novels in the library that the clerk wouldn't allow her to borrow because of her age. One by one, she snuck them to a table in the far corner and read material Mommy wouldn't have allowed.

As she lay next to her sister, the knowledge settled in her soul that what Uncle Pete had done was wrong. In Mommy's books, "the action," as Donnette called it, was always between "big people" and not children and their parents.

By the time Mommy died, Uncle Pete had had his way with Donnette more often than Casey could count. She tried staying awake, especially on Friday nights, and would flop around on her bed. Sometimes it stopped him. Sometimes it didn't. With tears streaming down her face, she listened to her sister's muffled screams and her listless sobbing after he left. Donnette sometimes refused her comfort, which made Casey cry harder.

"You don't understand. Go back to your bed," Donnette mumbled and pushed her away.

The rejection squeezed Casey's heart, and she wished Uncle Pete would die. She understood and grew accustomed to death, living in a farming district and being around Uncle Pete, who sometimes butchered the pigs.

When it came, Mommy's passing took its toll on Uncle Pete. He sank further into chain smoking and the rum bottle, and never made it out.

Losing Mommy and being unable to protect her sister hollowed Casey's soul and changed the way she viewed life. While she turned her angst inward and wrote grisly stories, Donnette channeled her grief into something useful when she became a nurse.

An illness that didn't have a cure shattered their lives, and Uncle Pete worsened their situation with his greed. That made him more evil than the devil in Casey's eyes.

CHAPTER 23

ALECIA

THE IDEA OF finding her biological parents took root early and ruled Alecia's life. Her sisters understood her obsession, and the lack of family history was the needle they used to stab her repeatedly when Mama wasn't around.

"Where Mama got you from? Seems God dropped you from the sky."

"Must be something wrong with you why your parents don't want you."

And the jab that hurt most: "Your mother was a prostitute, and your father was married. That's the only reason any woman would give away her baby."

A steady diet of frequent slaps and taunts defined her childhood. Mama never heard Maxine and Ophelia provoking her, but always happened upon them when Alecia attacked, screaming and pounding them with her fists. She couldn't grow up fast enough, and when it was time for college, she moved as far away as she could run. Now, she wondered why she returned to Orlando.

She nearly broke the speed limit after leaving Mama at the salon. Now, she perched on the side of the bed, scanning the bedroom. She'd let herself in with the key she still kept. Jamaican parents stored important papers securely in plastic because of the threat of storms and hurricanes.

Alecia had been everywhere inside the house but still couldn't find what she was seeking. She walked around the bedroom crammed with a huge bed, chest of drawers, and a dresser made from the same oak that carried a multitude of drawers.

Mama kept her papers in the chest of drawers, but Alecia had been through her stash several times and found nothing. Those bogus papers were useless. Mama claimed that she had "updated" Alecia's birth certificate at the Registrar General's Department on one of her early trips to Jamaica.

The closed closet drew Alecia, and she rose from the bed and walked out of her slippers. A line of clothing and storage boxes packed the shelf above. While wriggling her toes in the carpet fibers, she decided where to start searching. Mama's battered suitcase lay in the far corner above her head. It came down for her trips to Jamaica when she attended a funeral, wedding, or family reunion.

Alecia's eyes didn't stray from the brown suitcase, and the longer she examined it, the more certain she was that Mama might have hidden something inside it. She grabbed the step stool and lifted the suitcase, then hurried across the floor to throw it on the bed. The zipper across the front was the most obvious storage space, but Alecia didn't think she'd find any documents.

Running a hand over the fabric, she felt for any irregularity but still opened the zipper. The front panel was empty. She unzipped the entire thing, hoping that no dust would smear the pink bedspread. Her next move was to shove a hand inside various compartments, but she came up empty.

She was at the point of giving up when she peered at the side panel along the inside. One touch confirmed something was inside. With her throat tight, she tugged the stiff zipper. The loud sound it made startled her, but not enough for her to leave it be. A sheaf of folded papers filled her hand when she stuck it inside. She pulled them out and set them on her lap.

Was she ready to deal with whatever these documents contained? The question stopped her for a mere moment. With shaking hands, she unfolded them before she changed her mind, although that was next to impossible. Not after searching for years to find her roots. She was ninety-five percent certain of her mother's identity. All she needed was proof in black and white.

She frowned at the paper she'd opened—a one-page contract with her mother's spidery writing and another familiar scrawl above the second line. The agreement stated that Mercedes Emelyn Cookson was legally responsible for Alice Black and would not reveal the names of her parents under any circumstances. Stapled to the sheet was a makeshift receipt signed by Evadne Cookson to say she had received five thousand dollars, not from a person, but a company. Despite the name variation, Alecia knew Mercedes and Evadne were the same person.

The date on the document was six years after Alecia was born. An original copy of her birth certificate was among the papers. The one she'd always used listed Merrick Stone—her sisters' father whom Mama had divorced—as her father.

Dadda, as they called him, was a womanizer. In silence, Mama bore the humiliation of having his women calling their home to find him. When she secured her citizenship and was financially secure, she filed for divorce. Those papers were among the pile in Alecia's lap. With her phone, she took the pictures she needed and was about to put everything back when a photo fell to the floor. She grabbed it and peered hard at it as a smile broke over her face. This was more than she'd been expecting and would come in useful at the right time.

When she straightened, a pair of feet stopped to her left. The long, slender toes and impeccable pedicure confirmed that Ophelia stood next to her. Alecia swallowed hard, thinking she was about to retch on her sister's toes. She searched her mind for a lie to explain what she was doing, but nothing believable surfaced. Someone had told her that attack was the best form of defense, so she plowed ahead. "What are you doing here? Mama said—"

Ophelia scanned the bedroom, as though Alecia were a thief. "The question is, why *you're* here searching Mama's things."

She reached into the pocket of her shorts. "Mama believes you're all that. Let's see what she thinks when she hears about you pawing through her stuff."

Waving toward the suitcase, Alecia said, "That's not quite true. I want to borrow the suitcase."

"That old thing? You must think I'm a fool. Didn't you come back from Jamaica weeks ago?" She scoffed. "Mama gave you everything, including the love that belonged to us, and you're still not satisfied."

"Aren't you supposed to be somewhere else?" Alecia asked, taking in Ophelia's tank top and shorts.

"That's none of your business. It's a good thing I came by before heading out." Ophelia dialed, then put the phone to her ear. "Otherwise, you'd have gotten away with invading Mama's privacy."

Pleading with her would be a waste of time, so while she left the room to talk to Mama, Alecia snapped another picture and prayed she'd find a good enough story to win Mama's forgiveness. She'd believe Alecia tricked her to have the leeway to search her things, which was the truth, although it hadn't been her intention when she offered the spa treatment.

Alecia wedged the picture back where she found it, drained by the mixture of dejection and triumph warring inside her. At some point, she'd return and see if she'd missed anything, but that hope died when Ophelia returned and held out one hand. "Mama said to give me the key." Her eyes glinted with malice when she added, "By the way, don't pick her up. She'll take a cab from the salon, and you're not to be here when she comes back."

CHAPTER 24

ADDISON

SHE DIDN'T TRUST anyone, so she left anything that might incriminate her inside the vault. In her home safe, she stashed the few files she selected. Hiding her annoyance, she scrutinized the agency contract. Nothing was going her way.

Neither that silent partner of Rachel's nor Vance returned her files, but no matter. Everything Rachel held was kosher, except for the dedication page they'd discussed the last time she was at her office.

Kirkland was on a call with a contact he claimed was working on her case. She'd had it with him because she needed results, especially after the morning she'd had.

At Rachel's funeral, folks she considered her associates looked at her sideways. She suspected they were saying she'd poisoned Rachel. Each time she approached a group of attendees, they went silent, which told her they'd been talking about her. On the third occasion, she stormed out of the crematorium and didn't care how or what anyone thought. The funeral wouldn't be more or less of an event without her.

The continued questions from the police made her even more uncomfortable. They were no nearer to making an arrest or putting the matter to rest, and their innuendos were irritating. Not to mention frustrating. Even worse, a closer examination of the outline for *Murder by the Book* made her hair stand on end. Emily's and Rachel's death mirrored her story ideas.

The discovery sent her straight to the bar, where she poured a glass of port and spilled half of it on the counter. She hadn't shared her suspicion with anyone and would wait before raising a false alarm and possibly embarrassing herself.

Kirk ended his call and laid the phone on his thigh. Addison hated him for rejecting her, but had lectured herself *that* day after he left her bedroom. He wasn't the only man on earth, but she needed his help now. When he finished the job he'd been doing ineffectively, she'd be rid of him. She wasn't being fair, but how much time did it take to find the people who were making her life unbearable?

"What did you find out about the old woman I asked you to track down?" She was proud of her even tone, when inside, she seethed with impatience.

"She still lives in Jamaica."

Fiddling with the pearl pendant nestled in her bosom, she asked, "Who's taking care of her?"

"A couple of grandkids."

"Men? Women?" she asked, still playing with the pendant.

"Two females. Denise and Michelle Barnes."

Although Addison peered at the titles on the wall, her mind churned in circles while she tried to recall a couple of names that eluded her. They weren't the same ones Kirkland mentioned.

"And what about the other woman?" she asked when her brain cells wouldn't give up the details.

"She left her village. Immigrated."

"Where is she now?" Addison picked up her phone. She hadn't heard it ping, but the made-up distraction helped her avoid the man across the desk. Kirkland must have at least a half-dozen questions, but hadn't asked one yet.

"Here in America."

She was sure the vein in her temple was beating hard. "Do you know where?"

"Orlando."

Why couldn't he give her details all at once instead of these short answers that gave the impression she was prying into someone else's business? Sighing, she asked, "Do you have an exact address?"

"Not yet."

Heat flared in her face, and she wanted to blast Kirkland over his slow progress, but held on to her temper. He wouldn't appreciate her loss of control, and her staff would notice them arguing—or, more to the point, her ranting at him. She respected Kirkland, but lately, the anger that ruled her life was cause for concern. This madness had to end. When she found out who was making her life miserable, she'd sue them for everything they owned in this life and the next.

That's if they don't kill you first.

The thought rattled her, and she pulled in a sharp breath but didn't have time to settle her mind before Kirkland spoke.

"Do you mind me asking why you want to find these people?" He tapped a pen against the file jacket in his other hand in a steady rhythm.

She wanted to tell him to mind his business, but said instead, "I used to represent them and want to be certain they're not the ones trying to ruin me." The lie surprised her, but then she'd always been clever.

The side of his mouth twitched, but he didn't break into a smile. She wanted to ask what he found so amusing, but she soon found out.

"Didn't know you had a literary career, other than as a writer."

"I've been in this business a long time."

He studied the file jacket, wearing a thoughtful expression, then he sat forward. "About the baby that influencer posted on her page. Is there any truth to that story?"

She swung the chair sideways to avoid giving him an answer. The muted chatter from her writers, who seemed to be in the middle of an impromptu brainstorming session, broke the silence. She had to be slipping for them to break into discussion without fearing she'd tear into them, but she had so much going on that she didn't mind.

They knew what to do, and that worked for her. She held in a sigh. For the first time in her writing life, her work-in-progress didn't feel as if it mattered, even with a fast-approaching deadline.

To her surprise, her eyes burned from all the memories that wouldn't stay locked away where they belonged. But she was stronger than that, so she shelved her mental wanderings and faced forward. "I don't care what you think about me, but what would you say if I told you it's true?"

He propped both elbows on the chair arms and laced his fingers together. "I'm not judgmental, so I'd guess you were young and in a situation you didn't know how to handle."

"How politically correct that sounds."

"What else am I going to say? You're paying me to do a job." He shrugged and offered a faint smile. "Irrespective of how I feel, your business is not my business."

And yet she suspected he was judging her, perhaps because of the time she spent scrolling through hundreds of comments online. The people who weren't speculating condemned her outright, knowing nothing about her and what might have led to the decision to abandon a child.

"That's correct." Despite her efforts, her voice wavered.

His tone was gentle when he asked, "Do you need a moment?"

In the middle of her nod, he rose and left the office.

Like a crack addict who couldn't help reaching for the next hit, she picked up the smartphone and went to the page she'd already visited more times than she could count. Two pictures were posted side by side. She'd deny any knowledge of a baby but admitted the image of the toddler next to her was startling.

The child was a miniature version of her.

CHAPTER 25

CASEY

DONNETTE WAS OUT when Casey got home, which was a stroke of good luck. She didn't want to lie about where she was going and earn more silence. Not after Donnette acknowledged she was alive this morning.

Casey hurriedly changed into casual clothing and drove out in the Civic. On the way to the farthest internet café she'd found online, she concentrated on staying present during the ride. Traffic hadn't built up as yet, and she enjoyed the sun when it wasn't at its highest.

Inside the ice-cold facility, she checked for cameras. Thankfully, they had none. When she sat in the semi-private cubicle, she reached inside her bag for her disinfectant spray. She misted the keyboard and sat in front of the screen for some time before taking any action. Since Donnette's episode, Casey felt she was moving through quicksand, but had come too far to stop moving now.

Fifteen minutes remained before she had to buy more internet time, so she quickly created an account on one of the apps where Addison had a presence. Then she navigated to a post created by an influencer who'd been following Addison's story and left a comment.

Keep an eye out because things are about to go crazy in Addison Comstock's world.

With five minutes left to spare, Casey left the café. On the way home, she backtracked over everything that had happened since their trip to Jamaica. Addison's house of cards was imploding.

She didn't doubt the rumors about Addison having a daughter. Abandoning that child sounded exactly like something she'd do because of her ambition.

At home, she walked into the kitchen to find Donnette at the sink. Casey wrapped her arms around her sister's waist and rested her forehead on her back. "I'm so sorry. How long are you off for?"

Donnette shrugged, then said, "A week, but I have a bad feeling about this."

Shifting to lean against the counter, Casey examined the toe of her sneaker. "I won't tell you it will be okay, but if it isn't, you know I'm here for you."

To her surprise, Donnette smiled. "That's a given." She scanned Casey's clothing, then said, "Dinner is all the food we haven't been eating, so go warm up something. There's plenty of leftovers."

Fifteen minutes later, they sat in front of the television with plates of mac and cheese and fried chicken. While she ate, Donnette watched the news, and Casey poked bits of macaroni and pushed them around the plate. Eventually, her mind sank to a painful place she hated visiting.

When she was in her eleventh year, her grandmother escorted a woman to their stepfather's house to see Mommy. The three-bedroom house stood in a deep corner of the narrow main road that led to the village square. Casey and Donnette had returned from school, changed out of their uniforms, and were in the middle of taking turns rolling down the gentle slope in the backyard.

The remembered sensation of the sun on her face and the prickly crabgrass against her skin drew a faint smile. From the elevated yard, they spotted the black car that brought the stranger to their grandmother's home and chattered about the possibility of riding in it. Their disappointment with the visitor coming on foot faded when they crept into the house. From the kitchen-cum-dining room, they peeked at her through the multi-colored beads hanging in the doorway.

The woman in the lovely dress and shiny black handbag came because of Mommy's writing. She hurried to her room and returned with a slab of papers, then sat with both hands in her lap, staring at the lady while she read some of it. The woman's eyes shone when she raised them to meet Mommy's. "This is good."

"So, you can help me?" Mommy asked, skimming the plastic flowers crowded into the vase on the center table and the tired plaid sofa.

A wide smile came to the visitor's lips as she nodded. "I'm sure I can. Will you allow me to take the manuscript with me?"

When Mommy hesitated, she rushed to say, "We can draw up an agreement, and I'll sign for it. I'm excited about the story."

"I–I'd prefer to think about this, please, and discuss it with my husband." The lines on Mommy's forehead gave away her worry, but her voice was firm.

"That's fine," the woman said. "Take your time. I can come back in a week. Does that work for you?"

Mommy clasped her hands, the way she did when praying. "Yes. Thanks."

Gran hadn't said a word, but when the lady walked out of the room, she mouthed to Mommy, "We soon talk."

Their mother hugged the papers to her chest with her eyes closed. To Casey, she was beautiful. She tipped her nose into the air, and a few curls trailed from the bun on top of her head. She'd tried brushing her hair to appear presentable when Gran yelled her name from the gate, but the strands escaped again. When Mommy stood, she announced, "My work is finally going to pay off."

"Your story's going to be a book now?" Casey asked.

Her dark eyes sparkled. "Maybe. That short story competition I won and the interview last week brought Miss Black here today."

On the evening it aired, the three of them, plus Gran, squeezed onto the couch to watch Mommy talk about her win and the book she'd written. She'd received a gift certificate and the trophy now displayed on their whatnot. Too bad that win hadn't translated into more for Yvette Finch than a couple of articles in the newspapers and the television spotlight.

Donnette gripped Casey's wrist, which erased the image of their mother.

"I can tell you're feeling blue, but it helps not to spend too much time wherever you went."

"Agreed. I could say the same to you." Forcing a chuckle, she gently loosed her arm. "We both need to splurge a little, but I fear you'll die before you start living."

Donnette pushed a bone to the side of her plate and puckered her lips. "And here we have the pot calling the kettle black."

Easing sideways, Casey patted Donnette's shoulder. "So, we both work too much. Is that such a bad thing?"

"If circumstances worked out the way they should have, we wouldn't have to grind so hard," Donnette grumbled.

"Bad things happen to good people as we know too well."

Sighing, Donnette laid her fork down. "I'm not ungrateful or anything, but maybe if cancer and heartbreak hadn't killed her, Mommy would have had the strength to fight. That book would have made her famous, and we'd have had it easier."

"We have a decent life, but Mommy deserved more than she got."

"That's for sure." Donnette stared through the window next to the television. "I don't know how you do it, though. Working for that woman."

"I'm trying to right the wrong she did to Mommy. That's how I can stand to be near her." Casey tried to keep the bitterness out of her voice without success. "She couldn't have shafted us without Peter Grimes. He's the one who sold our mother's work for next to nothing."

Donnette stood and grabbed the tray off Casey's knees. "Our stepfather was stupid and greedy. *That* woman knew better than what she did."

Casey wasted no more words. What Donnette said was true. Being trolled on social media was what Addison deserved. She didn't have a conscience and, in the intervening years, she hadn't grown one.

Shaking the dust off her feet was necessary for her to step into the world she'd graduated to after she robbed their mother. Along with that, she'd ditched her surname, which was too pedestrian but easy to trace to the people in the village where she'd been born.

Her reaction to being forced to acknowledge her wrongs and the truth about her come-up would be interesting.

Casey rose from the sofa and took a bottle of water from the refrigerator. "I have some stuff to finish. I'm in my room, if you need me."

At the desk in the corner of her bedroom, she activated her virtual private network and went to the website of Matteo West and Associates. Casey was well aware his "associates" included very few attorneys, but he was good at his profession. Otherwise, Addison wouldn't have hired him.

She'd done her homework on Matteo, who seemed to be an honest lawyer—if there was any such thing. His clients recommended him highly, and no scandals followed him. Casey would know soon enough what side of the fence he sat on in terms of morals.

She inserted the thumb drive and pulled up the scanned manuscript that included the dedication page with Addison's handwriting—a signed promise to represent Yvette Finch as her agent for the novel *Games People Play.* Back then, Addison had been Adassa Black. She was certain Addison still had the bound copy of the manuscript, which Casey sent to her agent's office. To keep Addison on edge, she'd allowed time to pass, but she'd have to acknowledge her thievery—sooner rather than later.

Casey wrote a carefully crafted email to Matteo. He was a smart man, so she didn't need to explain the attachment.

She did, anyhow.

Let Addison try to lie her way out of evidence she couldn't deny.

CHAPTER 26

ALECIA

"YOUR WRITING IS deteriorating." Addison slapped a printed copy of Alecia's last chapter on the keypad. "What is your problem?"

She could have said, "you," but didn't. Addison's mood was so rotten, she'd probably throttle her if she answered. Alecia was no longer afraid of her, but every word that came out of her vindictive mouth was a poison-tipped arrow that tore her flesh.

Everywhere Alecia went, rejection followed her, but not for much longer. With the information she held, she could earn a tidy sum for her story. Profiting off Addison had never been her intention, but maybe a book deal would compensate for the hell her life had become. Then again, she'd have to get past that blasted nondisclosure agreement she'd signed.

"Are you hearing me?" Addison yelled.

Her eyes were red as if she hadn't slept in a week, and a faint whiff of alcohol drifted to Alecia. Aside from all her other faults, Addison was turning into a drunk.

The pressure must be getting to her. A smile betrayed Alecia the moment Addison raised both hands. Her twisted features and claw-like nails reminded Alecia of an unwelcome night vision. The blood-red suit didn't help matters.

She woke when a stinging sensation spread across her cheek. Then the other burned, as well. Addison had backhanded her before she recovered from the first slap.

Gripping the desk, Alecia propelled herself out of the seat. "Bitch, you've lost your mind."

It was the wrong thing to say.

Addison yanked her in by the collar.

Struggling to stay on her feet, Alecia grabbed Addison's hands to pry them from her clothing. When that didn't work, she whacked Addison's cheek twice. That freed her, but Addison kept coming. Her eyes were wild, and Alecia was positive she'd gone insane.

What the hell?

Alecia backed up and pointed with a trembling finger. "I've taken your abuse for months, but I'm not the cause of your problems. *You are*. Maybe you should find a different way to handle your business outside of abusing people."

The team members came to life when Addison moved toward her. Kirk and Quentin held her back by both arms. The others gaped in their seats, imitating a school of goggle-eyed goldfish.

Addison's jaws flexed as she spoke through her teeth. "You work for me."

"That does *not* mean you're entitled to abuse me."

The blotchy red mark on the side of Addison's face satisfied Alecia, who guessed she had matching ones on her cheeks.

"Everyone, back to work." Addison tipped her chin higher and ensured they complied before her gaze settled on Alecia. "*You*, get out of my studio, and don't think I'm paying you because you have the rest of the day off."

While the others tried to find their rhythm, Alecia slapped the laptop shut and yanked her handbag out of the drawer.

"Leave the laptop," Addison commanded before striding into her office. She'd have slammed the door if it weren't tethered to a hydraulic arm.

Alecia wanted to howl. Her throbbing cheeks reminded her of the indignity of being slapped as though she were an out-of-control child. Maybe that was part of the reason Maxine and Ophelia hated her so. Mama hadn't slapped her once, and for many Jamaican parents, beatings for simple to serious offenses were a rite of passage.

On her way out the door, Quentin's gaze connected with hers. The sympathy in his eyes was almost palpable, but she ignored him. Instead of protecting her, he chose to be Addison's handler.

In the parking lot, she sat with the door of the SUV open while her mind ran in several directions. What would Mama say about what happened today? After she cussed her out and hung up, Alecia gave her time to cool off. Surely, she'd realize if she had shared the truth a long time ago, Alecia's need to keep searching would have been nullified.

Through the years, she hadn't taken her sisters' taunts to heart…until she was old enough to understand they were serious. When she was ten, Mama returned home one Saturday afternoon and didn't realize anyone else was in the house. Maxine and Ophelia were at the mall, while Alecia was in bed with a stomachache.

She'd been dozing when Mama came in, but was soon wide awake. The thing she'd never understood was why her mother spoke at the top of her voice on the telephone, the way half-deaf people did. Even with the instrument next to her ear, she'd act as though the other person was on Mars. Alecia dragged herself from the bed and was on her way to the kitchen when her name froze her footsteps.

"So, how Alecia?" the female asked. From the shortcut English, she gathered it was someone from "back a yard" as Mama sometimes called Jamaica.

"Doing extremely well in school. So proud o' her."

"Glad t'ings turned out so good, considering you still don't know her entire story."

"Yes, mi dear, but trust me, she was mine from the mother leave her wid me."

"Is a shame you agreed to take her for such a small amount, considering what the woman is worth today."

"True, but she's part of my bloodline now. I love her from the moment I see her, so everything is copacetic."

Alecia peeked into the kitchen where Mama was taking groceries out of a plastic bag and putting the items in the cupboards. The phone was in hands-free mode on the counter.

"Take good care of her, and give her a good education, just in case some of her mother's talent runs in her veins."

"Ah, mi dear Cynthia, thanks. We'll talk again soon. Kiss yuh mother for me."

"And kiss the girls for me."

With her heart beating out of time, Alecia stumbled to her room and lay on the bed. All this time, the evil twins were right about her coming to them like a stray. Who gave her to Mama? What a wicked act to give her to a woman with two rotten daughters.

Alecia didn't dare ask any questions because Mama might forget herself and slap her for listening to "big people" conversation. Only through eavesdropping, research, and a pinch of luck did she discover her birth mother's identity. Sheer underhandedness resulted in one hundred percent proof of her beginnings. Knowing who her father was would be perfect, but one thing at a time.

As far as Alecia was concerned, her mother sold her to Evadne, Emelyn, or Mercedes Cookson, or whatever the hell her name was. This was the thing about Jamaicans, nearly everyone had a pet name that they were called at home. The legal version was recorded on their birth certificates and used for official purposes. This practice was so ingrained that some children only discovered their government name when they entered school.

She didn't know Evadne wasn't part of Mama's official name until they came to America because that was what everyone called her, yet nobody could explain how she came by it. And now she, too, had another name. That document she found in the suitcase brought home another fact. Mama hadn't been honest with Alecia's birth mother when she used her pet name, Evadne, instead of her legal one on that contract.

Never mind, though. Soon, she'd expose their foolishness.

CHAPTER 27

ADDISON

MATTEO'S DARK-BROWN EYES flamed with disapproval. His stare was owl-like behind circular, steel-rimmed glasses, and steepled fingers hid his mouth.

"The entire thing looks bad. It sends a terrible signal to those who read your books and may not be as open-minded as you."

Frankly, she didn't care unless it affected her book sales, but of course, she couldn't say that. She'd never pretended to be an angel, but it irked her that people who'd probably never bought a book from her had so much to say about her personal life and what she was and wasn't doing. Thanks to that runt who believed attacking her because of Quentin would change anything. She wasn't even in a relationship with him. He had something she needed, and she took it. If he had objections, he wouldn't have been in her bed—even though her male employees understood she'd take revenge if they didn't comply with her wishes.

The first man on her payroll who tried to tell tales out of school learned she wasn't someone who tolerated having her name or reputation sullied. The day she overheard him snickering with a coworker about her insatiable sexual appetite, she not only fired them both but also ensured they signed a document that gave her the right to sue them if they mentioned her name. Harsh measures, but essential for someone who valued her reputation over most things, including her life.

She sipped club soda from a tumbler. The music from downstairs floated on the airwaves, reminding her that she couldn't be absent from her party for long. Each time she completed a book, she hosted a celebratory event.

If she had her way, she'd have canceled this one, but it was too late for Piper to call everyone. In any case, she needed something to pull attention from all the crap surrounding her name. Sighing, she picked up the glass again and was mid-swallow when Matteo shifted in the seat.

"That's not the only thing," he said, clearing his throat. "That page you showed me the other day? The entire manuscript turned up at my office."

The club soda went down the wrong way and damn near choked her. She held a napkin over her mouth as she hacked and her eyes watered.

"It's a plot to ruin my career. Why now, when I'm about to start marketing this new book?"

He raised both hands, then folded them again. "I can't answer that, but we need to discuss it."

"Agreed."

"Let's do it at eight o'clock on Monday."

"Why so long?" She tried to stay calm, but her petulance was obvious, even to her ears.

"I do have other clients, plus I wish to review the information that came to me. I need a copy of the book."

"Why is that necessary? Don't you trust me?"

"It's not a matter of trust. My reputation also hinges on what my clients do. Humor me, please."

After another sip of the bubbly liquid, she spun in her chair, opened the credenza behind her, and retrieved a copy. Trying for a joke, she asked, "Should I sign it?"

He was about to shake his head, then changed his mind. "Sure. Why not?"

Matteo picked up his briefcase and placed the novel inside. "I'm out. See you next week, and congratulations on your new book."

She flicked her wrist. "It won't be out for another year or so, but thanks."

"Are you heading back downstairs?" he asked.

"No. You go ahead. I'll be down shortly."

Addison crossed her legs and shook the glass so the ice cubes tinkled. Matteo likely wouldn't read far into the book, so she didn't have to worry. Plus, she was certain he wouldn't abandon her, whether or not her enemies gained any traction. Those envious people, whoever they were, needed to get a life and leave hers alone.

If they knew her struggles, they'd shut up and take several seats. She sank lower in the chair, preparing for the memories about to hit again. Club soda wasn't nearly enough to ward off the demons inside her head. She'd read somewhere the worst thing that could happen in life was to be born into a dysfunctional family. Addison had proven that in spades with the useless women who shared her last name.

After leaving home, she had traveled to her aunt's house in Clarendon. Minette had studied her overstuffed bags, then Addison's belly, while suspicion darkened her eyes.

"The most you can stay is two nights," she said, slapping a dish of greasy soup in front of Addison, whose stomach churned at the aroma of the red peas, potato, yam, beef, and pigtail.

The two-bedroom house could barely fit Minette's common-law husband and two children, who chased each other around the cramped living room. Addison didn't expect anything different, and after choking down the heavy soup, worked her way around to asking about Janet. Surely, her sister wouldn't turn her away when she needed help.

"Janet not really in the best of situations, but maybe she can put you up." A near replica of her older brother, the resignation in the downward curve of Minette's mouth was disheartening. The bags under her eyes and premature grays at her temples supported her story of a tough life.

Later that evening, she handed Addison a slip of paper with Janet's address. "Be careful. Kingston can be dangerous if you don't know the place."

Without phone contact, she had no choice but to take a bus into the city and ask around until she found the address. Minette had spent a couple of nights with Janet when she had business in "town"—as people living outside of Kingston called it—so she gave her general directions, but not much else.

The following day, she got off the country bus and found the taxi stand and a cab to transport her to the heart of the city. When she arrived at the address, she had to step over a trail of mucky green water to stand on the sidewalk. After stopping at several premises to ask questions, she found the correct address and hammered on the battered zinc gate held up by two strips of rubber that acted as hinges.

A querulous voice inquired, "What yuh want?"

Addison tipped her head back until a middle-aged female with plaits shooting in several directions came into view.

"'Morning. You know Janet Black?"

"Maybe. Yuh resemble her." The woman narrowed her eyes as if she suspected Addison of wrongdoing.

"She's my sister."

"Hold on." Instead of leaving her spot, she yelled, "Janet, somebody come to see yuh."

"Who dat?" her sister asked.

"Yuh sister." The woman ignored Addison in favor of a passing car.

The *slap-slap-slap* of Janet's flip-flops announced her approach, then a sound between a screech and a groan as the gate opened.

"Addy, what…why?" Understanding dawned, and she stepped aside while giving Addison a full body scan. "Come in."

"Thanks, Miss Mavis." Janet's tone was grudging and her face a blank slate as she turned around and cut through dirt and pebbles, which gave way to concrete. She climbed a half-dozen steps and pushed open a door with white paint flakes hanging in the spots that weren't bare. Janet had gained weight and was no longer the happy girl she'd been.

When they stepped inside the room, she pointed to a stool and stood with her back to Addison. "Put your bag over there."

When she was sure Janet had forgotten her, she finally turned and leaned on the sofa, as though to brace herself. "He raped you."

The effort to say the words sapped her strength, but she eventually whispered, "More times than I can count."

"How did you find me?" Janet stood with her arms folded and both feet apart, her posture no longer welcoming.

"Minette."

A bitter smile twisted her lips. "She couldn't help you, right?"

"So she said."

Janet sighed, then cleared her throat. "I can't either. My man's paying the rent and—"

"Remember, I rented that room to two people," Miss Mavis shouted from outside, as though she'd been eavesdropping.

Shrugging, Janet mumbled, "You see what I'm living with."

Tears blinded Addison, and she lowered her head. This wasn't going the way she expected. What was she supposed to do now?

Janet touched her shoulder, then lifted her chin with one finger. "I'll work something out with Miss Mavis, but you have to sleep on the sofa."

"I understand."

But she didn't.

A glance at the sagging couch sent goosebumps over her skin. She couldn't even tell what color it used to be. Their family wasn't dirt poor, but Papa had forced Janet into a life that wasn't for her. Her dream included wedding bells and a family house. Not shacking up with a man in a dank room in a tenement yard. From what Addison saw on the way in, at least six other families lived on the premises.

She wanted a place to bawl her eyes out, but didn't have that privacy.

To her surprise, Janet hugged her. A moment later, she stood back, holding Addison by both shoulders. Gently, she asked, "Addy, are you pregnant?"

The question started her tears in earnest. She wasn't sure, but hadn't seen her period in months. Her waist had been thickening, and the tenderness in her breasts terrified her. She'd reasoned that if she didn't focus on what was happening to her body, maybe the symptoms would go away. No matter what her heart said, her head kept playing a different tune.

The sadness on Janet's face was mirrored in Addison's soul when she finally admitted what she suspected. "I think so."

Janet took the Lord's name in vain. Something she'd never have done while living at home.

As it did each day, Addison's hatred grew for the unwanted life her father planted inside her. Too often, she recalled his thick fingers invading places they shouldn't have been and the urge to vomit each time he violated her. Plus, the nauseating effect of him breathing close to her ear. Her jaw trembled, but she bit down hard. Weaklings didn't survive in the world, so she wouldn't allow anyone else to take advantage of her. Once had been enough.

To Addison's surprise, the back of her eyes burned. Her hand jerked, and the muted tinkle of the last ice cubes cut her loose from the past. She wasn't that vulnerable girl anymore.

Standing, she straightened the linen lavender suit meant to segue seamlessly from work to evening wear for today's function. She went to the bathroom, inhaling the aroma of roses while she refreshed her lipstick and slipped it back into a pouch inside the drawer.

It was risky, especially given her suspicions, but everyone was aware she kept a kit for emergency makeup repairs in the ladies' room. None of them had poisoned her yet, so she was relatively safe. She chuckled at her joke, then her smile faded. Since the episode with Rachel, she'd been wary, but habits were hard to break, especially when they made life easier.

On the way out, she passed Casey who nodded but didn't say a word. Soon, she'd have to do something about that girl, who for some reason had become an irritant to her spirit. Each time a small detail related to Casey floated to her memory, instead of becoming clearer, it stayed out of reach.

She joined the crowd of well-wishers downstairs and snagged a glass of port from a passing waiter. She was on her second glass and chatting with one of the publicists from her publishing house when Marion came into her line of sight. Her smile froze, but her brain ran down several tracks.

Piper would not have invited her, so she was crashing a private event.

What's so important that she dares to show up here today of all days?

CHAPTER 28

CASEY

SINCE MORE OF Addison's dirt had come to light, the horrors of the past wouldn't stay buried. They lingered at the edges of Casey's memory and confronted her at the oddest moments. That was the case when forgiveness wasn't an option. It turned into poison that ate away one's bones and spirit. Yet, she didn't have a choice about the vendetta she carried.

Casey returned downstairs after passing Addison in the washroom. More than once, she'd considered doctoring her lipstick or the eyeshadow she kept in the ladies' room, but rejected those ideas as risky. Besides, a swift death would be too good for Addison. She deserved to suffer while watching her fame burn in the flames of her wickedness. After gliding around the room and chatting up the important people in attendance, she disappeared with her lawyer.

Mixing with a bunch of people she worked with and hangers-on she couldn't stand made Casey want to find a corner and avoid everyone. She picked up a plate and collected a glass of orange juice, a couple of vegetable spring rolls, a cucumber sandwich, and barbecued chicken wings, then went to the back patio.

The view was picturesque with a water feature built into the adjoining golf course several yards away. She took a seat, hoping the function didn't go on forever. If Addison was feeling generous, she might give them the evening off.

Casey's thoughts shifted to the savings that could keep her afloat for a year if she didn't have work, and her investment portfolio was profitable. The one thing she couldn't fault Addison with was her generosity. They might work under sweatshop conditions, but none of her writers could complain about compensation. Truth be told, Casey enjoyed writing, compared to the administrative jobs she'd held in the past.

How ironic that the same craft that could have saved her mother's life was now sustaining hers. The air shifted, and she inhaled a light, citrusy aroma. Kirk stood behind her.

"Are you stalking me?"

He moved into view, lowered himself to the chair on the other side of the wrought-iron table, and set his glass down. His easy laughter told Casey she hadn't offended him.

"What would you say if my answer was yes?"

She finished a spring roll and sipped orange juice. "I'd tell you not to waste your time."

"You're a hard nut to crack, Casey Mitchell."

"Others might not share the same opinion." She spun the glass in a circle, then ran one finger over the droplets on its surface. "Or is it that you haven't found whatever it is you're seeking?"

He didn't deny her roundabout accusation, and she respected him for it. A long swallow of what she guessed was Pepsi stretched the silence between them. "I'm good at what I do," he finally admitted. "Sooner or later, I get what I'm after."

His words carried the weight of a threat, yet his body language said something different. This man was still interested in her. Pity she couldn't touch him.

"If I'm reading you correctly, I'd say not this time."

He stood and downed the last of his drink. "That remains to be seen."

As she bit into a spring roll, the royal palms she sat under waved gently. Casey turned her face into the breeze as the tall trees transported her to Gran's house and all she'd lost.

When Mommy died, her grandmother told their stepfather she was moving them back to her house. That same day, he brought his mother over to stay with them. The thing that grieved Casey most was that after the doctor pronounced their mother dead and the hearse took her away, Uncle Pete also disappeared. The afternoon stretched into evening, with Gran and Ma Grimes bustling around as people came to pay their respects.

How Gran could stand to be in the same room with Uncle Pete after he stole Mommy's chance of having treatment—and a longer life—mystified Casey. When she asked about it, Gran gripped her shoulders and held her still. "Yuh may not understand now, but the Bible says vengeance belongs to the Lord. It also tells us He sees every tear we cry and stores them in His bottle. Yuh understand?"

Her explanation sounded nonsensical, but Casey nodded to escape Gran's tight hold. The rest of that afternoon, Casey and Donnette sat in their room, taking turns staring into space or drying the tears that wouldn't stop coming.

Night fell, and Casey prayed that by some miracle, Uncle Pete wouldn't return. She listened at the door while her grandmother and his mother argued over his whereabouts.

Hours later, right before Gran left for home, she kissed their cheeks and told them to behave. "Everything will soon be all right."

Casey didn't believe her, and when Gran left, they stayed closeted in the room as the night grew cooler. Her unease was justified because while Ma Grimes slept in his room, Uncle Pete came to theirs carrying the stink of stale rum.

Casey knew for certain then, the duppy or ghost stories their cousins used to tell while they huddled under the sheets were all lies. The dead had no power over the living. If they did, Mommy would have stopped Uncle Pete from taking advantage of Donnette while he wept that same night.

A few weeks later, on the Saturday morning after their stepfather died in his sleep—according to Dr. Moodie—they returned home. The taxi driver had barely pulled up as far as he could on the unpaved driveway before she and Donnette leaped out of the Toyota. Their cousins weren't excited to see them because the Mitchell sisters' return meant they'd have to share a room again.

As the old man hefted their two battered suitcases onto the veranda, Casey hid her delight. Although the pain of Mommy's death would always be a nasty cut that never fully healed, being with Gran was heaven compared to living with Uncle Pete.

Life happened on a repeat cycle—school, chores, homework, and frequent squabbles—but Gran "split justice" between the two sets of girls, even when they didn't see it that way. The relatively peaceful atmosphere in the Finch household lasted until the day Gran announced she'd heard from Casey and Donnette's father.

Aside from the occasional ten U.S. dollars that came by registered mail for each of them, they didn't correspond with Ansel Mitchell. The last time they had contact was on Donnette's fourteenth birthday in April. Before he immigrated to the United

States, they hadn't seen him any more frequently, but Casey had a special love for him.

Their grandmother never liked him, and from what Casey gathered, he didn't feel any differently about her. As an adult, Casey came to understand that no one would have been good enough for Amina Finch's prized daughter—even worse, a man who gave her daughter two children and hadn't married her.

"That good-for-nothing man" was what Gran called him whenever Mommy complained about him. Donnette and Casey jokingly referred to him that way, although she knew it was wrong, until Mommy caught them and put an end to their disrespect.

Gran would mutter, "I don't know what made you even look in his direction. Not all that glitters is gold." She reverted to patois, a sign of her displeasure. "Mi try to tell yuh, but yuh never listen. Now him gone to 'Merica and forget you and him children."

Mommy lowered her head and sighed while Gran ranted. Casey remembered him as a loud, pleasant man who made them laugh when he bothered to visit. She clung to the image of him hoisting her into the air and tickling her until she was breathless with laughter. Eventually, his face faded, and Uncle Pete replaced him. Gran didn't seem to approve or disapprove, but warned him to "take care of my daughter and her pickney dem."

Their stepfather did much more than her grandmother demanded. He also taught Casey that if she were careful, she could get away with murder.

CHAPTER 29

ADDISON

MARION BRUSHED PAST a young man who tried to speak with her and made a straight line to where Addison stood, exchanging small talk with an executive. She excused herself to avoid having anyone else caught up in their unpleasantness.

When they stood face to face, Addison knew their issues would come to a head today. She saw it in Marion's eyes. So much for thinking she'd take whatever Addison owed her mother and disappear quietly. The tight black dress, dramatic eye makeup, and ridiculously high collar cast Marion as Dracula's bride.

"I need to talk with you."

Hiking one shoulder, Addison said, "Speak."

"Not here. I've been trying to meet with you, but haven't received a response to any of my calls."

"That's because I'm busy."

"There's no time like the present. This won't take long."

Addison let out a heavy breath and raised her glass. "This way."

She went to the steps and led the way to the studio. All the writers and editors were at the party, so no one would hear their conversation.

At the top of the stairs, she faced Marion. "That is as far as you go. What I told you last time hasn't changed. Every document that Emily had, bless her soul, my lawyer also has in his possession." That wasn't exactly true, but how would Marion know any different?

"That's all well and good." Marion assessed her perfect nails, then raised her head. "But you don't want your mess on the street."

"Darling, so many leeches are coming out of the woodwork, trust me, one more definitely won't make a difference."

"Call me whatever you want, I won't disappear. Not after you put my mother into an early grave."

Addison raised one hand with her palm outward at face level. "Please. Not that again, for the mother you hated."

"Whatever, but you're going to pay me."

With the fingers of one hand, Addison moved her collar away from her neck. "Listen, and hear me good: I don't care what you believe you have on me, but I owe you *nothing*. My assistant transferred a sizeable amount to your account, which was more than generous. It's time for you to ease back into the woodwork, like the blood-sucking vermin you are."

Marion's cold stare was menacing as she approached Addison. "We'll see how fast you backtrack when I release your business to the media."

The weeks of anxiety and worry exploded in her chest. Addison was fed up with people threatening her from every direction. "Do whatever you want. Get out of my house, and don't come back."

"Our business isn't finished. I expect another payment, and I won't wait too long."

"You must think I'm stupid." Addison shook her head and pointed at Marion's chest. "I'm to keep sending you money with no end in sight. For what?"

"To keep me from spreading what you and my evil vampire bat of a mother did to swindle people out of their work."

Addison's vision went hazy, and her stomach pulsed the way it would if someone was squeezing it with a cruel fist. Perspiration dotted her forehead, but she stayed composed. "Get out. Now."

"I'll leave when I'm good and ready."

"Don't test me. You don't know who you're playing with."

"You're right about that." Marion scoffed. "No wonder you and my mother got along so well. The two of you are cut from the same cloth."

She approached Addison who inched closer to the steps, impatient for this poisonous weed to exit her house.

Wagging one finger, Marion warned, "Be sure to lodge my money by next week."

Addison's blood pressure soared, and she grabbed Marion's arm and urged her toward the stairs. "You've worn out your welcome. Just go!"

Marion tried dislodging her fingers, but Addison's nerves were shot. She held on tighter and shoved her toward the stairs. "Good riddance."

The younger woman stumbled and clawed at Addison's arm. Both of them screamed as they tumbled down the stairs.

Addison broke her momentum by grabbing one of the spindles when she sprawled on the landing. Her face and the back of her head throbbed, plus her vision was hazy. She couldn't catch her breath but raised her head as a sickening crunch confirmed when Marion crashed onto the marble tiles near the entrance.

Someone had taken an ax to her forehead. Addison's eyes refused to open, and she may have screamed from the agony when gentle arms lifted her, but all that emerged from her mouth was a series of groans.

Amina Finch's face swam before her, and Addison wanted to claw her way from this waking nightmare, but it wouldn't let her go. Her head hammered, but not hard enough to remove the condemnation she'd brought on herself seventeen years ago, sitting in that depressing house.

At the time, the old woman's eyes blazed. "Why yuh would do something so wicked?"

In the face of Mrs. Finch's displeasure, Addison had sat straighter instead of shrinking. How was it her fault her son-in-law took the payment that should have gone to her daughter's treatment?

These people were simple country folk and couldn't have known that Addison wasn't an agent, nor did they understand her intentions. *Games People Play* renewed her slowly dying passion for writing. Intuition and knowledge of her craft told Addison the book would be a bestseller.

Mrs. Finch's intensity was unnerving, and Addison steeled herself not to show any emotion. She also forced herself not to focus on Yvette. The manuscript now belonged to her, and there was no going back. They simply didn't know yet. As far as they were concerned, Grimes had taken the advance and nothing more.

"You can't hold me responsible for your family matters," Addison choked out.

The lumpy sofa and peeling wallpaper inside the younger woman's home made her skin itch, and she longed to leave. Coming back was a mistake.

When Yvette tried to speak, the tears in her eyes and the convulsive swallowing wouldn't let her get a word out.

Her distress hadn't moved Addison enough to change her mind. She needed that manuscript to revive her stalled career.

Yvette's mother gripped her thin arm as she addressed Addison. "Yuh come here and offered to help, and now, like a vulture, yuh waiting for the worst to happen."

"Considering that *he* came to me—"

"Did you and Peter discuss any business before yesterday?" Amina Finch's gaze was as cold as her eyes were hot, when she continued, "No, but both of yuh want to benefit from my daughter's work." Her voice shook as she spat, "And di money dat should have gone to my daughter's treatment is in dat man's pocket."

Snagging that book for less than she would have paid had she dealt directly with Yvette had been a bonus. Her condition had deteriorated rapidly since their second meeting, and the light in Yvette's eyes slowly died when Addison explained how long the process from contract signing to publication would take.

That realization on their part left Addison in a position of power, which changed the trajectory of their dealings. Despite her "blunder" with Grimes, she would still act as Yvette's agent and provide another small advance "to help the situation." The words slid off her tongue, and it was easy to believe the story she'd concocted for their benefit.

"My family can still use the money after I'm gone" was Yvette's comment, despite her mother's warning to end the agreement.

"Take sleep and mark death. Dis woman and Peter not different from each other." Mrs. Finch's grim expression and cryptic advice sent a shiver down Addison's spine, along with her next words. "When yuh dig one pit, yuh better dig two."

Three months later, Addison landed a deal for *Games People Play* that outdid every dream she'd ever nourished in her heart.

Again, she switched her strategy. Why give away more than necessary?

Yvette's family still didn't have money to treat her cancer, and Addison held out until Mrs. Finch agreed to take an even smaller sum out of desperation. By that time, Yvette was bedridden.

Addison proposed signing a new contract that would give her total control of the book, for a price, but Mrs. Finch refused.

The last time Mrs. Finch confronted Addison, the woman snarled, "Mark my words, yuh wickedness will catch up with yuh one day. The God I know will see justice served. Yuh will *never* be happy."

She wasn't willing to believe that day had come. The blaring of the ambulance sirens woke her from that hallucination, but the pulsing in her head continued like a battering ram against her skull.

Mrs. Finch's curse hadn't affected Addison's life much because she couldn't remember being happy outside of her writing. She should never have gone back to Jamaica. To return to the place where her lies and deception started was tempting fate, even if she hadn't advertised her visit or done much beyond the interviews she'd approved.

Addison mumbled when the EMT leaned in and asked her to open her eyes.

"Don't let her sleep," a voice urged from her other side, but she heard nothing as she fell into another nightmare.

CHAPTER 30

CASEY

A SCREAM JARRED Casey from a place she longed to forget. Her hand jerked, and the glass toppled. She dropped the napkin over the spilled orange juice and ran inside, cutting through the kitchen and into the vast living space.

A crowd milled around the steps in the foyer, and Quentin walked toward her, leading Piper. She sobbed as if someone close to her had died.

"What happened?" Casey asked.

"There's been an accident. Two people, including Addison, may be injured—or worse." He swept the back of one hand across his forehead and asked, "Can you call for an ambulance and maybe get these folks out of here?"

"Sure. Where's Kirk?"

She wasn't certain why she asked, other than that he seemed to be someone who knew what to do in emergencies.

Quentin pointed toward where the people stood gawking. "He's dealing with them—keeping them back and seeing what he can do for Addison."

Of course. That didn't surprise her. While dialing on her cell phone, she guided Piper by the arm to a recessed corner of the living room. A quick trip to one of the food tables, and she returned with a handful of napkins, reeling off the address to the emergency responder. When she hung up, she regretted not asking someone else to call. Still, an accident was an accident, and thankfully, she'd been nowhere near the scene when it happened.

"That woman is dead," Piper hiccupped between her words. "There's so much blood."

The police would eventually show up, if that were the case, and Casey didn't want them to remember she existed.

"Who is she?" Casey asked.

Piper pulled in her breath and shuddered. "Emily's daughter."

Casey closed her eyes and cursed her luck. Why did this have to happen today of all days?

"Can I bring you anything?"

"No. I'm fine." Piper dabbed her eyes, but the tears wouldn't stop coming.

"Will Addison be all right?" she asked, toying with a button on her shirt.

If there was any fairness in life, her boss would still be alive.

"I think so, but she might have a head injury."

Casey didn't respond, but made herself more comfortable on the plush cream sectional, knowing she'd be there a while. She didn't attempt to move people along as Quentin had asked. Too much on her mind. Nearly four hours later, when she finally arrived home, Donnette was using her laptop at the kitchen table.

"What's up?" Casey asked, reaching into the fridge for a bottle of water.

"I should ask you that."

"Addison had a function, and there was an accident." She pulled out a chair and collapsed on it. Sitting around for the entire afternoon had sapped her energy. She drank a third of the water and capped the rest.

Donnette had stopped moving.

"What's the matter?" A moment later, Casey sighed. "I wasn't even in the house when it happened."

"Good."

She couldn't share the part where Detectives Ince and Robinson showed up and rattled her cage. Although she couldn't tell them anything about Marion's death, they reminded her she wasn't in the clear. She didn't believe them because she was sure she'd seen a mention in the newspaper that Rachel's death wasn't considered suspicious. There was no value to them baiting her, but if it made them feel useful, who was she to stop them?

"What were you doing?" Casey asked to change the subject.

Sitting back, Donnette ran a finger over a sticker on the laptop. "Checking out some positions in case I'm not called back to work."

"Keep your chin up. You're an excellent nurse. They can't afford to lose you."

"That may be true, but you know how it is when companies focus on exclusive clients."

Unfortunately, she did. Reaching across the table, she squeezed Donnette's hand. "Sorry, Dee. If I could do anything to change the situation, I would."

"I know." Donnette turned her hand and gripped Casey's before rising and picking up the laptop. Her smile was weak, and Casey cursed herself for not being able to fix this problem, which she'd caused.

When Donnette's bedroom door closed, Casey folded her arms and lay her head on them. Her heart ached, but what could they do but wait to hear if Donnette still had a job? She hoped Donnette wouldn't think too much during this time at home. While Casey obsessed over Donnette's emotional health, she was concerned with Casey's physical well-being—ensuring that she ate and that her muscles wouldn't atrophy from sitting at the laptop for hours.

Casey would do anything for Donnette, even if it cost her own peace of mind. She spiraled back to the night of Mommy's death when Uncle Pete came and left Donnette crying. Casey wanted to comfort Donnette, but didn't because she'd tell her to go back to bed.

Gran kept saying, "Soon, everything will be all right."

Casey didn't know what that meant, and she didn't care.

If she did nothing, Uncle Pete might think about touching her one day, and she wouldn't be a victim. If Mommy hadn't been sick, how would he explain the bloody sheets on Donnette's bed or the bite marks on her skin where no one could see them?

When he wasn't hacking as if he would cough up his organs, he snored like a buzz saw. Knowing that, eleven-year-old Casey decided how she'd help Donnette. The night was still, and Casey's eyelids drooped, but she forced herself not to sleep. Counting the times Uncle Pete assaulted Donnette kept her awake. Her sister's even breathing, sometimes broken by soft moans, strengthened Casey's decision. She sat up and swung her feet to the floor.

Uncle Pete snored loud enough to shake the entire house. She inched forward, holding both hands out until she reached the doorway, avoiding the loose floorboard. Her fingers led her along the corridor wall, past the picture of the jug with the yellow flowers, then to his bedroom.

Her mother's mantra rang inside her head, and Casey whispered the affirmations Mommy taught them: "We are strong. We can do anything. We can achieve anything."

The continued gurgling and snorting stalled her feet for a few seconds. She pushed the half-open door, and a hacking cough forced her to scamper out and press her back to the cool wall. Her heart galloped the way it would have if she'd been running.

If anyone saw her eyes in the gloom, they would have been as big as an owl's, or *patoo*, as Gran called them. Now was not the time to remember how their hoots made chills dance up and down her spine, so Casey cleared her mind and focused on what she came to do.

She crept into the room, hunched over in her thin cotton nightgown. As her eyes grew accustomed to the shadows, she stood taller. His room wasn't as dark as theirs because of the streetlight in front of the fence.

Wrinkles lined Uncle Pete's face, making him seem much older than his forty years. The cigarettes and rum had sucked away his flesh and left him as thin as a skeleton. Since Mommy's illness, Uncle Pete drank more than he ate.

"We are strong. We can do anything. We can achieve anything." The whispered reminder gave her strength.

A rattling noise came from his throat, and she sprang back, thinking he was awake. But he'd been "drawing a gear," as her grandmother would have said.

She scanned the bed until she made out the lumpy pillow at the foot of the mattress. Taking her time, she gently lifted the pillow and brought it back to the side of the bed.

Casey didn't know how long she glared at the man who had stolen Donnette's smile. Of the two of them, she saw the good in everything and believed each problem had an answer. Now,

Donnette walked with her chin tucked into her chest and both arms crossed over her breasts, not wanting anyone to notice her.

Uncle Pete was responsible for that.

Casey almost sucked her teeth until she remembered where she stood. Her spine tingled, and she looked over her shoulder, then raised the worn pillow. A draft of musty air filled her nose from the sponge inside the pillowcase. Gently, the way she would have treated a baby, she laid the pillow over his face, then she pressed harder. Nothing happened in the next few seconds. Until he tried sitting up. With all the strength in her body, she held on until he stopped struggling. His chest rattled as a cough tried to escape.

Even when he was barely twitching, she kept up the pressure. She counted to fifty and continued stifling him. Sweat dripped into her eyes, her hands shook, and her back ached with the effort not to let go. She counted to fifty more. Breathing hard, she raised the pillow and stumbled out of his reach, but he didn't move.

Another shiver chased up and down her spine, and she turned to the doorway to be certain she was still alone. Guilt made her think someone was watching. According to Gran, God saw everything. Surely, He could forgive her for killing this wicked man to bring the smile back to her sister's face. For a time, she stood rooted to the floorboards, staring at his body.

What if Ma Grimes catches me?

The idea sent her scuttling around the bed to replace the pillow. She put it back the way she'd found it and turned the side she'd used up to the air. If he left any spit on it, by morning it would be dry. One last check before creeping to the door satisfied her that he was gone.

She stopped at the bathroom in the passage and washed her hands, rubbing them hard with soap to rid herself of his smell, then she flushed the toilet in case anyone was listening and climbed back into bed. For as long as her eyes stayed open, she scoured every corner of the bedroom.

The duppy stories left her fearful that Uncle Pete might come and spirit her away with him. She turned on her side and faced the door, just in case. Then she snuggled under the sheet.

The dead have no power over the living.

Sleep dragged her eyelids lower, and eventually, she gave in.

She woke the next morning to the sound of a scream echoing through the house.

CHAPTER 31

ALECIA

THE DOOR TO the landing banged against the wall, startling Alecia.

Addison stood in the doorway. The bright-red spots across her nose and cheeks contrasted with her pale skin and the fitted black suit. Her hand shook as she waved a sheet of paper. The butterfly bandages on her forehead were reminders of the tragedy with Marion that unfolded the previous week.

"Don't all rush to confess," she screeched as she advanced into the room.

Piper went pale and fingered the faux pearls at her throat.

Everyone else stopped moving.

As she stalked past each of the glass-topped desks, Addison held the letter-size paper so it was visible to all of them. Alecia bit her lip to contain her delight. The two side-by-side photos had been making the rounds since last night, and she'd been delighted to see the momentum growing, along with people's outrage.

She wasn't a social media addict—at least she didn't think so. According to Casey, Alecia needed to check herself. She scrolled blindly to destress after work, but didn't understand the fascination with other people's lives, nor the need to police their morals. She hadn't intended harm, but was shocked at the attention that came from the post she'd made about Casey being detained.

Addison was a different proposition. The obsession of the masses had served Alecia well. She hadn't dared to release anything else from her accounts, but Island Gyal had been more than willing to accommodate Alecia.

Connecting with her was easy. She was one of the few influencers Alecia followed because she enjoyed her content. She figured she could trust her, and she was right. As long as the information was credible, Ronique or Island Gyal would share it on her platform. More views meant additional dollars shelled out to her by the social media platform. The exchange worked for both of them, and Ronique had always been true to her word, never revealing the source of her data and pictures.

When Addison moved past Quentin, he winced and lowered his head. A flush covered his creamy skin, and he glared at Alecia. He probably regretted pulling Addison off her on Monday. The caption under the pictures made Alecia want to break into a grin.

ADDISON HAS BEEN KNOWN TO ROMP
WITH HER STAFFERS.
IT'S CLEAR SOME DON'T MIND THE ATTENTION.

The smug smile Quentin wore announced to the world he wasn't averse to Addison cupping him in a public place. Served him right. She might have forgiven him if he hadn't made a fool of her.

Her smirk wore off, and her stomach cramped as Addison came closer, her movements unhurried and deliberate as she sniffed out her prey. Addison stared her in the face and prepared to move on, then focused on her again.

Alecia brushed the hair out of her eyes, uncomfortable with the minute study.

A crooked smile came to Addison's face. "*You*, come into the office with me."

She stopped mid-stride and faced Alecia. "You know what? I've changed my mind. Let's do it here. Explain to me why, when I've treated you as a valued member of my staff, you'd do something so underhanded."

The years of abuse and intimidation held Alecia captive. Her mouth refused to open, despite the urgent signals from her brain.

"Answer me," Addison shrieked, "you worthless piece of shit."

Startled, Alecia stepped back and stumbled, but the insult opened the floodgates. "If I'm a piece of shit, what are you?"

"How dare you?"

"I dare because I have every right." Alecia folded her arms to steady herself. This was what she'd waited for, and the situation wouldn't overwhelm her. Not today.

Addison shook the paper in her fist. "What right do you have to try and destroy me with these made-up stories?"

"That isn't a figment of my imagination." She glanced around the room. "I'm sure everyone here would agree that's a slice of undeniable reality."

A slight rustle went up as the men shifted.

"What I do is *none* of your business, you little shit."

Alecia's nostrils flared, and she yelled, "It is, when you refuse to acknowledge the wrong you've done all your life."

"Since my business isn't yours, you have no right to judge me."

"Oh yes, I do." Alecia sucked in her breath and shouted, "You're the bitch who threw me away to chase your dreams!"

The studio reflected the silence of a tomb while Addison stared at her. "You," she whispered, crushing the paper. "Who are you?"

"You heard me. I'm *Alice Black*. What I want to know is if it was worth it."

Addison's eyes widened, and she braced her feet, then she grimaced and brought out that evil smile Alecia recognized. She clapped slowly. Each meeting of her palms echoed, similar to the crack of a whip. "Well played, my dear. And to answer your question, yes, my freedom was worth every minute." She pulled her shoulders back, scanned the room, then motioned to Alecia. "Come with me. The rest of you get back to work."

Her feet were as heavy as two metal blocks, and her head felt light, but she followed Addison as requested. She entered the office and let the door swing shut behind her. A hungry lioness had nothing on Addison. Her lips barely moved when she said, "How did you find out?"

"I–I overheard a conversation."

Not once did Addison blink when she asked, "How did you find me?"

"I didn't know who you were when I came here. Two and two added to the right number as I found out more about you." She paused, then added, "My research took time, but proved I was right. Since that conversation I mentioned, I've been searching."

"You're disgusting and dishonest. If you meant me any good, you'd have told me."

"But I'm *disgusting and dishonest*, remember?" Alecia spat. "Same as you."

Addison marched across the floor and stood behind her desk. "You no longer work here."

"Says you." Alecia forced a triumphant smile while her stomach tied itself into painful knots. "I have a contract."

"Not after I consult with my lawyer." She sank to the seat, and her lips curled. Her mocking gaze raked Alecia the way she would decomposing roadkill. "Get out."

Turning away, Alecia said, "I'm leaving, but I'll be back."

She didn't know what was goading her to be defiant. The moment she revealed her hand, Addison would throw her out. She knew that. And yet, she couldn't leave without settling one issue.

She cranked the door handle, then asked, "What was so wrong with me that you couldn't have kept me, or at least come back at some point?"

With the speed of a rocket launcher, Addison shot from the chair. Her face and neck turned a splotchy shade of red. "I didn't take you with me because I couldn't stand the sight of you."

Walking around the desk, she shouted, "My father raped me. *You* are the product of his repeated attacks on me. Why the hell would I want you? Seeing you now—and knowing what I do—brings back the worst part of my life. I should have stifled you when I had the chance."

Tears seared Alecia's eyes, and the weight of Addison's hate pinned her to the floor. She stepped back when Addison lowered her voice and smoothed both hands down her side. "I told you already, get out, and don't come back if you know what's good for you."

Swallowing hard, Alecia stumbled from the office. The studio was ice cold, despite the light sweater she'd chosen that morning. She approached her seat on shaky legs, fearing they'd give out. Breathing hard, she sat, then picked up her handbag. The clacking of keys was missing, and she took it to mean the entire team heard Addison's words.

When she rose, Addison glared through the glass wall. The feeling of being "less than" threatened to drown her, but she faced

Addison with a defiant stare and held in a sniffle. Through a wash of maddening tears, she left the studio. At the top of the stairs, her tears escaped, and she stopped to blot them on her sleeve.

She hadn't meant to reveal her identity today, but her temper got the best of her. Nor had she calculated the true cost of outing herself to Addison. But she'd done enough damage so that snake wouldn't bounce back as if nothing happened. Her image had taken a hit, and this fresh scandal with Quentin would keep people talking.

No matter that her stupid heart was breaking, rejection had made her tough. She would heal. In time.

Standing in the parking lot, she stared at the building. She'd given up a valuable part of her life for nothing. As she drove out for the last time, despite her taunt to Addison, Alecia wouldn't miss the studio, even if her soul said something different.

At home, she kicked off her shoes and fell into bed. More than anything, it devastated her to know she was the product of rape and that Addison had considered killing her. She'd have been more sympathetic after hearing her story, if she wasn't mean through and through.

The minutes crept on, and she fell into a doze and dreamed of being chased by a witch through a misty forest. The surrounding haze parted when the doorbell echoed through the condo. Frowning, she supported herself on both hands. Who the hell was at the door? Maybe if she pretended not to be home, they'd go away. But after a couple more minutes, it was clear the invader didn't plan to leave.

She dragged herself to the living room and used the peephole.

Casey stood outside, carrying a document box.

Alecia dragged her fingers through her hair and tested her breath with a hand cupped over her mouth before turning the knob. "Hey, Casey. What are you doing here?"

That might be a strange question between friends, but it reminded Alecia that she and Casey socialized over food, drinks, and at the salon more than they did anywhere else.

Casey raised the box she carried. "I brought your things from the office."

Hardly believing Addison would be that considerate, she stepped out of the way and asked, "Why?"

"Addison was serious about you not coming back. She tore through the entire place after you left. Gave us a speech about loyalty and whatnot while tearing us new…let me not say that. Where can I put this?"

A smile lifted Alecia from the doldrums, and she pointed to a chair.

"I have something to say." Casey tugged at her ponytail and shifted from one foot to the other.

"Why do I figure this is something I don't want to hear?"

She shrugged and ran a hand over the hairs that had escaped her ponytail. "I never told you before, but there's a reason I'm working for Addison, too."

Rubbing the back of her neck, Alecia stepped away. "Why are you telling me this now?"

Casey shrugged. "When was there ever a right time in that studio?"

"Good point." Standing akimbo, Alecia asked, "So, what made you choose to work in such a toxic environment?"

"It's hard to know what you're walking into from the outside." She tilted her head and narrowed her eyes. "It's weird, but now that the whole thing is out, you *do* resemble her. Same complexion, a certain something around the eyes, but you always wear bangs so it wasn't in-your-face obvious."

Which was why she'd had the procedure done. It became too painful to wake up every day and deal with seeing Addison's evil face in the mirror. The plastic surgeon gave in to her request because of the nasty scar next to her eye. Ophelia had helped her onto the dining table when she was five with instructions to fly, then threw her off, and told Mama it was an accident. Rough landings were a constant in her life.

Nodding, she admitted, "I wanted it that way, and it worked."

"We heard what she said." Casey sighed and bit her lip. "I'm so sorry—"

"It doesn't matter. I didn't expect her to hug or welcome me." She cursed the burning at the back of her eyes and tipped her chin higher. "I wanted it to hurt…the way she hurt me."

Sliding both hands into her pants pocket, Casey lowered her head. "So, about what I said earlier…I was working there, too, because—"

The doorbell played what was fast becoming an annoying tune, and Alecia held up one hand. "Give me a minute."

She marched the few steps to the door, didn't bother to check who was outside, and opened it to give someone a tongue-lashing.

Quentin stood on the welcome mat and pointed between her eyes. "You're as crazy as a loon, you know that? Of all the things you could have done, this is how you choose to get back at me?"

"I'm not the one who was grinning like a pet monkey being pawed by its owner."

"You have a case of sour grapes, that's all."

"You can say whatever you like. The fact is, you lied up and down that you weren't sleeping with her."

"Revenge or not, that was a low blow." Quentin waited a second, then sucked his teeth. "Even for you."

A red tide swam before Alecia's eyes, and she lost reason. What did he mean by *even for you*? This double dose of humiliation was the limit, and before she could stop herself, her fist shot into his face.

CHAPTER 32

ADDISON

MATTEO NEVER MADE jokes, but had to be kidding this time.

"What do you mean you can no longer represent me?"

Sighing, Matteo waved a hand over her file. "My firm is small, albeit profitable. This terrible publicity can sink the business I've worked hard to build."

Addison uncrossed her legs and set both feet on the floor. "You're not the only one who's built something out of nothing."

"But the *nothing* you started with didn't belong to you."

"Are you going to believe petty and vindictive people who have nothing else to do but tarnish other people's success?"

He removed his glasses, polished them with a soft cloth, and set them on the desk. Matteo rubbed his eyes, a diversionary tactic that maddened her. Everything was going wrong, and she couldn't move fast enough to get them back on track.

"It's more than that, Addison, and you have to level with me if you want my help. How can I represent someone I don't trust?

You can't lie to me and then expect me to take care of your affairs effectively."

She sighed as if dealing with an inconsequential matter. "What untruth did I tell this time?"

He put the glasses back on and stared at her with an unreadable expression. "I read the book."

"All of it? Where did you find the time?" she asked, while her heart did a nosedive to her ankles.

"I carved it out to compare notes between the novel and the manuscript. The book came from the file that belonged to Yvette Finch. Plus, a justice of the peace signed the agreement, along with both of you. That makes it more than binding."

"So? I paid for the rights, fair and square."

Matteo continued staring at her with a disturbing intensity. "Whom did you pay, and where is that contract?"

"At the bank."

"I need to see it." He picked up a pen and tapped it against the leather-top desk. "Why didn't you bring it with you since it would likely be part of our discussion?"

"I can send it to you. In the meantime, I need you to do some things."

His eyebrows pulled together, and he laid the pen down. "That depends, but let me hear what you have to say."

"I need to access Emily's files—I mean, the ones that pertain to me."

"If they aren't contracts or your manuscripts, they won't be released to you."

"Next, I need a cease-and-desist letter for that picture being circulated with me and that toddler."

"That's doable, but challenging. Do you know who first posted it online?"

"I think so."

"But it's gone viral. How can we control that?" He shook his head. "My advice would be to leave it alone and let it die. Every day, there's a new scandal, and people move on."

"Well, can you address one to someone who works…used to work for me? She's out there feeding this gossip."

"That, I can do. As long as you're certain she's guilty of what you're accusing her of doing. I'll need proof."

"Also, I need a general one."

Matteo's lips moved, but he didn't smile. "A cease-and-desist order doesn't work like that."

"I just want to stop people from saying my book isn't mine."

"In that case, you issue a statement. But I'd be careful with that because the manuscript I received seems to be the real thing."

"I don't care what it seems to be. *Games People Play* is *my* book. I have a copyright."

"That's fine, but if you're taken to court, and it's proven you didn't come by it legally, you'll have a problem."

"I have another situation," she said, removing a folded wad of paper from her handbag and stifling a sigh. "Marion's brother is suing me for wrongful death."

"When it rains, it pours," Matteo commented when she placed the document in his hands.

"No truer words have ever been spoken." She wanted a drink, but it was too early. If she asked, Matteo would tell her no, with his judgmental self. "So, what are we dealing with here?"

Matteo cleared his throat and tapped the sheet. "Well, in a wrongful death, what they're accusing you of is being negligent."

"How can they hold me responsible for her being clumsy and falling?"

"I'm sure they'll try to make a case, especially if you were drinking."

"I had two glasses of port."

"And you hadn't been drinking earlier in the day?"

She shrugged. "I doubt it. I'll have to search my mind."

"This is serious, Addison. Someone lost their life."

Matteo looked at her the way Eustace Black would, when he was about to hand down his version of discipline. The image of her father turned her stomach, and she brought her mind back to the current problem. Everywhere she turned, a new issue reared its head. It was enough to drive her mad.

While Matteo scanned the papers, she reminded herself these challenges were temporary and someday she'd laugh about them. Today, she'd hunker down and prepare for any blowback from this outrageous claim.

She'd been toying with installing cameras in the building since her troubles started. Good thing she hadn't put them in place yet because they would have captured her altercation with Marion. Perhaps the police would have charged her with manslaughter at the least. Marion got what she deserved for crashing her party to threaten her with fabrications.

The police, when they arrived, had been sympathetic but professional. They hadn't accused her of anything, but told her she shouldn't leave town. While watching her keenly, they asked about the mark on Marion's arm. She'd shown them where Marion grabbed her. Then, she explained that she'd been trying to prevent her from falling and held on to her, but they both took a tumble.

They visited again and brought up Rachel's death, questioning her about that, too. She'd insisted it was an unfortunate accident. The cause of Rachel's death was a heart attack brought on by anaphylaxis. Once more, suspicion crowded her mind.

Two instances of murders from her book were too many to ignore, yet she still hesitated to mention it to Kirkland or anyone else. Who on her team had the temerity to pull that off? All along, she'd underestimated them. If she had to guess, she'd say Casey.

Simply because she hadn't pressured her as much as the others. Addison didn't know how she'd react when pushed to her limit. Unlike Erik, who went red in the face but didn't fight back.

This stupidity with Marion's brother, Gerald, was galling because Emily had shared her disappointment over her children. Neither of them gave a hoot about each other, but the smell of a possible payout had them sniffing around like hyenas. The lawsuit would soon be in the papers because everything she did was news. These days, the reports were more bad than good, but as she'd come to learn, all publicity was worth something.

"What if he gets hold of my files Marion was using to threaten me?"

"I'll do what I can to access them, but again, if they're copies of contracts between both of you, it's legal for him to have them."

"What about a press briefing? I've been meaning to do one for the longest time."

"I'd hold off on that as well. You don't want to call that level of attention to yourself with controversy swirling around you."

She leaned in to say, "One more thing."

Matteo's expression said, *What now?*, which made her want to hurl her phone at him. "Rachel's partner is still holding on to my files. Please get them, as I've been unable to reach him."

"Bear in mind what I said about the files Marion was holding on to. The same principle applies here."

Addison wanted to stick out her tongue, but that would be childish. He was a real killjoy.

She sent a message to let her driver know she was ready. These days, she made them wait close by to avoid being trapped by the paparazzi. "Touch base when you've cleared up some of this mess."

Matteo rose to walk her out, gently squeezing her arm. "In the meantime, try not to create any fresh ones."

In the front office, she said goodbye and left. She'd taken a few steps down the sidewalk when someone shoved a phone next to her chin. "Miss Comstock, given your recent misfortunes, what would you say about the future of your next book?"

Addison chose not to respond. Where the mini mob came from, she didn't know, but she walked faster to escape the small gathering. Years ago, she gave up trying to figure out how they always found her. The attention was good for her career, so she wasn't bothered by it, other than the ridiculous questions being asked. She'd been pussyfooting around long enough about hosting a press conference to tell her side of the story.

Two minutes later, she sat inside the vehicle arguing with Theo.

"It's not that I'm refusing to do what you ask. I don't think it's a sensible plan after all that's been—"

"What if I did a podcast with one of those people with a large following? That might help."

"You're *not* listening. That's *not* a good idea either."

The driver met her eyes in the mirror, and she reminded herself to say as little as possible.

"Why isn't it?"

The horn blasts told her Theo was on the street, so she pressed the phone closer to her ear.

"You won't come across as sympathetic, so I'd leave that alone unless you've had a crash course that will make you seem softer and more approachable."

"That's such a crock, and you're full of sh—"

"See what I mean?"

Addison stubbornly held her silence, cutting her eyes at the traffic when he added, "Until I come up with a short-term strategy, I'd suggest you let me do my job."

"It seems everything is getting worse," she whispered, then set her jaw to stop it from trembling.

"Let me worry about it. Give me twenty-four hours."

"Fine."

She was anything but and fumed over his silly advice. While he was busy doing whatever he did when he wasn't taking care of her business, her life was falling apart. What did Theo know about PR matters anyway? He'd simply been following Rachel's directions in the past couple of years.

A call to Piper to issue instructions improved her mood. Theo could go to hell. She'd do what she damn well pleased.

CHAPTER 33

CASEY

"SOMETIMES I WONDER if Mommy's death put you over the edge."

"Why would you say that?" Casey asked as she placed her feet on the floor and set her tablet aside.

"This." Donnette shoved the phone under her nose and let it fall in her lap.

Casey's network profile picture stared back at her from a post that claimed she was a failed writer with a crab-in-a-barrel syndrome and wanted to destroy Addison.

She didn't have words to respond to Donnette's accusation because she didn't know who would be this spiteful. She'd been careful with each piece of information she shared online and ensured nothing could be traced back to her. Addison couldn't possibly launch an attack without proof she'd done anything. Still, she'd ignored Casey since the police escorted her from the office two weeks ago—as if that solved anything.

Alecia and Rochelle were the only people, aside from her cousin in Jamaica, who might suspect her of attacking Addison. If it came down to a process of elimination, she'd point a finger at Alecia. Her nightmare with Quentin had made her unstable.

Donnette had disappeared, so Casey reached for her phone. The ringer was off since she left the office, and Rochelle had sent her several messages, the last of which read: *Have u fallen off the planet?*

Alecia's phone rang without answer, which wasn't surprising if she was hiding, but Casey warned herself not to assign blame with zero proof.

She flopped on the sofa with the iPad on her chest. When she checked again, two hundred comments had blossomed to nearly five hundred. Casey was being cancelled, and she barely had a presence on the internet.

How the hell do people get caught up in issues that don't concern them to the point of spewing vitriol about someone they don't know?

Addison would be delighted to have a light shining on someone else.

If any of this madness found its way to Donnette's employer, she'd be out of a job.

Casey wanted to weep. How did this happen?

With a hand stretched over the back of the sofa, Donnette demanded her phone.

"I'm sorry," she mumbled while handing it to her.

"You're saying that a lot lately."

Casey pulled one hand through her ponytail and turned her head. "At least, this time you're talking to me."

"I know this wasn't intentional, but still." She came around the sofa and sat next to Casey. "Do you remember how it was when we came here?"

"How could I forget?"

"We're all we have. I wish you'd remember that."

Both of them would rather have been with her grandmother than land in Orlando, a place where Casey felt like a tiny fish in the ocean. Everything in America was bewildering and super-sized for someone from a small district in Ocho Rios.

"Why do we have to go?" Casey asked Gran when the time to leave the island drew closer.

"Because your father filed for the two of you." Gran sucked her teeth. "How many times do I have to tell you the same thing?"

"But we don't want to go nowhere." Donnette sat on one of the patio chairs, hugging her knees. "We love it here."

"Can we come back if we don't want to stay?" Casey asked, knowing their situation couldn't be that simple.

"You're going to be citizens in a foreign land. Things aren't that simple."

Foreign made it sound as though they'd be swallowed in the belly of America. Everywhere outside the island was classified that way, no matter which country was involved.

They moped for days and pleaded not to go, and Gran telling them she didn't have a choice meant nothing. Casey had already lived in one too many places, and now they'd be moving farther than she could stand. This time, Gran wouldn't be a mile or two away. What if their father tried the same thing as Uncle Pete? How would they escape?

The "filing" wouldn't go away, no matter how hard she prayed or wished it would.

Visiting the U.S. Embassy meant rising long before daylight and sleeping on the ride to Kingston. They'd been groggy for the interview, and Casey prayed for a miracle that they'd be rejected. Then there were the medical exams and other appointments for presenting documents, which meant missing school.

Neither she nor Donnette understood why their father considered it a good idea to make them live with him after ignoring them for most of their lives.

Gran had shrugged when Casey asked. "Maybe it's his conscience."

"All of a sudden?" Casey had pulled her head back, knowing that wasn't possible.

"The Master can change anyone at any time." Their grandmother spoke with authority, and neither of them dared to contradict her.

When their father escorted them to America, he'd been patient while they clung to their grandmother outside the airport. Casey was sure her heart shattered into a thousand pieces, the way it had done as her mother declined and then died.

"The ride will be a short one." Ansel Mitchell smiled to reassure them, but his gesture did nothing to comfort Casey. She wanted to ask why he hadn't left them alone, but Gran's influence was strong. She'd drilled it into their heads to be polite. "I don't want your father to think we raised you like wild animals."

At the time her remark was funny, until the day they sat on the airplane. Casey couldn't find one thing to laugh about.

Gran had said they couldn't take everything with them, but Casey wouldn't leave her mother's battered laptop.

"Pack your things, but you can't carry all your *jing-bang*," Gran ordered.

She was adamant they couldn't arrive in America with items their father and his wife would consider rubbish. Hearing Donnette's laughter made their grandmother's comment less offensive. Her sister was good at pretending, but Gran had noticed how she'd changed.

Donnette leaned in and kissed Casey's cheek. "I'll be in the shower. Try not to find any more trouble while I'm in there."

She chuckled but followed Donnette's progress out of the room, sad without knowing the reason. Perhaps it was their history that wouldn't leave her alone. When she'd decided to act, she hadn't bargained on the memories that constantly plagued her.

Many months had slipped by since Casey last saw her father. Whenever he came to mind, somehow, he'd call to ask why they couldn't reach out now and then. She wondered why he bothered, but forgave him. She loved him more than she'd ever been able to explain to herself or anyone else, despite the harrowing chapter of their life that unfolded when they touched down in America.

Erica Mitchell was pleasant enough when he brought them home from the airport. In a whispered conversation, Donnette and Casey discussed the fact that their father had a type. She was of East Indian descent and was slim with smooth, milk-chocolate skin. Their father proudly declared she was pregnant with a son. When she showed them to the room they would share, she'd shut the door between them and their father to school them on the house rules.

The smile she wore when they stepped inside the house disappeared as she settled on a ladderback chair. "Ansel and I have rules. You will help with the cooking and cleaning. I won't tolerate any sass from either of you. When your brother is born, you'll help take care of him."

The two girls exchanged a look, at which point she added, "If you can't abide by our rules, there is always child services. They take care of delinquents."

Casey's skin itched because none of this sounded the way a welcome message should. Their stepmother reeled off an additional half-dozen instructions, which meant nothing to them. Her American accent was strange to their ears and hard to follow.

After she left, their father brought in their meager belongings and left them to unpack.

Sitting on the double bed, Donnette tugged her hair. "You think we goin' make it here?"

Casey threw her suitcase on the bed to disguise the lie on her lips. "We'll be fine. You'll see."

That night was the most peaceful they experienced in their new life.

Aunt Erica didn't abuse them physically. She was better with mean threats and remarks.

They settled into school, with Casey getting into frequent squabbles because she refused to be bullied. Fighting Donnette's battles, plus the frequent threats from Aunt Erica about being sent away if they didn't comply with her rules, grew exhausting. Casey missed Gran and Mommy more than ever. They didn't complain in their letters because if their grandmother contacted their father, Aunt Erica might have made their lives more difficult.

Their baby brother arrived six months later. Casey went from being part of a two-person housekeeping crew to a full-time babysitter when she wasn't in school. And some days she didn't go because Aunt Erica was too tired to take care of her son. If Carson cried a moment too long, Erica screamed at Casey, then locked herself in her bedroom. Her crying fits were legendary.

Then the day came when the baby wouldn't stop crying, no matter what Casey did.

Aunt Erica marched out of her room, yelling, "What are you doing to him?"

"Nothing."

Her stepmother's wild eyes, uncombed hair, and snarling mouth made her retreat.

"Then why won't he shut up?" She pointed to Carson in his seat. "And why aren't you holding him?"

"Because I had to put him down to warm his bottle." Her words were more forceful than intended, and Aunt Erica objected.

She grabbed Casey by the arm, and the bottle fell to the floor. "You're lying. I'll show you what liars deserve."

Stomping to the bathroom, she dragged Casey along. Her stepmother was strong for someone who spent her days lying in bed. Next to the bathtub, she flung Casey to her knees and dunked her head in the water she'd left in the baby bath. The force of her face hitting the water burned her nose and blinded her. She was sure she'd die each time Aunt Erica held her head under the surface.

The punishment ended when Donnette ran into the bathroom, holding Carson and begging Aunt Erica to stop. She whacked Casey across the face, then pushed past Donnette, who still carried her backpack hanging off her other arm.

Aunt Erica yelled, "For the love of all that's holy, make him stop screaming."

When the bedroom door slammed, Donnette and Casey stared at each other, dumbstruck. They hurried to their room, and once Carson was quiet with the bottle in his mouth, Donnette asked, "What happened?"

"His crying got to her."

"She's crazy." With Carson in her lap, Donnette dropped one arm around Casey's shoulders. "Don't worry. Things will get better."

Casey's voice wobbled as she stared through the window. "I don't see how."

"Trust me, they will." Her quiet insistence made Casey even more hopeless. She was the determined one, not Donnette.

The carpet shimmered, and tears rolled down Casey's cheeks. She was not one to cry easily, but she was tired. Tired of being a house slave, tired of missing school, tired of Aunt Erica's nonstop demands, and tired of her father's blindness. Since Carson's birth, he appeared by six o'clock each evening to spend time with him. Other than a casual question now and then about how his daughters were doing, Ansel Mitchell lived in dad heaven with Carson.

Always a voracious reader, Casey diagnosed Aunt Erica with postpartum depression. The knowledge didn't change her situation, but Casey learned to cope.

A library card gave her a passport to freedom. The first time she stepped inside the building, it transported her to a different planet from the postage-stamp library at her old primary school. She turned into a frequent visitor, and the staff came to know her.

Her world shifted and spun into space the day she picked up Addison's book off a return cart. The familiar face on the back of a paperback with a brief biography fascinated her. Casey scanned the blurb and frowned at the book's title. A copy of Mommy's manuscript was among the things she'd removed from Uncle Pete's house, and another remained on the laptop.

Only then did she understand the real significance of Uncle Pete's action. How could he have sold the novel for next to nothing when the agreement between Addison and Mommy was for representation to publish the story? She flipped the book over and confirmed the title was the same. A scan of the inside told her all she needed to know.

The name on the manuscript differed from Addison's new name, but it didn't matter. Casey didn't ask about the book on the return cart. She went to the relevant shelf, grabbed the copy she found there, and checked it out.

She shared nothing with Donnette until she'd read the book, then compared it to the pages they kept in a worn, brown envelope. When Casey was certain she was right, she forced

Donnette to read the paperback copy, then brought out their mother's manuscript for a comparison.

Donnette's reaction was unexpected. She flung herself across the mattress and sobbed until her eyes were red and puffy. No matter how many ways Casey asked, Donnette wouldn't say what was wrong. Casey drew her own conclusions. Life would have been different if Addison hadn't robbed their mother of her work.

The many revenge scenes Casey fantasized about would have horrified their grandmother. On the day she discovered the book, Casey decided no matter how long it took, or what she had to do, she'd recover her mother's story and expose Addison.

CHAPTER 34

ALECIA

"YOUR MOTHER IS a snake." The fluorescent light cast shadows on the hard planes of Addison's face. Her flushed skin reflected the fury boiling below the surface.

"I don't doubt that." Alecia's response was swift and intense, but Addison was too angry to recognize her jab.

"Evadne, Mercedes, or whatever she calls herself is playing with fire." With each word, she tapped the desk hard.

"What does that have to do with me? Why am I here?" Alecia scanned the office and scowled at the display wall with Addison's book covers. She'd poured her soul into writing at least three of them.

Kirk broke her concentration when he sat upright and put his phone on one leg. He opened a file, as though far removed from their argument.

"More to the point," Alecia said, bobbing her head toward Kirk, "what is *he* doing here? Is he your village lawyer?"

She'd used the term deliberately, to imply Addison couldn't handle business on her own. The description and role fit him, never mind that he'd joined the staff last.

"That's none of your business." Addison swept a hand over an open file. "What you did probably encouraged your mother's stupidity."

Alecia jerked forward, offended by the accusation. "I don't know what you're talking about, but I don't appreciate your tone."

The woman couldn't know that aside from being a snoop, Alecia lived an upright life. And now, she'd joined the ranks of criminals because Quentin couldn't stay out of Addison's clutches and had the nerve to file assault charges.

Kirk shifted again, irritating Alecia with his presence. This late in the evening, why was he here if not to pander to Addison's sexual whims and vomit each detail he'd been sucking up all week from those around him? But that wasn't her problem anymore.

She faced the woman who'd brought her into the world, then dumped her like garbage. Her chest tightened, but she slowed her breathing to regain control.

"Of course, you wouldn't welcome what I have to say." Addison sat back, the way a queen would when addressing her subjects. The burnt orange dress with a high collar suited her.

"I'm talking about how you got that woman to try and dig more money out of me."

"If you'd say exactly what you mean and stop wasting my time, I'd be out of here faster."

"Don't pretend you aren't part of her scam." Addison flung an envelope on the desk that landed with a thwack. "Open it."

Inside it was the same agreement she'd found at Mama's house, plus pictures of Addison's book covers, and another sheet of paper. Her mother's handwriting was unmistakable. Another few seconds clarified why Addison was so mad.

No one could say Mama wasn't smart.

Alecia threw the papers on the desk. "Seems to me, you dug up an ant hill with your threats."

"It wouldn't be necessary if people stayed out of my business." Addison scooped up the folded sheets and crushed them in one hand. "We had an agreement."

"Which has nothing to do with me." Alecia shrugged and prepared to rise. She didn't work for Addison, so she didn't have to take her insults. Also, Addison couldn't force her to stay.

Stabbing the desk with one finger, Addison groused. "I contacted you to ensure she wasn't the one spreading my business and violating our contract, but she *did* by telling you about me. I should sue her for everything she has."

"She did not," Alecia insisted. "I found out everything on my own. The fact that you sold me to her." She glanced at the papers. "And you've just told me she's getting her own back. Can't say I blame her for trying to have you cough up what your conscience should have told you was due to her."

"That's the problem with you people." Pointing with one of her manicured nails, she snarled, "You think because you know, or are related to someone, they owe you a living."

"Have I ever asked you for anything?" Alecia left the seat, flipping her hair over one shoulder. She'd had enough of Addison, and her jaw trembled with the effort not to spew some choice curse words. On her way to the door, she turned. "I'd rather die than ask you for anything."

Addison grimaced and spread her arms. "That didn't stop you from trying to claim me."

Her words struck Alecia with the force of an arrow. She swallowed hard as she gripped the metal handle that swam before her eyes. What did she expect when she told this Jezebel she'd meet her at this late hour? Addison wouldn't want the staff to remember Alecia existed—as though she could erase her because she didn't work there anymore.

"Tell your disgusting mother she won't see another penny from me."

The insult pierced Alecia, and she retraced her steps.

Kirk stood and moved between them.

"She may be disgusting, but you're downright wicked." Strolling closer to the desk, she shook her head. "You don't care about what you did. You're vain enough to think you're better than her, but you're ten times worse. You could have made her life less difficult if you wanted. Instead, you tracked her down to be certain you don't have to compensate her for taking care of what was your responsibility. *You have no soul.*"

Satisfied with getting her licks in, she glared at Kirk and stomped toward the door.

"Don't you dare contact me again," she said and headed for the stairs.

She barely made it down standing upright and clutched the rail for support. All her energy fled, along with any fight she had left. She'd keep going because it was what she'd taught herself to do all her life. Behind the wheel, she went to her phone gallery and tapped the picture she'd snapped from among Mama's papers.

A chubby and happy toddler, she sat on Mama's lap with her fingers stuffed halfway inside her mouth. Mama clutched her around the waist with both hands, her face creased by a wide smile. A much younger Addison stood stiffly beside them, halfway in and halfway out of the shot. Giving her up had been a kindness, and now Alecia regretted her relentless search for the truth. Knowing where she came from brought her nothing but pain.

She didn't know what she hoped for when Addison asked her to come to the studio, but with her track record, she should have expected exactly what she received. Another rejection that made Alecia question her life and worth.

CHAPTER 35

CASEY

TODAY'S EVENT WAS hush-hush, but it couldn't happen without the team knowing. They circled the room, talking up the book and making Addison look good. The crowd grew quiet as Addison approached the rostrum. She'd thrown this meet-and-greet together in days, nearly driving Piper to the edge of a breakdown with impossible demands and screaming fits. Addison was spiraling.

"Good afternoon, everyone." Her demure smile belied the tantrum she'd thrown an hour ago because the florist was late with the centerpieces. Casey and Maddy helped Piper set them on each table because the decorator and her team had already left.

The gathering of mainly female guests returned the greeting and settled down in the hotel ballroom, which featured a blue-gray Persian carpet and an elaborate chandelier. Addison was always innovative, so she invited book club leaders and first readers to attend through her publisher. She'd billed the function as a semi-casual affair, so the publisher's representative sat with a few other executives. Addison had vetoed a head table, which went against the atmosphere she wanted to create.

"I know you received very short notice for this meet-and-greet," she continued, "but I hope you enjoy your time here. We have some fun planned for this afternoon, starting with the gift bags you've received."

The guests *ooh*ed and *aah*ed as they pulled the bags toward them and peeked inside. Addison provided a sampler of her books, as well as a signed copy of one novel for each attendee. In addition, she included bookmarks, an expensive pen, a nifty reading light, and a lip balm. As the attendees ruffled the crepe paper inside the bags, Addison gently cleared her throat.

"I'll tell you a little about this new book, then my publicist will share how we'll ensure this next release is a special one, especially since it will be my fortieth book. Imagine that?"

A sprinkling of applause went up, along with a murmur of approval.

Casey stayed with the team members who sat around two tables at the entrance, allowing for easy entry and exit from the room. A time or two, guests who recognized her gawked in her direction. Clearly, they'd seen the mess online, and Casey still wondered what brought it on.

Addison went for the dramatic and was elegant in a fitted black dress with chunky silver jewelry that popped. Her hair was pulled into a smooth bun high on her head. A pair of silver hair sticks held the style in place. Her makeup was flawless, but her hollow cheeks were evidence of the combined anxiety and the meals she'd stopped eating. Casey couldn't remember the last time Addison passed through the staff kitchen.

Another round of applause rose when Addison stepped down, and Theo replaced her at the podium. Casey sat forward while he gushed about the "cool stuff" that Addison's fan club would be privy to once the PR machinery rolled out. The excitement in the air was electric, and Addison's satisfied smile pulled one from Casey.

She tipped her head to Rochelle, who winked from across the room. The timing of Alecia's departure from the team was ideal. Casey would have had a challenge explaining what Rochelle was about to do. She was an avid reader and also connected to one of the book club leaders. Even if she weren't, Casey would have ensured she received an invitation.

"And now for the question-and-answer session," Theo announced. "After that, we'll share what you can do to help this next book be a success."

Addison beamed and returned to the mic. She pointed to a woman on the opposite side of the room.

The young brunette asked, "How soon will reader copies be available?"

"That's way down the road, but we'll provide updates through my newsletter and the fan club, so stay tuned."

Another woman raised her hand. "Are there any plans to write a screenplay for your last book?"

"It has been optioned, but the process is lengthy." She opened both hands and quipped, "Until then, we'll continue to do what we do best: write good books."

After being signaled by Addison, Rochelle rose. "*We* know for sure, but how can potential readers trust the quality of your work, seeing that you're being called out everywhere on social media?"

Talk about a pregnant pause.

Addison stood frozen as the seconds ticked by, which gave Rochelle space to continue her seemingly innocent questions.

"It's being said that you may end up in several legal battles surrounding your first bestseller." Rochelle paused with a finger to her cheek, as though trying to recall an elusive detail. "*Games People Play*. That's it."

"Young lady, you're out of line." Addison lifted a shaking hand. "Get out! Right now. Security!"

Nobody came since the security personnel were stationed out front.

"One more question," Rochelle said, sweeping her braids over one shoulder. "How do you plan to compensate the owner of the book if the rumors turn out to be true?"

Addison's face flamed an ugly red as she yelled, "Get her out of here—now!"

When no one moved, she stepped off the podium, clearly intending to complete the task herself.

Theo leaped from his seat, veered into her path, and guided her away from Rochelle with a hand around her arm.

"If you don't remove that bitch, I swear I'll strangle her myself."

The idea of Addison describing anyone that way when she was the ultimate witch amused Casey. When she chuckled, Addison's attention settled on her. The smile slipped off her face, and she avoided connecting with Rochelle.

"I'll handle this," Theo murmured. "Take a few minutes if you need them."

Addison stalked past Casey, who watched Theo delivering a smooth apology at the podium. A wave of disappointment swept over the guests, who murmured while he spoke.

"I'm sorry, but given what has happened, we'll have to end today's proceedings early." He bowed and clasped his hands as if he'd delivered a sermon. "As Addison said, check for more information in the club or her newsletter. We'll be in touch soon."

At the edge of her vision, Casey spotted two men in navy suits. Upset or not, Addison had sent for the cavalry. At a nod from Theo, they made a beeline for Rochelle, who stood from the table and picked up her handbag. She strode ahead of them, bold and sassy, and winked at Casey. They'd catch up later.

"What the hell just happened?" Jon asked, scratching his head.

Quentin and Kirk exchanged a glance, then focused on Casey, who shrugged. "Ask Addison. I'm sure she knows."

The women filed past them, speaking in hushed tones. All the food Piper ordered would go to waste. Another thing to make Addison mad. She'd probably douse her temper in a glass of wine or that port she drank by the gallon.

"Can you guys help me clear up this stuff?" Maddy's cheerful voice cut into Casey's musing.

"Sure."

They moved around, collecting the leftover bags and placing them on a dolly. When they gathered the last of the centerpieces, Quentin and Jon said they were leaving.

Casey grabbed Quentin's arm. "Can I talk to you for a second?"

His forehead contracted in a frown, and he hesitated. "Yes, of course."

"This won't take long," she said, pulling out a seat.

She hoped he wouldn't refuse her invitation and was relieved when he sat. Since earlier in the day, she'd been mulling over what to say to him. She went with what came to her lips. "Alecia was way out of line, and you're within your rights to file charges. The only excuse I can offer is that she was under immense stress when it happened."

Quentin lifted one eyebrow. "What if I had hit her when she got in my face? Would you excuse me?" When she hesitated, his mouth puckered. Then he said, "I didn't think so."

She squeezed his forearm. "I'm asking a lot, I know, but with what has happened, I'm begging you to reconsider. After the way Addison treated her, she's not in a good place. Imagine how you'd feel if *that* happened to you."

After a long silence, during which she met Kirk's eyes over Quentin's shoulder, he nodded. "I'll drop the charges, but there's a condition."

"What's that?"

"When she can cough one up, which needs to be soon, she'd better apologize."

She didn't know how to swing that miracle, but what he asked wasn't unreasonable. "I'm sure she'll be okay with that." Quentin's raised eyebrows forced Casey to admit, "You know her too well, but I'll convince her. Thanks, Quentin. This is good of you, considering…"

"I know." In a terse tone, he said, "Don't think I'll forget that apology, and by the way, I'm sorry about all the bad publicity lately. You don't deserve it."

"Thanks, and remember, this will pass." She patted his shoulder. "You're the best."

This time, she got a cheeky grin as he rose. "Trust me, that I know."

Her phone pinged, and she reached into her jacket pocket and pulled it out. The message was from Donnette, asking how soon she'd be ready.

Should be good in another fifteen minutes. I'll be out front.

She crossed the room toward Piper, who was speaking with Theo. "Just checking if you need any help before I leave," she said.

"I'll be fine. The hotel will deal with everything else. Jon and Quentin are helping to transport the gifts."

"Sounds good. Talk on Monday."

In an alcove near the lobby, Casey relaxed in one of the huge armchairs, watching people. Now wasn't the time to savor Addison's embarrassment.

The handbag in her lap vibrated, and she pulled out the phone. Rochelle's text with a smiley face greeted her. Effective much? I'm persona non grata with that witch, but for you, I'd do it again.

Thanks, chica. Casey bit her lip as she added to the text. Pity you can't do anything about the people online who are still giving me hell. I had to delete my profile. The abuse and threats were too much to handle.

She watched while the ellipsis moved on the screen, then Rochelle's message came in. Time will take care of it.

The phone beeped again, and Donnette's text flashed on the screen. I'm pulling up out front.

Be there in less than a minute, Casey messaged back.

She hurried through the door and sat in the Civic, which Donnette borrowed to run errands. Her skin prickled, the way it did when someone was watching her. The car pulled away, and she scanned the area outside the lobby.

On the far side of the entrance, Addison sat with one of the publishing house reps. She looked past Casey, then back to her.

If Casey had to guess, she'd say Addison's mind churned at a mile per minute, fitting together a puzzle. Her memory was excellent. Time and a little more reflection would fill in the missing pieces.

Smiling, Casey wriggled her fingers in a wave Addison didn't return.

No matter. Your reckoning is coming.

CHAPTER 36

ALECIA

CASEY WAITED FOR her inside Tito's, a café that served all-American food.

The restaurant was ultra-modern with fiberglass tables and chairs in bronzes and creams. Whenever she ate there, Alecia imagined spaceships and intergalactic wars. The food was good and the prices reasonable, so on some Saturdays, they ate there after their salon visits. The place wasn't full, so she located Casey within seconds and thanked the hostess for her help.

Casey had secured a table in a corner next to the plate glass, where they could people watch—something they had in common because of their writing. Alecia studied couples and families, so the restaurant was an ideal place to watch them interact.

"How have you been?" Casey asked cautiously, setting aside her phone.

"Don't worry." Alecia sat and placed her cell phone on the table. "I promise not to do or say anything inappropriate."

She couldn't be sure, but Casey may have hesitated before she chuckled. Across her chest, the white lettering *In Flux* against a purple tee mocked Alecia. That's exactly what she was going through. Didn't know whether she was coming or going, and resentful as hell of all the people in her life. Couldn't figure out exactly what she'd do after this disaster, but knowing she had to decide.

"That wasn't what I was thinking, but anyway…" Casey patted her hand, then squeezed it.

"It is what it is." Alecia caught the eye of one of the waiters and motioned for him to come over.

"Good afternoon, ladies. My name is Richard. What would you like?" The tall, rosy-cheeked young man reached into his apron pocket for a pad and pencil and prepared to take their order.

"Bring me some orange juice, unless you have something stronger." Alecia sent a wink and a wicked smile in Richard's direction.

He laughed and handed them menus. "Unfortunately, we serve nothing with alcohol."

"It's all good," Alecia said, requesting orange juice.

"I'll be back in a moment," Richard said, then stepped away.

Before Alecia arrived, she figured eating would be a challenge. Now that she was here, she had an appetite. The unpleasantness with Addison came creeping back, but she pushed it aside, telling herself it didn't matter.

Casey must have picked up on her mood because she asked, "How did the meeting go?"

"The way it would with that woman involved." She fiddled with the napkin while her stomach sank. "You were right, by the way."

Casey went still with the glass of lemonade halfway to her mouth. "About what?"

"That little fart, Kirk. He was at the meeting, but don't ask me why." She tore a strip off the napkin, then laid it down. "He didn't say or do anything, except guard her, in case I had a mind to do some damage. As you suspected, he's her spy. There's no other explanation."

After a deep drag from her straw, Casey raised one eyebrow. "Good thing we never talked about her with him around. It says something about her that she'd feel the need for an ear to the ground inside her own office."

"True." The clatter of falling cutlery made Alecia pause for a few seconds. "The way things are going, her glass house is set to shatter."

"You may be joking, but it makes me wonder."

She hung her purse on the chair, then realized Casey was watching her. Not wanting to answer any questions, she raised one of her own. "The other day, you told me you had something to share. What was it?"

Casey licked her lips, then took another swig of lemonade. "It was about Addison."

Richard's return with her drink and his request for their order sidelined the conversation. She couldn't wait for him to leave, but when he did, Casey stirred slow circles in the lemonade, frowning at the glass.

"It's okay if you changed your mind about telling me." Alecia heard the resentful edge to her voice and hoped Casey missed it.

She released the straw and sighed. "It's a long story, and I don't know how or where to start."

A burst of unexpected laughter surprised Alecia. "Come on, you're a writer. If you were to give me the highlights, or better yet, an elevator pitch, what would you say?"

Still, Casey didn't speak. Instead, she held her silence, then eyeballed Alecia while making up her mind. "That's a good one. Lemme see."

She brushed at her chest, then let both hands fall to her lap. "What about this? Famous writer steals work from the less fortunate and passes it off as her own."

With both elbows on the table, Alecia leaned in. "You're joking, right?"

Moving her head side to side, Casey said, "I wish I were."

"Whose writing?" Alecia's heartbeat took off at a gallop. "Yours?"

Casey dragged her teeth over her lip and shook her head. "No. My mother's."

This couldn't be true, *but* from Casey's background and character, the story didn't sound far-fetched. Plus, that puzzling entry in her journal about her mother getting recognition now made perfect sense. She needed details. "For real, for real?"

Nodding, Casey smoothed the frown line on her forehead. "Yeah. I found out some time ago."

In a few sentences, she filled in what had happened. The story was bare bones and left much to be explained.

Sinking farther into her chair, Alecia sensed this news was too good to be true, coming when it did. She sprang forward, suddenly alert again. "And you never said a word?"

Casey hesitated while she tugged at her ponytail—or her fuzzy tail, as she sometimes called it. "I had to be sure."

"You had to be sure, or was it that you're so secretive you kept it to yourself?"

When Casey didn't respond, Alecia let out a soft puff of air. "I don't even know how to feel. Because if you trusted me, you would have said something."

Raising one hand, Casey said, "Back it up a little. We're in the same situation. You *knew* Addison was your mother, and you said nothing."

"Wait a minute. Put yourself in my position. What would you have done?"

Casey went back to playing with her straw. "This wasn't something I could share. I had to figure out the information I gathered. See if everything fit together."

"I had the same struggle," Alecia said, peering at Casey. "This just proves something I learned early in life: You can't trust anyone but yourself."

Hand to her chest, Casey declared, "I won't take offense because of what you've been through with Addison. I understand how difficult it must have been to find out you were related to her."

"Not just any relative." Alecia swallowed a mouthful of orange juice and had to clear her throat to prevent herself from choking. "My mother, no less."

She chuckled, although she wasn't the slightest bit amused. "To be honest, I've always wondered about you. I realized the other day that I know next to nothing about you. And now this—"

"It's the same for me where you're concerned. I guess it's easier to keep secrets when life forces you into certain situations."

"So, exactly how long have you known about Addison?" Alecia asked.

Her friend's eyelids flickered. She wouldn't tell the entire truth.

"A while." Casey didn't miss a beat and shot back. "How long have you known she's your mother?"

Alecia's mouth tipped into a sneer, and she sipped orange juice, observing Casey over the rim. "A while."

Other than a twitch of the lips, Casey didn't give away anything. "So, what's the plan after this?" she asked.

Shrugging, Alecia turned away and watched Richard approaching with their food. "I can farm out my services. Aside from secretarial skills, there's ghostwriting for other people. The truth is, after what I've gone through for the last few years, I–I'd prefer to avoid people."

Richard deftly placed the hamburger before her and moved across to Casey with her fish sandwich. "Bon appétit. Let me know if you need anything else."

"Are you going to continue working for her?" Alecia blew on a fry, waiting for what Casey would say.

"Not for much longer."

The fry Alecia bit into was still hot, which forced her to huff a little, then she asked, "So, the tidbits that have been popping up about Addison, do they have anything to do with you?"

Casey added a pinch of salt to the fish and closed the sandwich. "Maybe. Maybe not. The fact is, other people seem to have a beef with her. She's everywhere these days."

"And you're being cagey. As usual."

"That's because I've learned to keep things confidential. At the studio, we couldn't trust anyone, so I guess it's become a habit."

Alecia laid down the French fry and wiped her fingers when tears stung her eyes. She tried, but couldn't keep the bitter note out of her voice. "Everything around Addison is deceptive and eventually turns poisonous."

The first taste of the hamburger she'd been drooling over turned to ashes in her mouth, but she continued chewing. Before her next bite, she said, "Did I tell you Quentin filed assault charges against me?"

"You messaged me." Casey cracked a smile. "You *did* beat him up badly. He's a good guy for taking your abuse and not slapping you silly."

She pictured him protecting his face while she punched him everywhere within reach.

"Whose side are you on?" she grumbled.

"Both of you." Casey licked a drop of mayonnaise off her lip. "Which is why I talked him into dropping the charges."

"When?"

"Yesterday, after Addison's circus went south."

"Thanks, but right now, I don't care. If I had the chance, I'd beat him up again for making a fool of me."

Casey's face was expressionless when she lowered her chin and hiked one eyebrow. "Talk about being unrepentant, not to mention ungrateful."

"Would you forgive him if he'd pulled that crap with you?"

When Casey didn't respond, Alecia said, "I didn't think so."

"Anyway, I told him you'd apologize."

Alecia pulled her head back. "What did you do that for?"

"It was the one condition he mentioned for withdrawing that assault charge."

"Fine." She flapped one hand. "I'll do it sometime."

"Just as long as you don't make me a liar."

Around them, the scent of French fries, steak, and fried chicken was thick. Animated conversations filled the air.

Dabbing her lips, Alecia asked, "You sound sure Addison stole from you, so what are you doing about it?"

If she had to describe it, she'd say Casey's face twisted for one second.

"I plan to deal with it at the right time."

Alecia cut into her burger, a weird habit that followed her into adulthood from the times Mama used to cut them into four pieces for her.

After picking up her phone to read a message, Casey bit into the fish sandwich.

"By the way, which book did Addison steal? To be truthful, this doesn't surprise me because she has no morals."

"The first big one." Casey motioned to Richard, then added, *"Games People Play."*

After Richard came and left, having supplied them with additional paper napkins, Alecia picked up where they'd stopped. "She's all about her contracts and confidentiality clauses, so be sure when you're going after her, you have an air-tight case."

Nodding slowly, Casey said, "Trust me, I will."

Her comment dampened Alecia's mood, but she sounded almost normal when she said, "Trust. A word we throw around lightly, but it's clear neither of us had the confidence to share our situation with each other."

"True that. But as they say back home, not everything that's good to eat is good to talk."

"Some of those proverbs are so cryptic, you can't even dissect them."

"Right."

They laughed as they would have months ago, then continued eating. After they shared an enormous slice of blueberry cheesecake and split the bill, they stood in the parking lot next to the RAV-4.

"I'm heading back to the studio to put in some writing and then heading home."

"Thanks for coming, chica."

After sucking her teeth, Casey chuckled. "Stop with the thanks. You needed me. I came." She pulled Alecia into a hug and spoke next to her ear. "You've gone through so much this past week. Rest a little before you think about work." She pulled back and held Alecia's hands. "The one thing we can thank Addison for is that she pays well, although she's the worst employer I've ever had."

"Same here." She embraced Casey again. "I've always seen you as still water that's much deeper than it appears from the surface. Here's an oxymoron, if you prefer something fancy: You're a quiet storm. You'll have a long and bitter fight, but I hope you win. You deserve it."

"*Awww*. Thanks. This is more for my mother than anything else." Casey sniffed as she stood back. "Her name deserves to be on the book she wrote."

"I agree with you." Alecia clasped her hands and moved them in time with her advice. "Fight for your mom's legacy. It's the right thing to do."

CHAPTER 37

ADDISON

"NO INTERRUPTIONS, PIPER," Addison said, walking past her desk. "You know what? You're free to go now. Have a good afternoon."

Piper's pale face flushed. "Thanks, Addison."

"Don't thank me yet. You may have to make up the time another day."

Her face fell, and Addison chided herself. Her staff probably hated her, but it didn't matter. She paid them, not the other way around. The port she'd had in her suite mellowed her a little—just enough to help her fight the coming battle.

These days, she was drinking too much. The deaths of Emily and Rachel had sent her too far down a path that was turning her into a lush. As early as the morning, she wanted to dip into the bottle. And then there were the pills, which didn't work well lately. Not even the men satisfied her anymore, and that was saying something. It was a matter of time before the team started talking about her drinking. That's if they weren't discussing it already.

The studio was empty, except for Piper, who couldn't gather her things fast enough, and the enemy who waited in her office. From Casey's work habits, Addison figured she would stay late today, although it was a Saturday. She'd had trouble focusing earlier, and when that happened, she waited until the office was quiet and completed the writing or brainstorming for her chapters. She'd been relieved when she reappeared after lunch.

Addison shut the door, strolled to the desk, and took her seat. Piper had disappeared, as expected. She kept her pitch low when she said, "I know who you are."

If Casey was surprised, she didn't let on. She'd probably been expecting this confrontation.

"Huh?"

"You can drop the act. Seeing you with your sister yesterday triggered my memory."

To give Casey her due, she didn't move a muscle. Even on the weekend, she dressed well. A sleeveless linen pantsuit with a flared hem and high-heel sandals should have come across as ridiculous on a Saturday, but she made it work. The matching gold earrings and necklace completed her outfit. She carried herself well, considering her early life. How remarkable that she'd come into Addison's orbit—unless she had deliberately sought her out.

"Really? That's interesting."

"Yes. I remember the two of you peeking out from behind that ratty bead curtain." With mocking laughter, she continued, "You both had such wide eyes and gawked as though I was the most beautiful thing you'd ever seen." Addison picked up a heavy gold pen, wondering what kind of weapon it would make if she had to defend herself.

"Did you search for me?" she asked, genuinely curious to hear Casey's answer.

"What do you think? If someone had stolen your birthright, what would you have done?"

Addison placed the pen parallel to the edge of the desk pad. "Let's cut to the chase, shall we? Is there any point in offering you hush money?"

She could be this bold because Casey had no way to record her. The phone she could use was in her handbag in the studio.

"I refuse to answer that."

Folding her hands together, Addison stared at her nails. "These jabs at me online, I'd guess they were your attempt at revenge."

"I'm not admitting anything other than to say that the evil we do has a way of popping up when we least expect it. Nowadays, all it takes is a word here and there for social media addicts to run with it." She smiled, barely moving her lips. "Whether or not the story is true."

"Since I can't offer you anything for the work, what agreement would make you happy?"

Casey's face twisted as she spat, "*The work* you so glibly mentioned was what made you rich and sent my family into the pit of hell. You could have done the right thing, but you were so greedy to have it all, you helped rob my mother of her life."

"Surely, you don't blame me for her death?"

"You and Peter Grimes."

"As I told your grandmother so many years ago, I believed he was her legal representative. He. Was. Her. Husband."

"And you saw nothing wrong with making a deal with two people for the same book? You're a real piece of work, but we both know that."

Addison sat forward to assert control. "You don't disrespect me in my space."

Casey's smile was full of spite. "Knowing what I do about you, I'd say I've earned the right."

Rolling the pen between her fingers, Addison tried another tack. "Since we're at a standstill, what do you suggest?"

Casey stood, smoothing her shirt. "I'm not making any deals with you. You're going to admit publicly what you've done and compensate me and my family with all the royalties you've accumulated over the years from my mother's writing."

Forcing laughter, Addison snapped, "Come now. You know that won't happen. If I do that, everything else I've written will be under suspicion."

"And they should be. When was the last time you wrote anything? Do you even remember how?"

"Don't be rude. You're still my employee—"

"Not for long, Addison." She leaned in and smiled, but she wasn't amused. "Nothing will satisfy me, other than seeing my mother's name on the cover of the book you stole."

"There's too much at stake." Addison's hand went to the pendant at her throat, but she lowered it to the desk and sat straighter. "That's a pipe dream."

Casey's fixed study chilled Addison. She had the intensity of someone capable of murder. The unanswered questions about Emily and Rachel's death hovered, and she opened her mouth to throw an accusation, but Casey bested her.

"If you know what's good for you, you'll come up with a plan, starting now, because I won't wait forever for you to do right—although it's not in your nature."

Slowly, Addison rose from her seat. "I know this must be hard to swallow—"

"What? You living high off my mother's work? Damn right."

"Listen to me, you little scavenger. None of you would have known how to take the book to the heights I did." She wagged her finger, then pointed at Casey. "Tread carefully because I have the handle in this situation, and you have the blade."

"Are you threatening me?"

"Not at all, but remember, I have the assets and resources to handle a court case that may take forever to settle." She paused for dramatic effect. "Do you?"

"We'll see about that, won't we?" She moved toward the door, shoulders squared and her spine perfectly straight.

"I'm warning you, Casey, stop this foolishness. I can destroy you…if that's what it takes to end this."

She held on to the door handle, and a malevolent smile curved her lips. "Let's see you do your best."

Addison sank into her chair, conscious of the faint scent of apricots left from Casey's perfume. This was bad. She'd barely wrapped her head around one thing before another attack came out of the woodwork. At this rate, the one person who'd be making money out of her was Matteo, but she had to reach him, and fast.

Through the glass, she watched Casey, who sat and leaned down to retrieve her handbag. When she straightened, their eyes met, but nothing in her face hinted that they'd just argued. Addison had learned that such people were dangerous. They could strike you down with no hint of anger or resentment. She held herself still, willing Casey to go home.

The moment she did, Addison tugged at the small cabinet next to her desk to ensure she'd locked it, then picked up her cell phone. She checked the landing to be certain she was alone before she stepped out. She'd been smart to design the office with glass walls. How ironic that she had to watch her back in her own space. She wasn't afraid of death, but the unrelenting challenges made her jittery.

She went left and continued to her suite. After locking herself in, she poured a glass of port from the bar and kicked off her sandals. She scooped them up, entered the bedroom, and changed into a shift. Instead of crawling into bed, she returned to the living room and switched on the television.

Having settled on her favorite news channel, she sipped from the glass and then lay her head against the back of the navy cuddle seat. When her stomach rumbled, she squeezed a cushion to her chest. She didn't remember eating anything today, but no matter. She'd ask Randolph to bring her something light later.

All her life, she'd been self-contained, didn't need anyone, and believed those who did were weak. She'd weaned herself off depending on other people when she left Janet and her parents behind, and now the whole blasted lot of them wouldn't stop popping into her mind. Of course, the blame belonged to Casey and Alecia. The thought of that ingrate soured her stomach. She'd done the best she could have, given her circumstances.

The television noise faded while her mind trekked to the darkest period in her life.

Her time with Janet was short, thanks to Janet's boyfriend, Calvin, who insisted she had to contribute toward their expenses although Addison wasn't working. Miss Mavis kept threatening to increase the rent with three of them living in the small space.

"Dis is not our agreement," she muttered. "Either come up wid more money or move out."

The lack of privacy and being uncomfortable all day every day didn't agree with Addison. To ease her misery, she journaled and renewed her love of writing. Nothing she did took away the horror of being pregnant by her father. His crime against her had killed her secret dream of being a famous author.

"I've found something," she told Janet on her return from a trip to Ocho Rios. "The job is in a guesthouse, and it's enough for me to live on."

Janet hugged Addison tight and kissed her cheek. "I'm sorry how things worked out, but I know you'll go far. You're a fighter."

The minimum-wage job took her back to the North Coast. Near enough to be reunited with the familiar and far enough that she didn't have to be in contact with her family. The rented room in a stranger's house was enough to satisfy her needs.

Writing made the real world fade away and her imaginary universe come alive. Leonora Charles was everything her parents were not and brought her through the horror of being a teenage mother without losing her mind.

"Keep your head up," she'd say. "You're not the first, and you won't be the last."

In the evenings, Addison studied the two prized craft books she'd bought with her pay and perfected her stories. In that time, Leonora watched over the child Addison hated as much as the menial work the guesthouse provided. She wasn't meant to exist as housekeeping staff and would do whatever it took to escape the drudgery of that lifestyle.

Eventually, she bought a secondhand laptop and learned how to self-publish her work. A year in, she drove to her cousin's house. Evadne and she were related through their mothers, but hadn't been close. After two more visits, and assessing what offer to make, Addison freed herself of the burden her father created.

"What did you do with Alice?" Leonora asked each day after Alice disappeared. "A baby can't just vanish. At least tell me if she's all right."

Addison refused to say how she'd solved that problem. Eventually, she gave in and told Leonora the baby was with her relatives, but their relationship was never the same. That was all right with Addison, who took a loan to finance what wasn't exactly an adoption. Years later, she formalized and sweetened the agreement with another payment.

Loosed from her shackle, Addison spent everything she made selling her books. Her luck turned when a publisher agreed to give her a contract, and Addison hit stardom with Yvette Finch's book. Then, she turned her focus to making it to America, the land of opportunity. As with everything else she wanted to achieve, she worked until she lived that reality.

She couldn't deny Casey had a right to be upset, but she'd been warned.

The television cut to an ad, and Addison rang the kitchen on the intercom. "Randolph, can you rustle up a salad for me?"

"No problem."

"Thanks. I'm hungry, so hurry."

She eyed the port in the bottom of the glass and decided against drinking more. For what she was about to do, Addison needed her wits about her. If nothing else, Casey was busy and bold—to try and expose her at a major event, plus use her plot twists against her, she deserved a medal. But Addison didn't have that to offer. Instead, she'd teach Casey a lesson she wouldn't ever forget.

CHAPTER 38

CASEY

THE SALMON-PINK SUIT did little for the pale woman with suspicious eyes, who sat across from Casey, tucked inside the curve of a kidney-shaped glass desk. Her closely cropped blond hair combined with ice-blue eyes brought a fairy to mind, but Casey didn't delude herself. Amy Tiege's scrutiny was hard and assessing. The acquisitions editor who dealt with Addison's books had seen much and was fazed by little.

When Casey finally got hold of Amy, who'd been at Addison's event last week, she hinted that she had incriminating evidence of theft and was about to seek the media's help to get justice. The insinuation ensured she was "squeezed in" to see an executive editor. The appointment after office hours didn't matter to Casey. Any time of day suited her fine.

"So what..."—Amy pointed to the envelope with the manuscript Casey laid on the desk—"is that supposed to be?"

"The original version of *Games People Play* that Addison Comstock stole from my family. My mother wrote that book."

Casey let that sink in before hammering home her point. "I've brought it to you out of consideration, you might say, so this publishing house won't come out of this mess seeming careless and dodgy."

"Since our contract requires that writers declare the work they're offering belongs to them, how does that affect us?"

Casey put both feet on the carpet. "Given the rumors making the rounds for at least a month, it would have been prudent for Asdack Publishing to at least verify if any of it were true. I'm sure you've heard what's being said."

Amy flashed a smile, which vanished as quickly as it appeared. "I'm sorry. I'm not on social media."

Liar.

Every professional in the literary world kept abreast of market trends and emerging talent, and all of them owned social media accounts.

"Even if you aren't, I'm certain the company has a public relations and marketing department."

She made a face, hinting Casey was out of her depth. "You seem to know a lot about the literary landscape. Are you a writer?"

"I don't mean to be rude, but that's not important right now. I'm not trying to claim any of Addison's work for the attention." She laid one hand on top of the manuscript. "This right here will prove everything I've said."

"You'll have to give me some time while one of my assistants—"

"No." Casey kept her tone firm but not aggressive. "This *cannot* wait. Since you have doubts, you may contact Addison or her lawyer."

When Amy gasped, Casey nodded. "Yes. He also has a copy, which I sent."

"Couldn't you have handled this some other way?" Amy spoke as though dealing with an unruly child.

"You do what you must when you know the people you're dealing with." Casey lifted a small recorder from her handbag and pressed the play button. "Maybe this will convince you."

As Amy listened to the conversation Casey had with Addison on the weekend, the color seeped from her face. She gripped both chair arms and folded into the seat. "Maybe I can assess the manuscript and do the comparison sooner."

Closing her handbag, Casey sauntered to the door. "You do that."

In less than ten minutes, her phone rang. Addison's face appeared on the screen, and she debated whether to answer. Curiosity won, and she swung into the parking lot of a fast-food restaurant. If she worked anywhere else, Casey would have considered herself fired, but her contract stated that if they parted ways, they both had to give two weeks' written notice. Each day was like crossing a bed of nails on injured feet. What didn't help was Addison staring at her through the glass, attempting to intimidate.

Casey was waiting for Addison to fire her. She refused to walk away with no severance pay and also risk losing her benefits. She might despise Addison, but Casey wasn't a fool. Either Amy had reached out to Addison, or she would try to "soft soap" or bribe her again.

"Yes, Addison. I'm heading home."

"Come back to the studio. I need to speak with you urgently."

"You're talking with me now, aren't you?"

"This discussion must be face to face."

Nothing good could come of this impromptu meeting, but Casey figured she might as well deal with whatever mess Addison had orchestrated. Stewing on it overnight would sap her energy. If

Amy contacted Addison, which was a given, she'd be in a hellish mood. Casey snorted to cover a chuckle. Her boss had been in a terrible state for some time.

"It will take me at least half an hour."

"That's fine. We…I'll wait."

"Who is we?" Casey asked, frowning at the drive-through line at the burger joint.

"A slip of the tongue. See you soon."

When her stomach churned, she sighed. What could Addison do to her that hadn't been done already? She'd face her and deal with whatever came out of this farce of a meeting. She drove up to the restaurant's window and ordered a cup of lemonade and a bottle of water. Then she rolled back onto the road and took her time returning to the studio. The lemonade was the right mixture of tangy and sweet. The irony of how the drink compared with her life didn't miss Casey.

As she went past security and the Civic crept up the driveway, Casey prayed she wouldn't do anything she'd regret. Heaven forbid she forgot herself and clobbered Addison for saying the wrong thing. The next couple of weeks would be difficult, but she'd be fine. She'd handled all of life's vagaries so far, even when she felt she couldn't.

A few vehicles were still out front, but she thought nothing of it until she recognized Alecia's SUV.

She entered the foyer and took the stairs to the left. On the landing, she sucked in a breath, thinking she was getting out of shape. She shouldn't be this winded, but she blamed it on the sedentary lifestyle her job encouraged and the lack of exercise. She'd change that when she had more time to do exactly what she pleased.

Piper's desktop was clean as she left it at the end of each day. Spotting Alecia through the plate glass jolted Casey. Something about this situation didn't add up. Addison had banned Alecia from the studio, but she had been called to the same meeting.

What's going on?

Addison's grin was a visual representation of the proverbial cat who ate the canary. She waved Casey into the empty seat in front of her desk. Someone shifted to her right, which turned out to be Kirk. Really?

She tipped her head toward Alecia to acknowledge her before asking, "Why am I here?"

Addison rolled her chair forward and pulled a manila envelope to the middle of the desk pad. Her eyes seemed hollow, and her skin was paler than ever. Pulling her hair into a tight bun made her cheekbones more prominent, and the sleeveless black dress emphasized her weight loss. Addison opened the envelope and removed several sheets of paper held together by staples. She separated two heavily redacted loose sheets. Black rectangles covered most of the page.

Speaking directly to Casey, she grimaced. "If you guessed this document is my will, then you're correct."

And how would I know that?

Addison's attention shifted to Alecia. "Don't get excited. I don't feel any differently about you now than I did when you pulled that disgusting stunt with the photo. You proved I did the right thing by giving you away."

"Don't you mean selling me?" Alecia asked, breathing hard.

"Semantics, my dear." Addison laid two single sheets side by side on the desk. She ran her teeth over her bottom lip, then raised her head, addressing Casey. "Here's the deal: Irrespective of what you think, I acquired *Games People Play* in a legally binding agreement."

Casey's throat closed, but she forced herself to take one breath, then another. The demon across the desk hadn't shared anything she didn't already know, except for the part where she refused to acknowledge that she'd stolen another writer's intellectual property.

"As such," she continued, "I'm perfectly within my rights to update my will, which is what I did yesterday."

She tipped her chin toward Alecia. "*Games People Play* will belong to you and, of course, the corresponding royalties."

None of them moved, and the hum of the air conditioner and the ticking clock grew loud in her ears. Then they all spoke at once.

"What?"

"You're crazy."

"Huh?"

Casey held up one hand. "Help me understand this. You stole my mother's book and now you're willing her work to your daughter?"

"If that's how you want to put it."

Casey turned toward Kirk, who was frowning. "I don't know what you know or don't know, but can you tell this madwoman what she's doing is illegal?"

He dragged a hand over his jaw. "Addison, what about having someone take a—"

"Don't tell me what to do." She pushed both sheets toward Alecia and Casey. "You're here as a witness."

"Witness to what exactly?" he asked, opening both hands. "There's nothing right about this entire situation."

She didn't answer his question, but her satisfaction was clear from the way her eyes gleamed.

In an abrupt move, Kirk stood. "I don't want any part of your wrongdoing. Ladies, I'm out."

He walked away, and Addison called after him. "Kirk, despite that, I'm going to need a word with you."

Casey didn't need a bet to know what that word with him involved. She picked up the paper to speed-read the information. The language sounded legal, but this scenario was surreal. "If this is legal, why isn't your lawyer here?"

"That's none of your business." Addison pushed back her chair and stuffed the other papers inside the envelope. "Please show yourselves out."

Crushing the paper in her hand and standing from the seat, Casey faced Alecia. "So, if this is legal, will you accept what she's offering?"

Her slight shrug and slack jaw had the effect of a match on dry wood. "Really, Alecia? Are you serious? Your hesitation tells me everything I need to know."

Alecia scrambled to her feet, trying to form a sentence, but only guttural noises came from her throat.

Turning on her heels, Casey crossed the room and stomped down the stairs, twisting her ankle in her haste to leave the building. What the hell had just happened? Surely that was a scene from a soap opera or a dream? Maybe she'd wake up to find this had been a nightmare, but her mind dictated what was reality when someone gripped her shoulder.

"Casey, I'm just as shocked as you." Alecia's moist eyes connected with hers. "We should talk about this."

"What is there to say?" She shrugged out of Alecia's grip. "You should have told her to go straight to hell for trying to give you stolen goods."

"But—"

She stepped onto the wide porch, and when the front door closed behind them, Casey shook her head. "My brain can't even compute what just happened in there."

"It's not my fault. I–I didn't ask her to do that."

"You *didn't* refuse, and that tells me what kind of friend you are."

"Come on." Alecia followed her to the end of the veranda. "Don't tell me you'd give up what she's offering if you were in the same situation. You haven't given me tangible proof that the book is yours."

With both hands open, Casey asked, "D'you think I pulled an accusation out of the air because I hate Addison and want to hurt her?"

Alecia didn't reply or meet her gaze.

Disappointment flooded Casey's being and left her winded. "You really think I'm that kind of person?"

"I'm not saying that. What I *am* saying is maybe she had a change of heart and wanted to give me something to make up for the way she treated me."

Scornful laughter pained Casey's throat. "If you believe that, you're a fool."

Almost sobbing, Alecia cried, "You sound mean and bitter."

"I have a right to be." Casey couldn't bear to spend another moment with this woman she'd never known. "And to think I got Quentin to drop the charge against you."

She left Alecia wringing her hands and fell into the driver's seat of the Civic. Nothing that happened seemed to be based in reality, and she drove home in a fog, barely seeing the road ahead. In the front yard, she leaned against the headrest and closed her eyes.

Her frustration was a physical force that held her in a chokehold and ripped away her breath. To her surprise, a tear rolled down her cheek. Once again, she'd proven that some folks didn't understand the concept of friendship and loyalty when they truly mattered.

A while later, she mustered the energy to enter the house and make it as far as the sofa. She was half-asleep when Donnette walked inside and perched on the other couch.

"Hey. Another hard day in Addisonville?"

Casey shared what unfolded at the studio, but didn't know how to answer when Donnette said, "Knowing you, there's a plan circling somewhere in your head."

Undoing her belt, she warned, "You're all I have, so think about me while you figure out what to do. Please."

"Sure. I won't do anything crazy." Dragging herself upright, Casey rubbed her temples. "I'm going to hit the shower."

"Do you remember the affirmations Mama made us say every day when we were little?"

Nodding, Casey recited them with Donnette. "We are strong. We are intelligent. We are beautiful. We can do anything. We can achieve anything."

Tipping her chin with one finger, Donnette said, "Remember, time and patience solve most things. Talk to me later. Let me help you work through your plan."

They stood at the same time and hugged each other, as they used to do long ago when they first arrived in America and were lonely and lost. Another tear escaped from Casey, which she quickly brushed away. She held Donnette close a few seconds longer to compose herself and draw strength from their unity.

Despite Donnette's offer, she'd follow through alone. If anything went wrong, she wouldn't take her sister down with her. Addison might have ripped her sails to shreds today, but Casey still had enough ammunition to sink her ship.

CHAPTER 39

ALECIA

ALECIA WOKE WONDERING who died. A heavy ball of misery filled her stomach. Sleep abandoned her for much of the night, and today she resorted to makeup to repair the bags and creases under her eyes. On top of that, her emotions were all over the place. She spent the week alone, rehashing everything she'd done.

At first glance, Addison's gift could be seen as a belated gesture to acknowledge Alecia's existence—if she ignored good sense. But her heart confirmed that giving her the rights to the book was a way to stump Casey, plus pay her back for the rumors that Addison stole *Games People Play.*

Her first stop on leaving home was Casey's house, but no one answered the door. She headed for Tito's, where Casey and Donnette went for brunch sometimes. On the way, she rehearsed what she'd say to Casey, if that's where she was. She blew out a sigh when she spied Casey's Civic and ran over her apology lines.

The sisters sat at a table with a view of the street. Both wore sundresses and sandals and had tied their hair back with bandanas. Dull eyes and rounded shoulders told the story of their exhaustion.

She breezed past the hostess and pointed to Casey and Donnette. "I'll be over there."

Moving swiftly, she pulled up a chair and sat at the open end of the table, giving the impression everything was normal.

"What are you doing here?" Casey asked, but didn't seem to care what the answer might be.

"I came because…"

Casey raised both eyebrows at the same moment Donnette snarled, "What the hell d'you want?"

Alecia cringed, inclined to head back to the RAV-4, but it wouldn't solve anything. "I came to talk."

"The time to speak up was when you accepted stolen goods."

Casey's response was sour and delivered with a cutting look.

Biting her lip, Alecia searched for something to say. Nothing came to mind.

This awkward silence was new, and she hoped the damage to their friendship wasn't irreparable. She should have known no good would come of meeting with Addison again, but convinced herself another outcome was possible.

The thing was, Casey didn't understand the concept of never being enough. And come to find out, her father was also her grandfather. That did some serious damage to her psyche, but who the hell cared? Not her birth mother, and not the one who raised her and believed she should be grateful for the dregs that life handed her.

"I'm sorry, okay?"

The cup Casey brought to her lips fell into the sauce with a clang. "I don't give a f—"

Donnette grabbed her wrist in time to stop the expletive.

"Let me go, Donnette." Casey's nostrils flared as she faced Alecia. "Let me tell you something. You have *no* idea what this means to us. None. You don't know the agony we've gone through from the time we were too young to understand the evil Addison did and how handling that book the right way might have saved our mother's life."

She paused and grabbed the silver pendant at her neck with trembling fingers. This was the most passion she'd ever seen Casey display, and the hope of any reconciliation died as she watched her friend blink back tears.

Donnette wasn't as composed. She pressed a napkin to her face as she sobbed.

"And now after all of that…" A single tear trickled down Casey's cheek. "I'll have to fight my friend."

When Alecia tried to speak, Casey held up one hand to signal that she wasn't finished. "If you don't understand why I can't trust people, this is a prime example."

Despite the reluctance in her soul to offer up something, Alecia said, "Maybe I can convince Addison to change her will and—"

"You can't convince Addison to do shit." Scowling, Casey continued, "You can keep fooling yourself, but remember you're just a pawn in this game she's playing to pit us against each other."

"And you're letting her win," Alecia said bitterly.

"Don't get it twisted." After pushing her chair back, Casey stood. "Donnette, let's go."

To Alecia, she said, "You let her win the moment you accepted what's mine."

"But—" She jumped from the chair to stand in Casey's path.

"We're done, Alecia."

Casey wouldn't acknowledge or ask her to move. Instead, she turned her head to the window while a tear rolled down her cheek.

Finally giving in, Alecia shuffled sideways and collapsed in the seat.

They settled their bill, and she watched them enter the Civic through the glass.

Casey confronted her through the windshield, but without a hint of recognition or acknowledgment that she existed.

Sniffling, Alecia grabbed her keys and stood. On the way out, tittering from a nearby table distracted her. Ophelia's smarmy expression made her want to vomit. She kept walking while reassuring herself that her sister couldn't know what happened, but it didn't bring any comfort.

How was she at fault in any of this? As Casey said, Addison used her like a piece on a chessboard.

In five minutes—after repeating affirmations that no longer worked—she peeled out of the parking lot. Since Ophelia had busted her, she hadn't spoken to Mama. Three weeks. The longest stretch of time she hadn't been in contact with the woman who supported her in every way, outside of the times she downplayed Ophelia and Maxine's actions. Maybe if they treated her better, Alecia wouldn't have felt the need to fantasize about where she truly belonged and who was her family.

She tried calling Mama on the day Ophelia threw her out of the house and took her keys, but Mama hung up the phone and refused to answer after that.

Without being conscious of her intended destination, she headed to her childhood home. She didn't know what she'd do if Mama turned her away, but she had to take that risk. She needed someone. Addison had cost her a friendship, but she also contributed to her losses.

She stepped down from the SUV, thankful that Ophelia was behind her. She could talk with Mama without her listening in and making snide comments.

As always, Mama had the television volume turned up high.

She laid her fist against the door hard enough for Mama to hear. The sound cut off, and seconds later, Mama stood in the doorway. "What yuh want, Alecia?"

"Can I come inside?"

Mama stepped aside, barely giving her space to slide past. The living room hadn't changed, but she saw it with the eyes of a stranger. The space was neat, but the cluster of pill bottles on the center table gave away how regularly Mama sat in the same spot.

She perched on the edge of the sectional while Mama claimed her favorite spot in front of the television. A crime drama occupied the screen.

"Yuh just couldn't leave things alone, *eh*? Yuh had to search into what didn't concern yuh."

"It wasn't like that."

"Well, I hope yuh can deal wid what yuh found."

"It's not that I didn't know who she was. I just needed receipts." She regained some of her energy and straightened. "And speaking of those, why would you even reach out to her?"

"I didn't." Mama sucked her teeth and shook her head. "She's di one who find me and send some man to remind me dat our agreement was final. What she paid me to tek yuh was an insult, but dat didn't bother her at di time. In all deese years, I never contacted her, so why would I try to find her now?"

"You wouldn't have had to search far."

Mama sighed. "I wouldn't know who to look for or who she is now. Back den, she was Adassa Black, not dis fancy name she's wearing deese days. It's what was on yuh birth certificate. I had to apply for a new one with my name on it so I could bring yuh here."

"Isn't that fraud?"

"Fraud, my ass." Her attention went to the cell phone on the table when it beeped. "I did it because I love yuh."

She reached for the phone and tapped the screen several times. Alecia's instructions that banging on the LED display was unnecessary hadn't stuck. "And by di way, why yuh dealing wid yuh private business in public? Phelia send dis to me."

Alecia gasped at the familiar scene. She stood in front of Casey, and to the left, barely inside the shot, Donnette sat with the napkin covering her eyes. The caption sucked away her breath: *When you're so toxic, you poison your friends.*

"She doesn't know what we were talking about. Why would she do this?"

"Young people live for di screen, so what d'you expect?"

It would have been better if her sister had dealt her a physical blow. With the controversy swirling around Addison, Alecia didn't want anyone to connect them to her mess.

"Ophelia heard yuh fighting Casey over something Addison stole from her. That can't be true. I raised yuh better than that."

"How can you accuse me of anything when Addison told me you tried to bribe her into giving you more money for not sharing her story?"

"It's di principle of di t'ing." Mama sucked her teeth and folded her arms. "She was making all dis money and didn't once turn di back of her eyes to find out how we was doin'."

Mama's way of expressing herself was normally amusing, but not this time.

"*She paid you.* You signed a document saying that. You shouldn't have contacted her after that man or whoever visited you."

Mama stood and pointed to the door. "Yuh can't come into my house and tell me what I should and shouldn't do. You're the cause of all di passa-passa in dis family."

Pulling her head back, Alecia scowled at Mama. "*I'm* the reason your daughters don't know how to play nice? That's *your* doing. You never once corrected them when they were abusing me."

"That's what older sisters do."

"Stop chatting rubbish, Mama." Alecia rolled her eyes and picked up her key fob from the cushion. "That's not how normal people treat their siblings."

"Your problem is dat yuh spoil and expect everything to go your way."

Alecia had had enough and rose from the seat. "I'm leaving. I didn't come here for you to attack me."

"Then why yuh come?" Mama asked with her nostrils flaring. "Yuh lost yuh way?"

"No, but you've lost yours. You talk about people from the island having a third-world mentality, trying to hijack people, just like the choppers, lotto scammers, or whatever they call themselves. Yet, you're so greedy, you tried the same thing with Addison. I bet Ophelia put you up to it. She reads, so she knows who Addison is."

Mama avoiding her eyes meant one thing. She was right.

"You told Ophelia she's my…the woman who had me."

When Mama didn't confirm or deny the accusation, Alecia walked to the door, praying her stupid tears wouldn't betray her. She turned the handle and spoke around the mass that blocked her throat. "I have one question: Why do they hate me?"

Mama picked up the remote and turned the sound back on the television. "They don't hate you. They're jealous of you, but yuh know dat already."

"And you enabled them by not shutting down their foolishness."

"Mi tyad. Matter of fact, yuh exhaust me." Still staring at the television, Mama flicked her wrist the way she would with a pesky fly. "Go home."

The casual dismissal struck her like a blow to the stomach. She'd hoped Mama would forgive her and they could move on from this mess. What she wouldn't do was stick around for this kind of disrespect.

The child in her had hoped for much more than she received from finding her birth mother. Exposing Addison turned out to be a hollow victory, but at least she didn't have to face the assault charges. She didn't know what Casey would do, but when the time came, she'd deal with the consequences—the same way she'd dealt with the highs and lows in her life. As for an apology to Quentin, he'd die before receiving one.

Before she drove off, she picked up the phone. Her notifications had gone bonkers. She swiped the phone and opened her favorite platform. Island Gyal had posted several voice notes and was dissecting each on her podcast. Alecia's blood turned to sludge as she listened.

The book Addison willed to her meant nothing, yet the concept of owning something this valuable had turned Alecia's head. Now, that dream had burned to ashes. The blowback would be fierce. Her name linked to Addison's would taint her future as a writer. Any dreams of a writing career shriveled and died as the show progressed.

Perhaps it was what she deserved, but she'd hunker down and let the storm pass. Maybe then she could gather whatever unbroken pieces of her life remained and create something worthwhile—something just for her.

CHAPTER 40

ADDISON

THE PRESS BRIEFING she hurriedly called, against Theo's and Mikhail's advice, was underway, and she finally relaxed. Somewhat. Despite the damning recording, she stood tall and addressed the intimate gathering of chosen media folk Piper invited.

Aside from a bit of port to keep her frayed nerves under control, she was ready to speak, but careful to avoid connecting directly with any individual.

Theo hovered next to her, which comforted and irritated her at the same time. If luck was on her side, she'd be finished within twenty minutes.

"No doubt, you've heard a voice clip that was doctored to sound like a conversation between me and one of my research assistants."

A slight rumble came from the group, but she waved it away with an explanation. "These days, with AI, it's almost impossible to know what's real and what isn't, and I assure you what you heard isn't true in any way, form, or shape."

The space was silent, and she continued building on the layers of carefully curated information that would keep her head above water. If she could rise from this patch of trouble and publish the next book, she'd be back on track.

"I'll take a few questions at this time."

A young Latino raised his hand. "Miss Comstock, you're saying this bad publicity arose because of someone you had to fire. What about the other stories that have been popping up over the past few weeks?"

"Folks at the top of any sector become targets. That has been my experience over the years."

"But why have these rumors persisted? Do you know?" he asked, holding up a smartphone, which she assumed was recording the briefing.

"I definitely cannot say." She scanned the room and prepared to close down the questions when another young man put his hand in the air.

"Earlier today, that employee on the podcast claimed she had receipts, which she shared with the host. I reached out to her for an interview and—"

Her neck warmed, and she covered it with one hand. "What does that have to do with this briefing?"

"She agreed to meet me after this function, so—"

"What?" She lowered her hand and searched the room, but didn't see any sign of Casey. "So, why are you here if you intend to take the word of someone who is trying to ruin my reputation?"

"You did that yourself."

A tic danced beside Addison's mouth, and she scanned the space to be sure her ears weren't fooling her.

While he also did a visual search, Theo stepped in close and laid one hand on her arm. "Let me handle this."

From the back of the room, Casey advanced, carrying a handful of paper.

"How did she get in?" Addison asked sotto voce. "Remove her. Now."

Theo pulled out his cell phone, but her attention returned to Casey, who held up her hand. "The information I have here will prove this woman is a scam artist and a thief who refuses to do the right thing."

While she spoke, Casey passed a sheet to each person, and by the time the security guard entered the room, she was on her way out. She stopped in the doorway as though to thumb her nose at Addison one last time, and with a flick of her wrist, threw the rest of the papers on the chair in the foyer.

The young reporter hurried after Casey and disappeared.

Addison's attention returned to her guests. An eerie silence hung in the air, and for several moments, nothing and no one moved. Then the reporters surged forward, firing more questions than she could answer.

"What is the meaning of this?"

"How does this accusation change the status of this particular book?"

"How will you make restitution?"

"If this information turns out to be doctored, will you sue?"

"Did you actually write this book, Miss Comstock?"

She clung to the podium, hoping her knees wouldn't give out. After this meeting, her first task was firing the security firm. How had Casey made it past them? And how did these people expect her to answer their questions at this rate?

"I'm sorry." Her hand went to her throat, where her pulse beat to a staccato rhythm. "This briefing is over."

The reporters clustered in twos and threes as they walked out of the building.

When the last of them left, she climbed the stairs on unsteady feet and sat in her office, weighing scenes from the past hour. She wanted to smash something, but didn't have the energy. The only result she'd ever seen from acting out was that it cost her in terms of repairs. Not that it mattered now. She'd blundered, and it had cost her everything.

Casey had the luxury of walking in because Addison was too busy plugging holes to preserve her image and prevent her world from falling apart. She'd neglected to inform security that Casey was no longer part of the team. Her absence for the week could have meant she'd been on vacation. And today, she'd walked in and blown up everything Addison was trying to hold together.

She needed a drink, but she had things to do right now. The first was to ask Kirkland to come in and see her. When she finished that conversation, she thanked Theo and Piper, dismissed them, and settled in to wait.

Kirkland arrived within half an hour, and she directed him to a seat. His long-sleeve white polo and black jeans didn't give her any clues as to whether he'd been at home or not. He'd been an asset, although he hadn't prevented disaster from coming to her door.

"Are you all right?" he asked, sitting on the edge of the visitor's chair.

"Yes. Thanks for coming."

His doubtful expression confirmed his disbelief, but she was past caring.

Aside from confirming he'd met with Alecia's adopted mother, he had nothing new. At this point, she didn't believe she'd need him for anything else.

"Thanks for what you've uncovered." She put a check in his hand, then slid the book inside her top drawer. "I'll bet you didn't expect to find all you dug up."

He leaned back and nodded. "You told me you'd lived a colorful life."

"True, and as you now know, I've done some things most wouldn't approve of or understand."

"Thanks for this." While folding the check, he tipped his head toward her. "There's always the option of doing the right thing."

She relaxed in the seat and clasped both hands on her stomach. "That works for people who give a damn about others. I'm not one of them."

Her family and other hangers-on taught her that people were only after their own good, and kept her around only as long as they could have their way with her. In her book, survival meant using others or being used. She chose the former. Always.

Kirkland's handsome features didn't shift, except for a twitch of the eyebrows. When their meeting ended, he understood his job was over, but she stayed in the office gauging her options and next moves.

Two days ago, another woman had come crawling out of the dust of history to say Addison had stolen her book. A romance novel at that. *The audacity*. Theo had shut that down because she didn't know the woman. If they had met, she had no memory of it, nor the inclination to search her mind for unnecessary information.

Theo earned every dollar she was paying him this past week. No matter what they did, the social media mavens kept digging, and their followers lapped up their gossip and innuendo. The talk with Casey had been a mistake. Clips of it surfaced all over the internet.

She'd been arrogant to believe Casey would give up after acting the part of a garden snake that invaded her studio—and life—to lie in wait for the opportune time to raise her head and strike. Their hectic schedule caused her to forget the suspicion she harbored about her. Now, she was paying the price.

In desperation, Addison approved one interview, in which she said someone doctored the recording to imitate her. It didn't help. And the phones rang incessantly, day and night. On Tuesday, in a fit of rage, she sent the staff home and instructed them to return next Monday prepared to work harder than they ever had before. That was because she'd done nothing about replacing Alecia and Casey.

She'd never told them, but they were her best writers. The irony of it made her want to scream and go on a rampage—destroy them for wrecking her life. But she didn't have the energy. Her face was drawn and haggard under the makeup. She'd barely eaten anything all week, but had more than her fill of port, rum, and her pills when she needed to sleep.

In a stroke of luck, she'd finally gotten hold of Marcus Ryder, who told her in no uncertain terms he wouldn't be releasing any documents Rachel had been holding. His snippy response left her no choice but to have Matteo do whatever it took to retrieve the files being held by the agency. She didn't see that battle ending in the near future.

According to Matteo, Gerald hadn't withdrawn his suit and actually believed he had a chance of winning. Since the police had absolved her, she didn't care if he continued wasting his time.

After today's catastrophe, drumming up the energy for anything else seemed impossible, but she couldn't rest. One task remained for her to complete.

CHAPTER 41

ADDISON

"FIND CASEY." ADDISON could barely form the words she needed. She yawned and stretched on the sofa. "I need to meet with her."

"She may not come." He glanced at his watch. "It's late in the day."

"I don't care. Bring her here."

Kirkland backed out of the room, careful not to let his eyes wander.

Addison was beyond caring. She drank too much earlier, then eventually showered and came back to the living area for another drink and lay naked on the sofa to sleep off the liquor. Today's drink of choice was rum cream. None of that weak stuff made in Europe, but the real deal from home that could blow the top of your head off if you weren't careful.

She'd asked him to come back after their earlier meeting because she'd had time to think and had one last request—a talk with Casey.

Before closing the door behind him, Kirkland glanced at the circular table.

Let him look. It wasn't his business what she did. Life as she knew it was over anyway. Casey had seen to that.

Resignation settled over her again. This past week, she'd tidied up all her contracts and destroyed what she didn't want any other eyes to see. She'd also dealt with her financials and left Matteo in charge of managing her affairs, including her mother's care.

He'd harangued her about all the "wrongness" spilling out every which way. Despite his suspicions about her obsessive cleaning up, she blew him off. "Don't worry about me. Deal with my business. That's all I'm asking you to do," she ordered.

A sigh left her, and she rolled onto her side and cushioned her head under one arm.

Would Casey come? Maybe she would, to crow over her bittersweet success. After all, she'd do anything to acquire the rights to *Games People Play,* which still wasn't hers. If Casey had claimed she was her daughter, Addison would have believed her. She had an indomitable spirit, and Addison would have done everything possible in similar circumstances.

The one thing she now saw in Alecia—because she was looking for it—was the familial resemblance to the Blacks. She'd hidden behind the bangs and the makeup, but it was there. Alecia let her emotions drive her, but she didn't have the spirit of a true warrior, not like Casey. Perhaps rejection made her weak.

This evening, Addison would break Casey—or Casey would break her.

Maybe they would be the death of each other.

One last fight.

The thought provided a shot of energy, and she pulled herself upright. She padded into the bedroom, stopped at the closet that ran the length of one wall, and selected a silk robe with a Chinese collar, which she wrapped around herself and tied at the waist.

She washed her face and brushed her teeth. It wouldn't do to smell as though she'd fallen into a rum barrel. Next, she applied makeup in front of the mirror. She kept it to a minimum—just enough to make her seem attractive, but not overdone. Then she fetched a tall glass of water and one half full of port and returned to the couch to wait.

When the phone rang, she picked it up off the table. "She's here?"

Kirk's answer was curt. "Yes."

"It certainly took her long enough. Now that she's here, you can go."

"Are you sure?"

"She's already done everything she can to hurt me. She won't lay a finger on my body, if that's what you're thinking."

"I think I'll wait."

"If you wish, but it's neither here nor there to me."

The last thing she needed was his pity. She ended the call, wondering when exactly her heart had turned to flint. If she had to say, it might have been when her family refused to support and help her through the anxiety and terror of bringing a child into the world alone.

Parting from Alice, or Alecia, had been the easiest thing. She'd been careless in naming her, but Addison's wonderland came when she separated herself from the child she considered a little ball of misery. Everything about her brought back the pain of being assaulted by her father and discarded by her mother.

The only satisfaction that came from that part of her life was hearing news of Eustace Black's demise. Long after Addison's escape, an irate farmer attacked her father in the front yard. He chopped him all over his body with a machete, then reported to the police station with his teenage daughter. Eustace had raped her, too.

A firm knock came at the door, and Addison called, "Come."

"You wanted to see me?"

Casey was casual yet classy in loose black slacks and a close-fitting shirt in the same color. She'd put her hair into two plaits that rested just beyond her shoulders and tied the ends with elastic bands. The flashback of the two girls peeking at her seventeen years ago made Addison swallow hard. Casey had done this deliberately. The poky little house and the simple country woman, along with her stern mother, appeared vividly in her mind. The thorn in her flesh bore a striking resemblance to her mom, Yvette Finch.

"Yes." She waved toward the other end of the circular sofa. "Come in. Sit."

While scanning the room, Casey settled on the cushion and laid her cell phone on her thigh.

"How does it feel?" Addison asked, excited despite herself. Perhaps because she was finally facing a worthy opponent. Or so this moment felt.

"What?" Casey arched both brows, giving the impression she had no worries.

"Winning." Addison smirked. "And by the way, our conversation is not being recorded."

"Right." Casey moved her head from side to side and scoffed. "This was never about winning or losing. It was about principle, and we both know you have none."

"Come on. It must have given you a thrill to bring me down."

Casey studied her for a moment before she spoke. "Understand this: I don't take pleasure in destroying people. I do what I must. You made me an enemy when you took the thing that meant the most to my family and could have saved my mother's life."

Inhaling deeply, Addison picked her words with care. "Did I tell you he came to me?"

"No matter what Peter Grimes said, you'd already made a deal, but his was better, wasn't it?" She made a disparaging sound in her throat. "He settled for less. That's why you robbed my mother."

Addison swallowed a mouthful of port, then set the glass down, disgusted by her shaking hand. "My decision had *nothing* to do with cheating your family and *everything* to do with my success."

"Which you achieved on the backs of God knows how many other people." Casey's sigh reeked of impatience. "Why did you call me here? Surely it isn't to tell me what I already know. If you had a conscience, you wouldn't have tried to destroy my reputation with your shenanigans online."

"My name is my brand. I'll protect it to the death." Her pitch was higher when she spat, "You used my outline. Don't even try to deny it."

Casey didn't respond, other than to raise her eyebrows.

"*And*, you forced me to pull that move with the book."

Casey sucked her teeth. "Please. Nobody made you do anything. You have so much power, but instead of doing good, you choose evil. Every. Single. Time."

Instead of responding, Addison lifted one bottle off the table. "You're no different, because you've pulled out every stop to get revenge."

When her gaze returned to Casey, her greatest desire was to strangle her until she was dead. But that was a pipe dream. Funny how she'd termed Casey's wishes regarding her mother's work as exactly that, but here they were.

In a matter-of-fact tone, she said, "The media is camped outside my home. I can't go anywhere without people hurling abuse at me. My name is dirt in the literary world—"

Hand to her chest, Casey mocked her. "Surely your friends don't think you stole *all* the books that have your name on them?"

Friends? She'd never taken time to cultivate them, and in the early days, all the people she associated with gave in to jealousy. But Casey didn't need to know that. It was bad enough that she'd brought her world crashing down.

She flipped the cap off the first bottle. Her physician had kept her supplied with sleep aids and anxiety meds over the years, but in the last month she'd gone overboard. All of it was to no avail because she couldn't rest for more than a couple of hours each night.

"So, is that your exit strategy?" Casey asked, her tone incredulous when her attention went to the collection of pills.

"That's none of your business."

Casey's lips curved, and her eyes glowed. "If you expect me to be sorry for you, you're out of your mind."

"Did I ask for your sympathy?"

A handful of the white oval pills spilled into her palm.

"No, but it's clear you're a coward and need help." She tugged one of her braids. "This, you'll have to do on your own." She let the lull between them build before adding, "But, if you don't…are you prepared for the litigation that will come? I won't stop, you know? I will fight you *and* Alecia, to the death, if necessary."

Litigation she could deal with. She had more money than Casey could dream of, but that might not be the case if she had to pay damages and royalties from seventeen years ago up to now.

Games People Play made her and had come full circle to break her.

Casey was relentless. Crossing her legs, she continued, "Have you thought about the possible cancellation of your contract for this last book and maybe all the others, if people keep coming forward to say you stole their work?"

Perspiration covered Addison's forehead, and she closed her fist around the pills.

"Because, just so you know..." Casey played with the end of her plait and watched her keenly. "Your publisher reached out to me about the ownership rights to *Games People Play* and telling my side of the story. And in this era of cancel culture, a wave of your readers has already turned on you, but you know that, I'm sure."

Addison winced. Not having adoring fans across the world waiting for her next book was unthinkable. If she couldn't publish books, her life would be pointless. That was what made her famous. That was her raison d'être. She was nothing without her books. They were her, and she was them.

Soft yet insistent, Casey's questions continued like drill bits, digging past her skin and into the most vulnerable parts of her psyche. "How will you live knowing you've been blacklisted and nobody cares about you or your stories?"

Being relegated to a nobody made the final decision for Addison. She couldn't do that life. She tossed back the pills, then swallowed several more, and chased them with water. Then she picked up another bottle of pills.

"I didn't come here to witness your downfall. Irrespective of what you think, I'm not cruel. You, though, deserve everything that's coming to you." Casey shrugged on her way to the door. "Who knows? Life may improve when nobody knows who you are. Maybe you could even start over."

"I don't need any advice from you," she snapped. "Thanks to my team, people will always recognize my name, even when I'm gone."

"Don't be so sure your evil won't kill your legacy." Casey stopped and laid a hand on one hip. Her scorn was obvious when she added, "And by the way, the right circumstances made it easy to break up the unholy triad you formed with your Jezebel friends."

Addison's heart palpitated, and she laid a hand against her chest and whispered, "Are you saying you…I knew it. You crazy bitch."

Casey neither acknowledged nor denied that she was involved in Emily's and Rachel's deaths. "I hope you all burn in hell. When you arrive there, tell them I said hello."

"At some point, you'll join us." Addison smirked, although her energy ebbed.

"You don't have a say in what will be." Casey walked back to where Addison sat and studied her closely, as though memorizing her features. Then her lips twisted, and she leaned in close, speaking through her teeth. "Your name is mud. You. Are. Finished."

"Get out."

"That will be my pleasure. Carry on." Her gaze strayed to the bottles on the table. "Have a nice life. Or not."

CHAPTER 42

CASEY

"EVERYTHING ALL RIGHT?" Kirk straightened up from the column where he'd been leaning when she stepped onto the veranda.

"I'm good as gold. Don't know about her, though. It's not so simple when you have to face your sins in public." To ensure he didn't think about going back inside, she added, "Knowing her, she's in there scheming how to recover from this mess."

"It won't be easy to rise from this bed of thorns. It's bad."

Glancing at him, she chuckled, "That has to be the understatement of the year."

He walked with her to the Civic, and the gentle evening breeze brought the smell of vanilla and musk to her nostrils. When she unlocked the car, he opened the door.

"Why are you here?" she asked softly. "Now, I mean."

He didn't miss a beat when he answered, "Addison and I had some stuff to complete."

"Don't you mean people's business you've been snooping in for her?"

He shrugged. "It is what it is."

She gripped the top of the door and couldn't help the contempt that surfaced when she asked, "How do you work for people like that, though?"

"It's a job, same as any other, and as long as they operate within the law…"

She sat in the driver's seat and swung her legs inside. "Not all money is good money."

Kirk slid both hands into his pockets. "True, but she isn't running a criminal enterprise."

"Says you," she shot back.

His grin was unexpected, and his gaze softened. "Hey, now that my stint here is over, I was wondering if…"

"No." Casey shook her head for emphasis, despite the flicker of emotion that made her heart beat faster. "There's no way I would go out with you."

"Okay." He dragged the word out and stood back from the car.

Something in the downturn of his mouth and the long breath he expelled wouldn't let her go. She hesitated, but before the desires of her flesh changed her mind, Casey broke the spell by shutting the door.

She wound the window down to quip, "I could lie and say it was nice knowing you, but it wasn't, so I won't insult you."

"Understood, and I respect you for being honest." He saluted her, then strode to his black Elantra.

A tinge of sadness clogged her throat. She'd decided not to return his handkerchief and hadn't washed it either. Although she hadn't given Kirk any encouragement, she'd been feeling him. Pity he'd been Addison's stool pigeon, but she couldn't risk him knowing anything more about her than he already did. Nor would she ever be able to relax completely in his company. Not after the things she'd done in the name of securing her mother's legacy.

When he called earlier on Addison's behalf, her first inclination was to refuse. On the ride over, she'd hoped that Addison would do the right thing even after that meeting with Alecia. That was a stupid and vain hope.

Since then, she avoided thinking about Alecia. Didn't want her name to soil the inside of her head. Some people weren't worth the time it would take to dissect their character or the effort needed to understand their actions.

She hadn't been back to the studio after crashing Addison's press briefing and releasing that recording of Addison's attempted bribery. The idea came to her to carry the recorder because once Addison realized what she was up against, she'd want to bargain. It wasn't in her to make concessions, but pride dictated she'd do everything to save her damaged image.

As Casey left the premises and tooted the horn at the security guard, hope flared inside her, fighting the numbness trying to take hold. If her luck held, this chapter was closed, *and* if Addison had one shred of shame left, she'd continue what she started and finish the pills. They both understood there was no coming back from the scandal and disgrace. Not in today's cancel culture.

People were swift to hop on a bandwagon that had nothing to do with them. Social media had turned ordinary people into a dangerous and relentless horde, caught up in their feelings.

She'd gotten ahead of herself to tell Addison that the publisher would want her story and did it to sink another nail in her coffin and steer her toward the cliff where she was headed.

Addison had struck her as being stronger than the end she'd settled on, but in truth, Casey was relieved. The stress of figuring out how to bring closure to her mother's stolen work and balancing a job with Addison and her mercurial temperament wasn't easy to manage.

Added to that, Donnette's stagnation still weighed on her mind. Not that she was different. They were stuck in a time machine that had everything to do with their past and little to do with the present.

She drove home below the speed limit, and when she sat in front of the house, Casey bolstered her courage. Today, she'd discuss Donnette's stranglehold on the past. Her ten-year-old Suzuki Swift was parked in the driveway, another testament to her inability to escape from the prison she'd created for herself. She kept her possessions way beyond a useful time span and clung to the familiar. Anything to maintain a sense of control.

Some minutes later, Casey dropped her key fob on the table near the front door and followed the scent of red peas soup to the kitchen.

Donnette stood in front of the stove, adding sprigs of thyme and a scotch bonnet pepper to the pot.

It was out of character, but Casey dropped an arm around her neck and kissed her cheek. "Hey, sis. Thanks for all you do around here. That smells *soooo* good."

Laughing, Donnette said, "*Mmm-hmm.* It's not that you can't cook, it's that you don't."

"Why should I when you do it so well?" She removed a bottle of water from the fridge and leaned against the counter, sipping.

"One day, I'm going to take a trip somewhere, and we'll see if you won't have to prepare food for yourself."

Casey wriggled her eyebrows. "Really? In which lifetime is that going to happen?"

"That's where you're wrong," Donnette dropped the spoon in the sink, then lowered the flame under the pot. "I've been thinking a lot since our last talk."

She mirrored Casey's position and threw her head back to stare at the ceiling. "I didn't tell you, but I started therapy again."

"Really?" Casey tried not to sound too interested. That would keep Donnette talking.

"Yeah. Life has become empty. Dead. Boring. Same thing day in and day out. I don't have to ask why I need to do something different—help myself, as you keep saying."

Casey didn't comment because she'd done most of the talking over the years.

She faced Casey, propping one hip against the counter. "With you doing all you could to expose that serpent and the way you've risked everything for me, I figure the least I can do is listen to you and start living again."

"This is what families do for each other."

"Not all of them." She breathed in deeply and wiped the corner of one eye. "You know how I know you love me?"

Casey pursed her lips, holding back tears, too. "Nope, but I'm listening."

She gripped Casey's wrist and whispered, "I know what you did with Uncle…Peter Grimes."

Casey was certain her heart stopped beating, until it thundered in her ears and chest. She licked her lips, while the pulsing in her chest slowed. "You knew?"

With one hand, Donnette swiped at her cheeks. "I followed you, then I went back to bed and thanked God that hell was over."

A sigh erupted from Casey's chest. "Then to come to America and fall under the care of that wicked woman."

"Yeah, we've certainly been through some things, and you took care of me at every stage." She inched closer, dropped her arm around Casey, and laid her head in the crook of her neck. "And that is why I took care of Carson."

Casey swayed, feeling faint as her throat closed. "What are you saying?"

"Exactly what you think."

"But they said it was crib death," she murmured.

Releasing her, Donnette asked, "Who are we to say it wasn't?"

Casey wanted to ask a million questions, but held her tongue. Some things were best left unsaid.

A half-smile curved Donnette's lips. She understood what was going on inside Casey's head. "You didn't deserve any of what she put you through. I figured if I removed the thing that made your life miserable, the situation would improve. And it did."

She sniffed, then continued, "It still bothers me, but I feared if she pushed you any more, you might have done what you did to *him* and ended up in the juvenile facility she used to threaten us—or worse, prison."

Casey didn't admit she was right, but remembered her relief when their brother passed suddenly. Aunt Erica never overcame her depression, and nothing their father did consoled her. Nor could he change her mind when she decided never to become pregnant again. They watched him grow older overnight because his two daughters hadn't been enough.

The house took on the atmosphere of a mausoleum. Between them, they managed the household and made the best of the hand they'd been given. When the time came, they escaped from that prison.

"Sometimes, I think God made a mistake with you being the younger of the two of us, but I believe Gran. He makes no mistakes." She stepped in front of Casey and cupped her cheeks. "This is the first and last time we'll talk about these things. Agreed?"

In a choked voice, Casey whispered. "Okay. Love you, sis."

"I love you more," Donnette said, gently pinching her cheek.

"We have one thing left to do." Casey blotted her eyes with both hands. "Get back what belongs to our mother."

"Now, to that, I say yes." Donnette eased back to ask, "By the way, how did the meeting with that woman go?"

"As well as expected."

Tipping her head forward, Donnette asked, "You didn't do anything to make the news or break the internet, did you?"

"Nope. I made suggestions I hope Addison will follow through on."

After throwing her a puzzled look, Donnette lifted the cover off the pot and sniffed the steam from the soup. "This will be ready in another couple of minutes. Go do whatever you need to do, then let's enjoy dinner."

When she was almost out the door, Donnette said, "By the way, I no longer have a job at the hospital."

Casey spun to face her. "Sis, I am so sorry. But how come…" She stopped, not wanting to say the words.

"I'm still speaking to you?" She shrugged. "I was angry and hurt, but no matter what I say, I'll never give up on you."

Nodding to avoid speaking or risking the tears that threatened to betray her, Casey left the kitchen. Inside the bedroom, she removed her sandals and lay on the bed. She should call their grandmother with an update, but not now. Right now, she was too exhausted, and time with Donnette was important.

Her mind flashed to Addison, but she was merely a blip on her radar—part of a painful past Casey prayed was finally over.

CHAPTER 43

CASEY

ROCHELLE DISTRACTED THEM on the weekend by taking them to see a movie. On Monday, Casey received an email from Amy, inviting her to a meeting on Wednesday. She dressed carefully in a black suit with white piping and matching sandals. She pulled her hair into a smooth bun at her nape. Amy had taken her for a joke when they first met. Today, she'd know Casey hadn't come to play.

Amy's assistant welcomed Casey when she arrived, but this time, instead of meeting at her desk, they sat in a conference room connected to her office. If Amy figured the impressive space containing a massive table would intimidate Casey, she had another think coming. Two minutes after they exchanged polite conversation, Amy's assistant also took a seat.

"Tanya's here to take notes." Amy opened a file and offered a faint smile. "Our team of editors went through both versions of *Games People Play*. We've concluded that it needs a second assessment."

Casey lowered her chin and raised one eyebrow, but didn't speak.

"However, we agree it seems Addison took some liberties with your mother's work."

"That's what you choose to call it?"

"You understand, I'm sure. We have to be careful how this matter is handled."

Uncrossing her legs, Casey asked, "Should I have come with an attorney? Since you didn't indicate the nature of the meeting, I didn't take that step."

Amy perched a pair of cat-woman glasses on her nose and flipped a sheet of paper. "It will be advisable later on when we're negotiating the rights, but there was another matter we wished to discuss."

"And that is?"

"Since the situation has changed—"

"It definitely has. As it relates to the negotiations, you should know Addison gave the rights to her daughter. Now, that matter has to be sorted out as well."

"That's…" Amy's ice-blue eyes widened. "Unexpected."

"But exactly what *I* expected from Addison, but I plan to see this matter through."

Amy set the file aside. "Don't tell me you haven't heard?"

The half-question, half-statement jolted Casey, although she knew what was coming. Moving her head sideways, as though curious, she slowed her breathing. "I'm not sure what you mean."

"Addison passed away over the weekend. Her publicist notified us."

"The team got an email on Monday." Casey nodded once, then stopped for a few seconds. "It was shocking because she was fine the last time I saw her."

Amy lowered her gaze to the file. "There was also a statement in the paper on Monday."

"I missed that." Casey sighed, as though deep in thought. She was careful to maintain a neutral expression while reciting the statement in her head.

We have been notified of the passing of Addison Comstock, a prolific USA Today *and* New York Times *bestselling author. Ms. Comstock passed suddenly over the weekend. She had just completed her 40th novel, which was submitted to her publisher a week ago. In recent times, Ms. Comstock was embroiled in controversy over her first bestseller, with claims made that another author wrote the book.*

Casey brought her mind back to the present when Amy's assistant rose from her seat.

"What was the other matter you wanted to discuss?" Casey asked.

"Once the copyright ownership is settled, Asdack Publishing wants to offer you a contract to write about your experience with Addison—what being a part of her team was like—and the process you'll go through to recover your mother's work. A sort of exposé. Who knows? It may help others in a similar position."

"Won't that be a conflict of interest for both of us?"

Amy's eyes crinkled as she smiled. "When there's big money involved, publishers find a way around pesky details."

She considered Amy's words while staring at the skyline. But that was an act. She'd already made a decision. To move past the gatekeepers, she'd had to resort to subterfuge. Now, a week later, the same company was prepared to capitalize on one of their authors' misfortunes.

"I'm sorry, but I have to refuse. My sister and I need time to figure out how to navigate through what's coming."

The light in Amy's eyes faded, and she stood. "Very well. If you change your mind…"

As they shook hands, Casey said, "Thank you."

What she didn't reveal was that she'd never write any such book. Gran always said it was best to let sleeping dogs lie. This was one such instance. She'd done so much wrong, she'd be foolish to dig up all the scattered bones that represented her misdeeds. She'd deal with them in time.

This crusade was almost over.

Though she'd harassed Donnette over the years about being stuck, she had also been existing. With Addison dead, her outlook was changing.

Maybe she'd even find love, if the right man came along.

She was sure of one thing.

It was time to start living.

GLOSSARY

Below you'll find a list of terms and their definitions.

chupid—stupid

dat—that

den—then

deese—these

di—the

dis—this

doin'—doing

duppy—ghost

fi—for

goin'—going

groanin'—groaning

gyal—girl

jing-bang—garbage

John Crow—vulture

passa-passa—quarrel

mek—make

mi—me

patoo—owl

pickney—child

probly—probably

siddung—sit down

soft soap—to fool someone with lies

talkin'—talking

tek—take

tiefin'—thieving

t'ings—things

tyad—tired

upstandin'—upstanding

wid—with

yuh—you

WWW.BLACKODYSSEY.NET

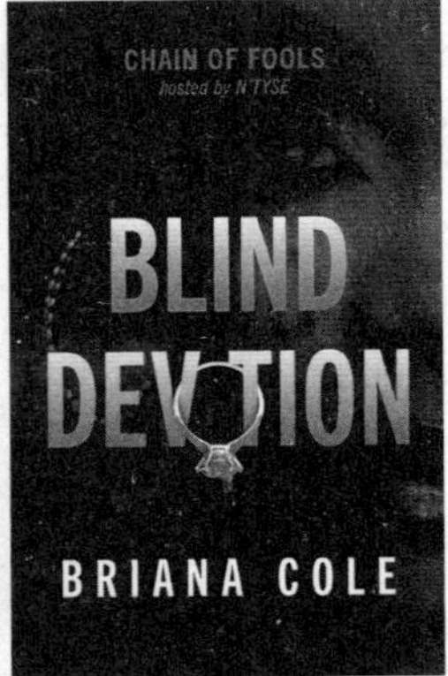